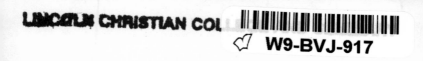

CLASSICAL LITERARY CRITICISM

PLATO (c. 429–347 BC) stands with Socrates and Aristotle as one of the shapers of the Western intellectual tradition. He came from a family that had long played a prominent part in Athenian politics, and it would have been natural for him to follow the same course. He declined to do so, however, as he was disgusted by the violence and corruption of Athenian political life, and especially sickened by the execution in 399 BC of his friend and teacher, Socrates. Inspired by Socrates' inquiries into the nature of ethical standards, Plato sought a cure for the ills of society not in politics but in philosophy. At an uncertain date in the early fourth century BC he founded the Academy in Athens, which was the first permanent institution devoted to philosophical research and teaching, and the prototype of all Western universities. He travelled extensively, notably to Sicily as political adviser to Dionysius II, ruler of Syracuse. Plato wrote over twenty philosophical dialogues and there are also extant under his name thirteen letters, whose genuineness is keenly disputed.

ARISTOTLE was born at Stagira, in the dominion of the kings of Macedonia, in 384 BC. For twenty years he studied at Athens in the Academy of Plato, on whose death he left, and some time later became tutor to the young Alexander the Great. When Alexander succeeded to the throne of Macedonia in 336 BC, Aristotle returned to Athens and established his own school and research institute, the Lyceum, to which his vast erudition attracted a large number of scholars. After Alexander's death in 323, anti-Macedonian feeling drove Aristotle out of Athens and he fled to Chalcis in Euboea, where he died in 322 BC. His writings, which were of extraordinary range, profoundly affected the whole course of ancient and medieval philosophy, and they are still eagerly studied and debated by philosophers today. Very many of them have survived, famously the *Ethics* and *Politics*.

HORACE, the Latin lyric poet and satirist, was born in Venusia in Apulia in about 65 BC. He was educated in Rome and Athens. In 44 BC Horace enlisted in Brutus's army and fought at Philippi as a military tribune. Ensuing poverty, he says, drove him to write poetry. Horace is said to be the most quoted author of antiquity, appealing to a wider range of readers of every age and at any age than any other ancient poet.

It has long been thought that the treatise *On the Sublime* was written by CASSIUS LONGINUS, who was a third-century AD Greek rhetorician and minister of Zenobia, queen of Palmyra. However, it is now generally ascribed to an unknown Greek author writing in the mid first century AD.

T. S. DORSCH was Professor of English at the University of Durham from 1968 until his retirement in 1976. He also taught at Westfield College, University of London, where he was Reader. His publications include the Shakespeare section of *The New Cambridge Bibliography of English Literature* (1974). Professor Dorsch died in June 1991.

PENELOPE MURRAY was born in Malaya in 1948, and was educated at Wycombe Abbey school and Newnham College, Cambridge. She held research posts at King's College, London, and St Anne's College, Oxford, and was a founder member of the department of Classics at the University of Warwick, where she is currently Senior Lecturer. She has written on a wide variety of topics in ancient literature, and her publications include *Genius: The History of an Idea* (1989), *Plato on Poetry* (1996) and *Music and the Muses: The Culture of Mousike in the Classical Athenian City* (ed. with Peter Wilson, 2004). She is working on a book on Orpheus.

Classical Literary Criticism

Translated by
PENELOPE MURRAY *and* T. S. DORSCH,
with an Introduction and Notes by
PENELOPE MURRAY

PENGUIN BOOKS

PENGUIN BOOKS

Published by the Penguin Group
Penguin Books Ltd, 80 Strand, London WC2R ORL, England
Penguin Putnam Inc., 375 Hudson Street, New York, New York 10014, USA
Penguin Books Australia Ltd, 250 Camberwell Road, Camberwell, Victoria 3124, Australia
Penguin Books Canada Ltd, 10 Alcorn Avenue, Toronto, Ontario, Canada M4V 3B2
Penguin Books India (P) Ltd, 11 Community Centre, Panchsheel Park, New Delhi – 110 017, India
Penguin Books (NZ) Ltd, Cnr Rosedale and Airborne Roads, Albany, Auckland, New Zealand
Penguin Books (South Africa) (Pty) Ltd, 24 Sturdee Avenue, Rosebank 2196, South Africa

Penguin Books Ltd, Registered Offices: 80 Strand, London WC2R ORL, England

www.penguin.com

First edition published 1965
This edition published 2000
Reprinted 2004
9

Copyright © Original translations by T. S. Dorsch, 1965
© Introduction, revised translations, new
material and notes by Penelope Murray, 2000, 2004
All rights reserved

Set in 10/12.5 pt Monotype Bembo
Typeset by Rowland Phototypesetting Ltd, Bury St Edmunds, Suffolk
Printed in Great Britain by Clays Ltd, St Ives plc

CONTENTS

INTRODUCTION   vii
1. *Homer and the Early Greek Poets*   viii
2. *Aristophanes*   xvi
3. *Gorgias and the Sophists*   xx
4. *Plato*   xxiii
5. *Aristotle*   xxix
6. *The Alexandrians*   xxxvi
7. *Horace*   xxxix
8. *Longinus*   xliv
9. *Epilogue*   l
FURTHER READING   lii
LITERARY CHRONOLOGY   lviii

PLATO
Ion   1
Republic 2   15
Republic 3   24
Republic 10   40
ARISTOTLE
Poetics   57
HORACE
The Art of Poetry   98
LONGINUS
On the Sublime   113

NOTES   167

1112 64

INTRODUCTION

Literary criticism is a label that covers a number of different activities. In the narrow sense in which it is customarily used today, it refers to the analysis and interpretation of texts; but in its wider application literary criticism is concerned with more fundamental questions about the nature and function of literature: what is literature? How is it created? What are its effects? How do we evaluate it? Literary criticism can include scholarly exegesis, evaluative judgement, prescriptive criticism, literary history, and theory, and thus might be broadly defined as discourse about literature. But literature itself is not a stable or self-evident category, so that discourse will inevitably vary with the changing nature of the literature that is its object. As T. S. Eliot observed, 'Our criticism from age to age will reflect the things that the age demands.'[1]

In the Western tradition, attitudes to literature have been profoundly shaped by the great writers and thinkers of classical antiquity. For it was they who invented much of the critical vocabulary and terminology which we still use today, and, as with so many areas of our culture, it was they who first formulated some of the most basic and enduring questions. Literary critics throughout the ages have returned again and again to classical themes, and it would scarcely be an exaggeration to say that the history of criticism cannot properly be understood without some knowledge of the key ancient texts from which later approaches to literature were developed. Principal amongst these are the works of the four authors presented in this volume – Plato, Aristotle, Horace and Longinus – all of whom have exerted a seminal influence on the discourse of criticism in the Western world.

Before turning to the texts themselves, however, some account needs to be given of the background from which they emerged. For literary criticism did not spring up as a ready-made entity in the fourth century BC. The point is well put by the critic Tzvetan Todorov when he says: 'Aristotle's *Poetics*, 2,500 years old, is at once the first work entirely devoted to "literary theory" . . . and one of the most important in the canon. The simultaneous presence of these two features is not without paradox: it is as if a man with an already greying moustache were to emerge from his mother's womb.'² That striking image reminds us that the *Poetics* is not only the starting point, but also the culmination, of a tradition. Many of its ideas have their roots in the literature of earlier periods, and behind it lies a whole inheritance of speculation about the nature of poetry which goes right back to the first-known Western poet, Homer. Indeed, the origins of criticism in Greece are deeply bound up with poetry, for it is in response to poetry that many of the fundamental doctrines of ancient literary criticism are formulated, and it is in poetry that the impulse to criticism first manifests itself. Theoretical discourse about literature and the critical analysis of it, what we might call criticism proper, is, of course, a subsequent development, but in order to understand that development we need to consider the ways in which poetry was envisaged by poets themselves in the 'pre-theoretical' period. For criticism has its beginnings in the reflections of the early Greek poets on the nature of their art.

1. *Homer and the Early Greek Poets*

When Homer invokes the Muse in the opening line of the *Iliad* ('Sing, goddess, the wrath of Peleus' son, Achilles'), that is already a signal that we are about to listen to a specialized form of discourse, one that is bestowed on the poet by the higher authority of a goddess, who gives him privileged knowledge about the famous deeds of great heroes of the past; and they in turn will be immortalized in the song which the poet himself is singing. The Homeric poems tell us much about the nature and function of poetry and of how the poet's role was conceived. From the invocations to the Muses, from the words spoken by Homer's characters, and from the descriptions of bards which are embedded in the *Odyssey*, we learn of the celebratory function of poetry, of the fame it confers by preserving the memory of past greatness, of the pleasure it brings to its audience, and of its power to affect the emotions. The bard himself is an honoured figure, respected not least because of his special relationship with the Muses, who love poets, teach them and give them the gift of poetry. But the bard is also a craftsman, esteemed by those whom he serves for his professional skills.

The attitudes that we find in Homer are taken up and developed by the poets who followed him. In the seventh century BC, the peasant poet Hesiod, for example, expands on the theme of poetic inspiration in his *Theogony*, and in a canonical and much-imitated account he describes how the Muses met him on Mount Helicon as he was tending his sheep, and singled him out to be a poet. They plucked for him a staff of laurel and breathed into him a divine voice so that he could sing of past and future, and celebrate the immortal gods. The immortalizing powers of poetry are particularly celebrated in the victory odes of the lyric poet Pindar in the fifth century BC, who, like all the greatest Greek poets, is painfully aware of the stark divide between gods and mortals, and of the transience of human life. Nevertheless, he believes that mortality can be transcended and that poetry above all has the power to achieve this transcendence: a man's glory dies unless it is remembered in song; language is more lasting than deeds; poetry is a treasure house which cannot be destroyed, a child which lives on after its parents are dead; it has a power even greater than that of sculpture, since it is not only everlasting in time, but can also travel across the boundaries of space. More than any other Greek poet, Pindar is conscious of being a chosen individual, and he speaks of himself as the prophet and herald of the Muses, who has special knowledge which sets him apart from other men. A frequent motif in his poetry is the superiority of natural talent over learning, a contrast which became a commonplace of ancient literary criticism: the question of which of the two, art or nature, was the more important was debated for centuries. In later ages Pindar himself was to become a symbol of overwhelming natural force, too great to be constrained by the conventional rules of art, the paradigm of wild and untutored genius. But for Pindar and his contemporaries, craft and inspiration were not incompatible: poetry depended on both.

Throughout early Greek poetry the major functions of poetry were to give pleasure and to preserve the memory of great deeds from oblivion; but poetry was also regarded as the source of ethical wisdom and practical guidance for living. In the oral culture of early Greece poetry was the prime medium through which the values of society were reflected and handed down, hence its prestige. From earliest times the moral and didactic functions of poetry were emphasized, and the poet himself was regarded as a teacher, an attitude which can be summed up in the words spoken by Aeschylus in Aristophanes' play *Frogs*: 'Children have a master to teach them, grown-ups have the poets.' It is only against this background of the central importance of poetry in Greek society that we can begin to understand the ways in which ancient literary criticism developed. For Greek criticism is not primarily concerned with 'literary' or aesthetic matters, but rather with philosophical questions relating to the moral authority and ethical value of literature. The mainstream of ancient literary criticism takes it for granted that poetry, and literature in general, is a form of communication, and that literature and morality are intimately connected.

The truth value of poetry was an important preoccupation of poets and their critics throughout antiquity. From Homer onwards, poets claimed to have special knowledge vouchsafed to them by the Muses, daughters of Memory. Thus, before the catalogue of ships in *Iliad* (2.484–92) the poet calls on the Muses to tell him who were the leaders and princes of the Greeks who went to Troy, for they, as goddesses, are eyewitnesses of events and know everything, whereas men depend on hearsay and know nothing. In the *Odyssey*, Odysseus praises the bard, Demodocus, for the accuracy of his song about the Achaeans' fate at Troy, saying that either the Muse or Apollo must have taught him because he sings as though he had himself been there (8.487–91). Hesiod depicted the Muses on Mount Olympus singing of the past, present and future (*Theogony* 36–9), and clearly the gift of poetry which the goddesses conferred on their chosen bards involved the power of true speech. Pindar often claims to have special knowledge from the Muses, as we have seen, and he insists on the truthfulness of his own poetry, calling on Truth, the daughter of Zeus, as a source of inspiration for his song.

But alongside this insistence on the truth was the consciousness that poets could also lie. For, whatever poets might claim about the truth status of their own poems, the existence of variant legends made it clear that truth could vary from poet to poet. Indeed, the agonal or competitive context of performance in early Greece positively encouraged poets to come up with competing versions of traditional stories, so that one poet's truth could easily become another poet's lie. Thus the poet of the *Homeric Hymn to Dionysus* prefaces his own account of the god's birth with a list of alternative versions of the story, all of which he criticizes as false: other poets lie, whereas he alone tells the truth. Pindar criticizes Homer for his seductive falsifications, and finds fault with traditional myths which deceive because they are 'subtly decked out with intricate lies' (*Nemean* 7.20–24; *Olympian* 1.28–9). And the lyric poet Stesichorus wrote a famous *Palinode* in which he rejected the traditional portrayal of Helen as a faithless wife, who deserted her husband and started the Trojan war: 'This is not the true story; you didn't go on the well-benched ships, nor did you come to the high towers of Troy' (fragment 192). According to Stesichorus, Homer was wrong: in reality it was only her phantom that went to Troy. But how do we, the audience, know which version of the story to believe? The only guarantee the poet can offer is the inspiration of the Muse. But once we are faced with the possibility that poets lie, how do we know that this particular poet's version of the truth is true? The Muse becomes an alibi for the poet's own invention.

The fluidity of Greek myth meant that at a basic level poets could be perceived as liars because the stories which they told were incompatible with each other. But the notion of the lying poet was more complicated than that. When the Muses met Hesiod on Mount Helicon and chose him to be a poet they said to him: 'We know how to tell many lies (*pseudea*) that are like the truth; but we also know how to tell the truth when we wish.'

These famous and enigmatic lines have been much debated. According to one interpretation, Hesiod is here distinguishing between two different types of poetry, Homeric epic and his own didactic style: the Muses tell lies to the poets of heroic epic, but speak the truth to Hesiod himself. Certainly the Muses' words, as Hesiod reports them, would seem to guarantee the truth of his own poetry, and although he makes no explicit reference to Homer, it is quite possible that he means to dissociate himself from the poetry of his rival. On the other hand he may be making a more general statement about the kinds of utterances that the Muses can inspire. But if so, what do the Muses mean? For the contrast which they draw is not a straightforward one between truth and lies, but between truth and 'lies which are like the truth', that is between truth and the illusion of truth. Their words seem to point to the illusory nature of poetry, or at least of certain sorts of poetry, and possibly even to its fictional status. The Muses, and by implication the poets whom they inspire, have the power to make us believe their stories, whether they are true or not, because they can make their stories plausible. They can speak the truth or they can make things up, but either way they will be believed. To put it another way, we might say that the contrast which the Muses make is not between truth and lies, but between truth and fiction. Part of the difficulty in interpreting this passage (and others like it) stems from the fact that the Greek word *pseudos*, which I have translated as 'lie', has a wide semantic range covering lies, falsehood, factual error, deliberate deceit and literary invention, or fiction. Some would argue that it is anachronistic to speak of a notion of fiction at this early period, and indeed the question of how far the Greeks at any time distinguished between lying and fiction in a way that corresponds to modern categories is highly complex. But the preoccupation with truth and lies which we find in so many of the early poets suggests that such issues were of central concern. At the very least we can say that the problematic nature of poetic truth is recognized from very early on in Greek literature.

There are also indications that already in the early period poets were aware of their ability to craft and fashion their narratives. They might claim inspiration from the Muses, but they did not present themselves simply as unconscious instruments of the divine. In the *Odyssey* (17.382–5) the bard is described as a *demioergos*, a worker who is prized for his technical skill, and there are frequent references to the poet's expertise in early Greek poetry. The art of poetry is traditionally described in terms of weaving and carpentry, and the increasing use of craft metaphors to describe the poet's activity from Pindar onwards is indicative of the importance attached to the craft elements in poetic composition. By the end of the fifth century BC the poet is regularly described as a *poietes*, a 'maker', and his product is a *poiema*, a 'made-up thing'.

Together with this idea of poetry as a made-up, crafted, object, a composition in the literal sense, goes an awareness of the poet's inventive powers. Indeed, the theme of storytelling is central to one of our earliest Greek texts, the *Odyssey*. Bards and their songs feature prominently in the poem, and Odysseus himself is presented as a storyteller *par excellence*, entertaining his audiences with a wide variety of different types of narrative, ranging from the ostensibly true, but fantastic, tales of his wanderings (the lotus-eaters, the Cyclops, the Sirens, Scylla and Charybdis, the cattle of the Sun, and so on) to the sequence of false, but plausible, stories he tells in the second half of the poem. Odysseus' bard-like qualities are self-consciously highlighted at several points in Homer's narrative. For example, like the ideal audience of the *Odyssey* itself, the Phaeacians sit silent and spellbound as they listen to Odysseus' tale (11.333-4), and their king, Alcinous, praises him for putting together his tale 'skilfully like a bard' (11.368). Odysseus' capacity to charm and enchant his audience is also underlined by the swineherd Eumaeus, who tells Penelope how the disguised Odysseus kept him enthralled for three nights and three days with the tale of his sufferings: 'Just as a man gazes on a bard whom the gods have taught to sing songs of loveliness to mortals, and whenever he begins to sing they would gladly listen to him for ever, so did this man enchant me as he sat in my hall' (17.518-21). The verisimilitude of the lying tales which Odysseus tells to Penelope is described in words which are very similar to those spoken by the Muses in Hesiod's *Theogony*, for he spoke 'many lies like the truth' (19.203). And at the climactic point of the poem when Odysseus strings the bow with which he will slay the suitors and finally reveal his identity, he is again likened to a bard: 'As when a man well-skilled in the lyre and song easily stretches the string round a new peg, fitting the pliant sheep-gut at either end, so without effort did Odysseus string the great bow. He took it in his right hand and tried the string, and it sang beautifully beneath his touch' (21.406-11). The repeated analogy between hero and bard, and particularly the emphasis on Odysseus' bard-like storytelling abilities, suggests that the *Odyssey* poet himself is fully aware of his own role as the artificer and shaper of his poetic narrative.

The *Odyssey* is thus a highly self-conscious poem, which celebrates, amongst other things, the delights of poetry and song: as Odysseus himself says, there is no greater pleasure in life than to listen to the bard at a feast, when the tables are laden with meat and the wine flows (9.5–11). That pleasure is regularly described as a form of enchantment, often with erotic overtones: Odysseus enchants his listeners, just as Calypso and Circe enchant their captives with their spells (1.56–7; 10.291, 318, 326); Penelope enchants the suitors with her loveliness (18.212, 282) and in the opening book of the poem she herself describes the bard's songs as 'enchantments', a word which is repeatedly used of the alluring power of song and its seductive charms. Song and sexual seduction are brought together most vividly in the image of the Sirens, the divine singers who lure sailors to their deaths by the loveliness of their voices and their omniscient knowledge (12.39–54, 158–200). As with the spells of those other seductive females, Circe and Calypso, the pleasure that the Sirens offer is one that brings with it a forgetfulness of self; but in their case that forgetfulness is deadly. Poetry enthrals, but the nature of its power is ambiguous: it can tell the truth, but it can also persuade us that false things are true; it offers us pleasure, but at the time it destroys our judgement.

Poetry also has the power to arouse intense emotions, and we find both Penelope and Odysseus weeping as they listen to the voice of the bard. Penelope cannot bear to hear Phemius singing of the homecoming of the Achaeans because it stirs up her longing for her husband (1.336–44), and Odysseus himself is twice reduced to tears when Demodocus sings of the fall of Troy. The first time (8.83–95) he covers his face with his cloak to hide his grief, but the second time (8.521–31) he melts, and sheds tears like a woman bewailing her husband as she watches him dying in a defeated city: the graphic and beautiful simile not only describes Odysseus in terms more suitable to Penelope (thus underlining the reciprocity between husband and wife), it also shows us that poetry has the power to make a man cry like a woman. Perhaps we can see here, too, a prefiguration of the paradoxical pleasure of tragedy, that the depiction of suffering can give pleasure. There is certainly an awareness in Homer of the pleasure of remembered suffering: so Eumaeus suggests to Odysseus that they take pleasure in each other's grim sorrows by recalling them, 'for a man finds joy even in suffering, once it is over' (15.399–400); and when Odysseus and Penelope are finally reunited, 'after they had taken their pleasure in delightful love, they took pleasure in tales, speaking each to the other'. She told him of all that she had endured in the halls at the hands of the wicked suitors, and he told her of all the sorrows that he had endured, 'and she rejoiced as she listened, and did not close her eyelids in sleep until he had finished his tale' (23.300–309). This emphasis on the affective power of poetry, first articulated in that of Homer, is one that remains central to Greek poetics: as we shall see, it played a major role in Plato's attack on poetry, and in Aristotle's defence of it; it also formed the basis of Longinus' theory of the sublime.

It will be clear from the material I have considered so far that Greek attitudes to poetry were shaped long before the advent of literary criticism or literary theory. For Greek poetry contained within it a self-reflective and critical spirit which was there from the beginning: the earliest critics were the poets themselves. This critical impulse was fostered no doubt in part by the competitive instinct which permeated all aspects of Greek life, including poetry and song. Hesiod praises the benefits which a healthy rivalry can bring, when potter vies with potter, carpenter with carpenter, beggar with beggar, and poet with poet (*Works and Days* 25–6), and he boasts of the tripod which he won as a prize for his victory in a poetry contest at the funeral games in honour of Amphidamas in Chalcis, which he subsequently dedicated to the Muses. Funeral games and festivals were important occasions for the staging of poetic contests such as Hesiod describes, and would have involved audiences as well as poets in the process of judging and evaluating rival performances. The competitive nature of Greek poetic performance continued to be a feature of Greek culture, and, with the emergence of drama in Athens in the sixth century BC, poetry and the judging of poetry become a matter of major civic concern. Tragedy and comedy were performed before vast audiences at popular festivals in honour of the god Dionysus, where dramatists would compete for the coveted first prize. The plays were judged by a panel of citizens chosen by lot, but every member of the audience could be regarded as a potential critic. Poetry itself features prominently as the object of satire and debate in Old Comedy, and particularly in the plays of the most famous comic poet, Aristophanes. Literary pastiche, caricature and parody are staple ingredients of all his comedies, and two of his plays focus on tragedy as their central theme.

2. Aristophanes

In the *Thesmophoriazusae*, produced in 411 BC, Aristophanes portrays Euripides as a stereotypical woman-hater who has repeatedly slandered the female sex in his tragedies. He has discovered that the women of Athens are plotting their revenge on him, and tries to persuade the young and effeminate tragic poet Agathon (familiar to us also from Plato's *Symposium*) to join the women and act as a spy for him. In the opening scene of the play Euripides and his kinsman, Mnesilochus, visit Agathon, whom they find hard at work on his latest tragedy, dressed in drag and in the very throes of creation. When Mnesilochus comments on Agathon's outlandish appearance, he replies:

Come, come, my aged friend, do I detect a note of envy in your criticism? I refuse to be riled. I wear my clothes to suit my inspiration. A dramatic poet has to merge his whole personality into what he is describing. If he is describing a woman's actions, he has to participate in her experience, body and soul . . . If he's writing about a man, he's got all the bits and pieces already, as it were; but what nature hasn't provided, art can imitate . . . Anyway, it's terribly uncultured for a poet to go round looking all wild and hairy. Look at Ibycus, and Anacreon of Teos, and Alcaeus, with those exquisitely tempered harmonies of theirs – they all wore the proper ministrel's sash, and their movements were graceful, like mine. And Phrynichus, you actually went to his recitals perhaps: what a handsome fellow and how beautifully dressed – and that's why his dramas were so beautiful too: what you write depends so much on what you are, you know.[3]

The whole scene offers plenty of scope for verbal and visual humour, much of it obscene, which Aristophanes exploits to the full; but beneath the hilarity there lurk some important ideas about the nature of the relationship between the poet and his work, which become key issues in later criticism. Agathon justifies his bizarre appearance and conduct on two grounds: firstly that in order to create convincing drama the poet must identify himself with the characters whom he portrays, indeed he must as far as possible become those characters; and secondly, that poetry will reflect the nature of the poet who composes it. We also have in this passage the first occurrence in extant literature of the key critical term *mimesis*. Here it is obviously used in the sense of 'dramatic impersonation', and, significantly, in the context of a male poet impersonating a female character. This scene prefigures Plato's development of the notion of *mimesis* in book 3 of the *Republic*, where issues of gender are similarly implicated; but Plato is deeply worried by the process involved in the kind of male performance of female characters which Aristophanes' Agathon so blithely advocates.

A number of Aristophanes' plays contain detailed and sophisticated parodies of scenes from Euripidean tragedy, but tragedy as a genre receives its most extensive and far-reaching treatment in the *Frogs*, a play produced in 405 BC, on the eve of Athens's disastrous defeat at the hands of Sparta in the Peloponnesian War, and shortly after the deaths of both Euripides and Sophocles. The play opens with Dionysus, the god of drama, determined to go down to Hades to fetch back Euripides; when he arrives there, however, he finds that a great contest is about to take place between Aeschylus (long since dead) and the newly arrived Euripides for the Chair of Tragedy, which he is asked to judge. A large part of the play is taken up with the competition between Aeschylus, the embodiment of rectitude and old-fashioned values, in literature as in life, and Euripides, the representative of cynical modernity and all its wickedness. Euripides attacks Aeschylus for his long-winded and incomprehensible language, his turgid imagery and his grotesquely inflated style, and claims that Tragedy was in a terrible state when he inherited her – swollen, overweight and unhealthy. But he has put her on a diet and slimmed her down, restoring her to health by filling his plays with characters who act and speak in an intelligible way, like ordinary human beings. Aeschylus defends himself on the grounds that the heroes of his tragedies and their heroic subject matter have taught the Athenians to be honourable, patriotic and brave, and that lofty themes must be expressed in lofty language. Euripides' plays, by contrast, focus on unsavoury topics like sex and crime, and are peopled with adulterous women, cripples and beggars, dressed in rags and with the diction to match. In a scene of brilliant stylistic parody both poets criticize each other for their incompetence in the composition of prologues and lyrics, and finally try to settle their dispute by actually weighing lines of poetry in a pair of scales. Though Aeschylus' diction predictably turns out to be more weighty than that of Euripides, Dionysus is reluctant to choose between them. Switching tack, he says that he needs a poet to save the city, and will take back with him the one who can best advise the Athenians on their perilous situation. But in the event he cannot decide on the basis of the political advice which each poet offers, and chooses Aeschylus simply because he feels like it. The arbitrary nature of Dionysus' decision suggests that there is little to choose between them in terms of their poetic stature.

The literary contest is remarkable both for its detailed stylistic parodies of the two tragedians (which presupposes a certain level of familiarity with both of their styles on the part of the audience), and for the views of poetry which it sets before us. There can be no more potent witness to the importance attached to poetry in Greek society than this play. For despite their differences, Aeschylus and Euripides both agree that the duty of the poet is to educate. When Aeschylus asks Euripides what qualities he looks for in a good poet, the latter replies unhesitatingly, 'Technical skill, and the ability to give advice, to make people better citizens' (1008–9). Aeschylus himself enlarges on this idea, enumerating the various ways in which poets, from earliest times, have been of service to society: Orpheus instructed mankind in religion, Musaeus in healing and oracles, Hesiod in agriculture, and Homer in the arts of war. (This theme became something of a commonplace in later literary criticism, as we can see from Horace's *Art of Poetry* (391ff.), where the same argument is developed with a similar list of examples.) Aristophanes' play itself stages the role of the poet as teacher by offering serious political advice to the audience through the voice of its chorus:

> We chorus folk two privileges prize:
> To amuse you, citizens, and advise.
>
> (lines 686–7)

They then go on to urge that the Athenians who had been deprived of their citizenship after the collapse of the oligarchic revolution of 411 should be reinstated so that all Athenians could fight together to save their city. Aristophanes' play, whose central theme is the search for a poet to teach and advise the city, appropriates for comedy the didactic function that Aeschylus and Euripides regard as the hallmark of tragedy.

But perhaps more significant than any explicit statements about the poet's role as teacher is the implicit assumption, shared by both Aeschylus and Euripides, that poetry, and particularly drama, profoundly affects people's behaviour. Poetry, says Aeschylus, should be morally improving, and drama should offer good role models for people to follow. His own depiction of the heroic valour of the men of old encouraged similar behaviour in his audience: who could have watched the *Seven Against Thebes* without wanting to go off straight away and slay the enemy? And his *Persians* instilled in the audience the desire to win. But Euripides has promoted selfishness, idleness and cynicism amongst the people, and harmed the city by making adulterous women the subject of his plays, thereby encouraging the women of Athens to behave in the same way.

'Did I invent the story of Phaedra?' asks Euripides.

'No', replies Aeschylus, 'such things do happen, but poets should keep quiet about them, not put them on the stage.'

Both poets assume a direct connection between literature and life: the argument that what you see on the stage is in any way separable from what you do in everyday life does not occur to either of them, nor is there any suggestion that aesthetic experience may be different from other kinds of activities. This is comedy, of course, and should be treated with the appropriate pinch of salt; but, as we shall see, Plato agrees wholeheartedly on the crucial importance of role models in literature, and the question of how far people's behaviour is influenced by the depictions of art remains a subject of lively debate today.

The dramatic festivals at which tragedy and comedy were performed involved the citizen body as a whole, and it is clear that poetry played an integral part in the life of the community. Other playwrights apart from Aristophanes also treated poetry as subject of comedy (the titles of other plays we know of include *The Muses* and *The Poet*, and we have comic fragments on literary themes), but the *Frogs* has a special place in the history of criticism. In it we have parody and criticism of tragedy, but also parody of criticism itself. This is particularly evident in the scene in which each poet finds fault with the other's prologues, where we are given a lengthy demonstration of the detailed criticism of poetry and language which had become fashionable in intellectual circles. Euripides objects to the tautology in Aeschylus' line, 'Lo, to this land I come and do return', and Aeschylus retaliates by ridiculing Euripides for saying that Oedipus 'became' the most unfortunate of men, he *was* so all along, and so on. Dionysus, in true layman's fashion, pronounces the criticism brilliant, but adds that he doesn't understand a word of it (1168).

Much of Aristophanes' satirizing of Euripides, both in the *Frogs* and elsewhere, centres on his newfangled intellectualism and the sophistic spirit which pervades his plays. Like the Socrates of the *Clouds*, Aristophanes' Euripides embodies the new mood of scepticism, with its subversive attitude towards morality and tradition, which characterized Athenian society in the late fifth century BC. That mood was particularly associated with the sophists, itinerant teachers who travelled through the Greek world offering instruction on a variety of subjects, which included the study of language, the analysis of poetry, and, most significantly for the history of criticism, the techniques of oratory.

3. *Gorgias and the Sophists*

One of the most famous and influential of these early teachers of rhetoric was Gorgias of Leontini, who visited Athens in 427 BC and amazed the Athenians with his dazzling speeches. In his *Encomium of Helen*, a rhetorical display piece in defence of Helen of Troy, he produces a number of reasons why Helen should not be blamed for eloping with Paris. One possible line of argument, developed at considerable length, is that she was persuaded to do so by the irresistible power of speech, *logos*. Speech, Gorgias claims, is a great master, with the power to stop fear, remove sorrow, create joy and increase pity. All poetry is speech in metre, and everyone recognizes the remarkable ability of poetry to arouse the emotions: 'Those who hear it feel the shudders of fear, the tears of pity and the longings of grief, and through the words, they experience in their own souls the successes and misfortunes which affect the actions and persons of others' (section 9). The effects of speech on the mind are similar to those of drugs on the body: just as some drugs are beneficial, and others harmful, some speeches give pain, others pleasure; some induce fear, others confidence, and some 'poison and bewitch the mind with an evil persuasion' (section 14). The mind is powerless to resist; therefore if Helen was persuaded by speech, she acted under compulsion and cannot be blamed for her actions.

In this passage Gorgias articulates a number of ideas which have an important place in the development of literary critical theory. His description of the way in which poetry works on the emotions clearly influenced Plato's views on audience psychology and the dangerous effects of poetry, which he too describes as a *pharmakon*, a drug, and the emphasis on pity and fear in Gorgias' analysis anticipates Aristotle's association of those emotions with tragedy. The emotional power of poetry had been recognized from Homer onwards, but in Gorgias' formulation the characteristics traditionally associated with poetry are applied to speech in general. The view that poetry is simply 'speech in metre' (later refuted by Aristotle) need not be taken as a serious attempt at a definition of poetry, since Gorgias' purpose here is not to distinguish poetry from prose, but rather to establish that, because both use words, whatever power poetry has, prose will have too. However, if poetry is treated as a branch of *logos* like any other, it inevitably loses its privileged status. The blurring of the boundaries between poetry and oratory, and the view of poetry as simply one of many modes of discourse is one that is characteristic of the rhetorical tradition which came to dominate classical theories of literature in later ages. And the question of what, if anything, differentiates poetry from other forms of literature is a perennial issue in the history of poetics.

The rapid development of prose and the rise of new genres of discourse in the fifth century BC had decisive consequences for the evolution of literary criticism. As we have seen, the earliest critical reflections are by poets, and are integral to poetry itself. But with the emergence of prose, criticism becomes a secondary activity, separable from the object of its study. The sophistic study of language and the practical training of orators which dominated education in Athens in the late fifth century BC brought with it a new approach to literature, which now included prose and verse alike. Exegesis of poetry, such as that parodied in the prologue scene of the *Frogs*, was a regular feature of sophistic education, and teachers of rhetoric habitually used material from the poets to illustrate grammatical and stylistic points. But the purpose of such study was not to understand the theory and practice of poetry *per se*, but rather to teach budding orators how to speak persuasively in the practical context of assemblies and law courts. The analysis of poetry thus becomes subordinate to the demands of rhetoric.

The other great challenge to the supremacy of poetry came from the newly emerging discipline of philosophy. Already in the sixth century BC the Ionian philosopher-poet Xenophanes had criticized epic poetry on moral grounds, saying that Homer and Hesiod attributed to the gods 'all things that bring shame and reproach to men: theft, adultery and deceit' (*fragment* B11). He ridiculed the traditional, anthropomorphic conception of deity, pointing out that each race attributes to such gods their own characteristics ('The Ethiopians say that their gods are snub-nosed and dark, the Thracians that theirs have blue eyes and red hair', *fragment* B16), and that animals would also make gods in their own image, if they had the ability to do so. It was doubtless in response to such criticisms of immorality that others rose to Homer's defence by offering allegorical interpretations of his poems. This practice is said to have begun with Theagenes of Rhegium, allegedly the first man to write about Homer. He explained, for instance, that the battles of the gods represented the opposition of elements or qualities such as dry and wet, hot and cold, heavy and light, fire and water. Apollo symbolizes fire, Poseidon water, Artemis the moon, Hera the air, and similarly with abstract qualities, Athena represents wisdom, Ares folly, Aphrodite desire, Hermes reason, and so on. This kind of allegorical interpretation of works of literature, and particularly the poems of Homer and Hesiod, was well established by the end of the fifth century BC, and was to have a long history, notably in that branch of criticism inspired by Stoic and, later, by Neoplatonist philosophy. At the heart of allegorical criticism was the desire to find ways of defending literature against the strictures of moralists and philosophers, such as those first formulated by Xenophanes in Greece in the sixth century BC. His criticisms anticipate Plato's attack on the poets in the *Republic*, and can be seen as the beginnings of what Plato himself described as the 'ancient quarrel between philosophy and poetry' (*Republic* 607b).

4. *Plato*

With Plato we move into a different register. For the first time poetry is the subject of a sustained philosophical critique, which raises fundamental and enduring questions about the nature of literature and its justification. Plato wrote no treatise devoted specifically to poetry, yet his engagement with poetry was intense and life-long, as we can see not only from the dialogues in which poetry is explicitly discussed (notably the *Ion, Protagoras, Republic* and *Laws*), but also from the frequent references and allusions to poetry throughout his work. Many of the dialogues themselves have affinities with poetry in their use of imagery, myth and dramatic technique, and the poetic nature of Plato's style has been recognized since antiquity. There was even a tradition (romantic, but in all probability false) that Plato had written poetry himself in his youth, but abandoned his early passion when he met Socrates and turned to philosophy. Certainly Plato writes about poetry like no other philosopher, before or since; for he is deeply imbued with poetry, and deeply attracted to it, yet determined to resist its spell. Hence the paradox that the most poetical of philosophers banished poetry from his ideal state.

Plato's notorious hostility to poetry strikes the modern reader as very odd: in the *Republic* he is concerned not merely with censoring poetry, but with removing it altogether, and his target is the entire heritage of Greek literature. Though hymns to the gods and encomia to good men will be permitted in the ideal state, there will be no place for the epics of Homer, or the tragedies of Aeschylus, Sophocles and Euripides, long since canonized as high art. Why is Plato so afraid of poetry that he has to abolish even its greatest masterworks? One factor that we need to remember when considering this question is that poetry in Plato's day was not simply a minority interest indulged in by the leisured few, but a central feature in the life of the community, as we have seen. Greek education was centred round poetry (together with its accompanying elements of music, song, and dance), and it was through the medium of poetry that the values of society were transmitted. Poetry played a central role not only in the education of the young, but also in the lives of adult citizens through their participation (both as performers and as audience) in the various public festivals at which drama, lyric and epic were performed. The vehemence of Plato's attack can thus be seen at least in part as a reaction against the moral authority and cultural prestige of poetry. For his project is none other than to replace poetry by philosophy as the central educational discourse in Athenian society.

But Plato's critique of poetry is not merely of historical interest – for Plato was the first thinker to formulate major questions about the function and role of art in society, and his writings on poetry, music and the visual arts are fundamental texts in the history of Western aesthetics. Many of the questions which we still debate today were first raised in Plato's work. What is poetry, and indeed art in general, and how does it operate? What is and should be the function of imaginative literature in society? Is it dangerous in that it encourages emotions and feelings which ought to be kept in check, or is it therapeutic in that it allows us to give vent to our emotions in a harmless way? Should there be censorship? Is literature (which now, of course, includes television and film) a form of escapism or does it deepen our insight into the nature of people and the world around us? How can literature justify itself? These questions might seem to us somewhat academic when confined to poetry, but if we ask them in relation to popular entertainment and the mass media, the closest modern analogue to poetry in classical Athens, the force of Plato's critique is immediately apparent. In fact, many of the arguments used by critics in relation to television, for example – that the depiction of violence and antisocial behaviour encourages similar behaviour in those who watch it, that television is primarily concerned with gratifying large audiences irrespective of quality, that it presents us with dubious role models – are strikingly similar to those which Plato uses against epic and tragedy.

Like all the poets before him, Plato is acutely aware of the pleasure that poetry affords its listeners; but for him that is the source of poetry's greatest danger. In the *Republic*, pleasure is the key factor in determining what makes poetry 'poetic' (387b), but pleasure has nothing to do with value. Poetry – and particularly tragedy – aims solely at the gratification of its audience and not at moral improvement. And since the ignorant masses invariably enjoy what is bad for them, poetry is dangerous precisely in proportion to the pleasure it gives, and must therefore be censored accordingly. In the *Laws*, where Plato is more concerned with the practical possibilities of establishing a workable society, he takes a more positive view of pleasure, and there is much emphasis on the constructive role of poetry, music and dance in the education of the young and in the cultural life of the citizens as a whole. But though poetry has its place, it is to be strictly subordinated to the purposes of the rulers. All the city must sing, but the main task of poetry and song is to turn the soul towards virtue (*Laws* 664–5). When poems are performed at public festivals, the Minister of Education will select composers on the basis of the excellence of their conduct in the community rather than on their artistic ability; no one should dare to sing an unauthorized song, 'not even if it were sweeter than the hymns of Orpheus' (*Laws* 829c–e). Only the morally virtuous will be allowed to compose poetry. Pleasure is not an appropriate criterion by which to judge poetry, because poetry should always be subservient to the aims of morality.

A large part of poetry's appeal for Plato stems from its ability to arouse the emotions. In the *Ion* (535d–e) we are given a vivid description of the rhapsode's emotional state as he performs his recitals from Homer: his eyes fill with tears, his hair stands on end, and his heart pounds, and when he looks down at his audience he sees that they too are affected in the same way. As I have said, the emotive power of poetry had been recognized from Homer onwards, but Plato was the first to cast doubt on the value of this power. In the *Republic*, one of the central arguments against poetry is that it is psychologically damaging, for it appeals to an inferior element in the soul, and encourages us to indulge in emotions which ought to be kept firmly in check by the control of reason (606d). By engaging our emotions and activating our natural desire to weep and wail at misfortunes, epic and tragedy disable our rational responses and make us incapable of judging and reflecting on the performances we are experiencing. Poetry, by means of the natural magic inherent in its throbbing rhythms and seductive melodies, draws us into an emotional identification with the characters it portrays in a way that threatens the health of the psyche. And the worst of it is that poetry has the power to corrupt even the best of men in this way, since surrendering to our emotions is so intensely pleasurable (605c–d). Hence the only defence against poetry is to banish it altogether, like a lover who tears himself away from a passion that is doing him no good (607e).

One of Plato's most important and influential theories about poetry is that it is a form of *mimesis* or 'imitation'. The word *mimesis* has a wide semantic range, covering impersonation, copying, imitation and representation, and Greek draws no clear distinction between these meanings. Plato's own use of the term is highly flexible: mimetic language is used not only of the arts of poetry, painting, music and dance, but also, for example, of the relationship between language and reality, and of that between the material world and its eternal paradigm. The precise connotations of the word will vary according to context, but broadly speaking we can say that *mimesis* and its cognates indicate a relation between an existing entity and something which is made to resemble it. We first encounter the term *mimesis* in the *Republic* in book 3 (392c) when Plato is considering the question of what kind of literature the future Guardians of his ideal state should study. Having considered the content of such literature, he then moves on to its form, or manner of presentation. Plato distinguishes between two different types of narration which he calls *diegesis* ('narrative'), when the author speaks in his own voice, and *mimesis* ('imitation'), when he speaks in the voice of his characters. Both epic and tragedy involve *mimesis* in this sense, in that they require the reciter (whether actor, rhapsode or schoolboy) to imitate or impersonate the characters whose words he speaks. When someone speaks in the voice of another he makes himself like that person not just in voice, but also in character: he adopts his looks, his gestures and even his thoughts, so that in a sense he almost becomes that person. The role models of literature thus have a direct influence on the lives of those who come into contact with them, for what we enact and see enacted will affect the kind of people we become.

The notion of *mimesis* is further developed in book 10, this time with reference to the Platonic theory of Forms, according to which a metaphysical hierarchy is established, consisting of the ideal world of Forms, the sensible world of particulars, and imitations of the sensible world (595c–597e). Taking painting as the paradigm of *mimesis*, Plato argues that the painter is like someone who picks up a mirror and carries it around with him, instantly creating images of everything that he sees (596d–e). But what he produces are insubstantial reflections of objects in the sensible world, which are themselves less real than the Forms, which alone have true existence. Since poets are also imitators, they, like painters, are condemned to operate at the third level of reality, their products being nothing but worthless imitations which reflect nothing true (597e, 600e). The theory of *mimesis* put forward here, which depends on the example of painting, seems rather different from that expounded in book 3 in the context of what kind of poetry the Guardians ought to perform. There *mimesis* involved a deep identification on the part of the imitator with the object of his imitation, whereas now *mimesis* is defined as the superficial activity of copying appearances. Plato seems to oscillate between regarding the poet's *mimesis* as dangerous, but potentially beneficial, if properly regulated (398a–b), and condemning it as trivial play (602b). This ambivalence arises partly from the fact that the products of *mimesis* can be evaluated in two distinct ways, either in terms of the objects imitated (whether they are good or bad), or in terms of the quality of the imitation (how good the likeness is, how nearly it approximates to reality). As far as Plato is concerned, existing poetry fails on both counts: poets imitate the wrong kind of behaviour and therefore corrupt the souls of their listeners (605c–608b); but they are also incapable of producing a true likeness of goodness and the other moral qualities because they do not know what goodness is (598d–600e). Hence Homer and his fellow poets are to be banished entirely from the ideal state.

The *Republic*'s view that poetry is nothing but a worthless imitation with no grasp of reality would seem at first sight to be incompatible with the more positive image of poetry that emerges from other Platonic dialogues. In the *Ion*, Plato pictures the poet as a god-like being who pours forth beautiful poetry when inspired by the Muses' power. And in a famous and highly influential passage in the *Phaedrus*, poetic inspiration is described as a form of madness bestowed by the Muses:

Taking a tender and virgin soul it rouses and excites it to Bacchic frenzy in lyric and other sorts of poetry, and by glorifying the countless deeds of the past it educates the coming generations. Whoever comes to the doors of poetry without the madness of the Muses, persuaded that he will be a good enough poet through skill (*techne*), is himself unfulfilled, and the sane man's poetry is eclipsed by that of the insane.

(*Phaedrus* 245a)

But despite this eulogy, later on the dialogue (248d–e) the life of the poet is rated sixth in order of merit after the philosopher, the king, the man of affairs, the trainer or the doctor, and the seer. The contradiction between Plato's low rating of the poet's life and his earlier exaltation of the recipient of the Muses' power suggests that his attitude to poetry and poets is ambivalent, just as it is in the *Ion*, where the point about inspiration is made in a not altogether flattering way. For the corollary of the notion of inspiration is that poets have no understanding of their art. Poets are traditionally regarded as teachers in Greek society, but they are unworthy of this role: their work is not based upon rational principles, nor do they have any knowledge of the things which they claim to teach. The negative implications of inspiration are very clearly brought out in the one passage in the entire Platonic corpus where the themes of inspiration and imitation are brought together. In Plato's last work he refers to

an old story . . . that when the poet sits on the tripod of the Muses, he is not in his right mind, but like a spring lets whatever is at hand flow forth. Since his skill is that of imitation he is often forced to contradict himself, when he represents contrasting characters, and he does not know whose words are true.

(*Laws* 719c)

Here the poet is pictured as divinely inspired, but also as a mindless imitator of the characters whom he portrays: either way, the poet is unaware of what he is doing and is therefore incapable of judging his productions. It is the poet's lack of knowledge which Plato consistently attacks, whether that attack is veiled in the ambiguous language of praise, as in the *Ion* and *Phaedrus*, or is more explicitly hostile as in the *Republic*.

Plato's attitude to poetry is neither simple nor consistent: when he banishes poetry he does so in terms which suggest the renunciation of a sinful love in the interests of a higher good; equally, when he speaks of the poet as divinely inspired, that image does not carry with it an unambiguous respect for the poet's message. The ambivalence of Plato's presentation of poets and poetry in his dialogues has generated an extraordinary variety and range of responses, and, paradoxically, given rise to a tradition which elevates the poet's creative powers to an almost god-like status. By ignoring the ironic resonances of Plato's concept of poetic inspiration and by re-interpreting the famous 'mirror' motif of *Republic* book 10 as a means of exploring the relationship between nature and art in a positive way, later writers, and particularly those inspired by Neoplatonism, were able to respond to Plato's provocation by developing a defence of poetry which was constructed out of Plato's own work. Thus, for example, Plotinus, the influential Neoplatonist philosopher of the third century AD, transformed Plato's view by declaring that the artist bypasses the sensible world and looks to the Forms themselves, enabling him to create works of beauty which improve on the imperfections of nature. And the long tradition of apologias for poetry from Aristotle's *Poetics* to Sir Philip Sidney's *Defence of Poetry* (1595) to Shelley's essay of the same name (1821) can all be seen as responses to the challenge that Plato issued when he banished poetry from his *Republic*.

5. *Aristotle*

For Plato poetry is not an object of study in itself; his concerns for poetry and art are ultimately subordinated to his larger philosophical aims, whether epistemological, ontological or ethical, hence his discussions of poetry are always embedded in some wider context. With Aristotle's *Poetics*, however, we arrive at the first work of theoretical criticism devoted specifically to poetry in the Western tradition. Aristotle, Plato's pupil, was no poet. His treatise is written in a spirit of scientific detachment, and he treats poetry no differently from any other field of inquiry, whether it be politics, logic or biology. Poetry is for him an independent art with its own internal logic, and his emphasis is primarily on its formal aspects without reference to the social, political or religious dimensions which had so preoccupied Plato. Poems are, so to speak, objects in their own right which can best be understood through the analysis of their structure and form. As Aristotle makes clear in his introduction, the *Poetics* is intended as an investigation into the nature of poetry through the classification of its different kinds and the analysis of their function and purpose. Though it contains elements of prescriptive criticism and description, it is primarily a work of aesthetic theory, whose object is to understand how poetry operates and the way in which it achieves its effects.

The *Poetics* is in part a response to Plato's strictures against poetry, and the Platonic background is crucial to our understanding of Aristotle's arguments. Whereas Plato views poetry as an inspired, and therefore irrational, activity, Aristotle treats it as the product of skill or art, which is based on rational and intelligible principles. For Plato the poet has no knowledge, and the imitations which he produces are mere reflections of the external world, at third remove from the ultimate reality of the Forms; for Aristotle there is a close relationship between imitation and learning, both at the simplest level (human beings 'differ from other animals in that we are the most imitative of creatures, and learn our earliest lessons by imitation', *Poetics* 1448b), and at the much more sophisticated level where the 'universal' situations of poetry are said to be more philosophical than the particulars of historical narration (1451b). Since poetry presents us with 'the kinds of things that might happen' in human life, it gives us a generalized view of human nature from which we can learn more than we can from particular facts. Plato regards poetry, and especially tragedy, as morally harmful in that it stimulates emotions which ought to be suppressed; according to Aristotle, the ability to engage our emotions is an essential feature of tragedy, and one that is positively beneficial in its effects. Pleasure, which for Plato is the source of poetry's greatest danger, is for Aristotle an intrinsic part of our response to poetry, since all human beings instinctively take delight in 'imitations' (chapter 4).

Aristotle takes over from Plato the idea that poetry, together with other arts such as painting, sculpture, music and dance, is a form of *mimesis*, but, unlike Plato, he nowhere explains what he means by this term. Scholars worry about whether it should be translated as 'imitation', or, alternatively, as 'representation', but Aristotle's usage includes both of these meanings. The range of ideas covered by *mimesis* in the *Poetics* is changeable and varied, and no single English term can do justice to the flexibility of Aristotle's usage. What we can say, however, is that an artistic 'imitation' of the kind that Aristotle discusses appears to have the following characteristics:[4] it represents or stands for the object imitated, it is produced by the act of imitating, and it is similar to the object imitated. But *mimesis* is not merely an aesthetic phenomenon. According to Aristotle, the instinct for imitation is a basic element in human nature: we have a natural propensity to engage in imitation, we learn from it, and we instinctively take pleasure in works of imitation. As he explains in chapter 4, we enjoy looking at representations, even if they are of things which we would find painful to see in real life, because we enjoy recognizing the similarities between the image and the thing which it represents. Perceiving likenesses and working out resemblances is a positive pleasure for human beings because it satisfies our natural desire to learn. Hence the enjoyment of imitative arts like poetry and painting is rooted in human nature, and the pleasure they afford has cognitive value.

The notion of similarity or resemblance between art and its object is crucial to Aristotle's conception of *mimesis*, and both poets and painters are specifically referred to as 'image makers' or 'makers of likenesses' (1460b7–8, chapter 25). But that is not to say that *mimesis* involves the notion of mechanical copying. The artist can present things as they are, as they seem to be, or as they ought to be (1460b10–11), hence what he offers is a re-fashioning of nature or experience rather than a straightforward copy (whatever that might be). Indeed, in chapter 9 Aristotle explicitly rejects the idea that tragedy mimics reality, when he says that the poet's function is not to describe what has happened, but rather the kinds of thing that might happen. Facts are the province of the historian, whereas the poet aims at verisimilitude. Aristotle's idea of poetic imitation is thus not unlike the modern category of fiction in that what the poet describes is, so to speak, a reality that he imagines. What is crucial for Aristotle, however, is that the poet's imitations should be plausible, that is, that the events which are dramatized should be of the kind that could happen because they are, in the circumstances, either probable or necessary. Tragedy represents the probable rather than the actual, but in doing so it deepens our understanding of the world in which we live. The paradox is well put by the critic A. D. Nuttall when he says: 'An art which treats no actual existent can nevertheless deal with the world we all inhabit. Drama is something simultaneously real and unreal, real at the level of possibility, unreal at the level of actuality.'[5] For Aristotle the poet is a 'maker' (the literal meaning of the Greek *poietes* from which our word 'poet' derives), but specifically a maker of imitations, and the work which he produces is poetry by virtue of the fact that it is an imitation in the verbal medium rather than because it uses metre. *Mimesis* is thus what distinguishes poetry from other kinds of discourse.

The *Poetics* promises a discussion of poetry in general through the analysis of its different kinds or genres, but the text as we have it focuses predominantly on tragic drama. Epic is briefly discussed in chapters 23–5, and a second book on comedy is lost, so that the *Poetics* is, in effect, a treatise on tragedy. Tragedy, according to Aristotle's celebrated definition in chapter 6, is 'a representation of an action that is serious, complete, and of some magnitude; in language that is pleasurably embellished, the different forms of embellishment occurring in separate parts; presented in the form of action, not narration; by means of pity and fear bringing about the *catharsis* of such emotions'. The requirement that tragedy should represent an action that is complete and of some magnitude is further developed in chapter 7, where Aristotle emphasizes that it must be a whole, with 'a beginning, a middle, and an end', by which he means that the action must have an ordered structure so that events follow on one from another in a logical sequence, and not simply at random. This basic need for organic unity is further brought out by the parallel with living organisms: 'Whatever is beautiful, whether it be a living creature or an object made up of various parts, must necessarily not only have its parts properly ordered, but also be of an appropriate size, for beauty is bound up with size and order.'

Another essential feature of tragedy concerns the effect that it has on its audience. Pity and fear are the emotions characteristically associated with tragedy because we feel pity for the undeserved suffering of others, and fear when that suffering is experienced by people 'like ourselves' (chapter 13). But what does Aristotle mean when he speaks of the *catharsis* of these emotions? This idea is mentioned only once in the *Poetics*, without any explanation, but it also appears in the *Politics*, where Aristotle says: 'What I mean by *catharsis* I will state simply now, but more clearly in the *Poetics*.' But this promised discussion is nowhere to be found. All we have to go on is the single reference in chapter 6 of the *Poetics* and the brief account in the *Politics*, which occurs in the context of a consideration of the uses of music. Music, says Aristotle, has a variety of beneficial functions: it can be used, for example, for the education of the young, for relaxation and leisure, and for *catharsis*, which he explains in the following way:

The emotions which violently affect some minds exist in all, but in different degrees, for example, pity and fear, and 'enthusiasm' too, for some people are subject to this disturbance. We can see the effect of sacred music on such people when they make use of melodies that arouse the mind to frenzy, and are restored to health and attain, as it were, healing and *catharsis*. The same effect will necessarily be experienced in the case of those prone to pity or fear, or any other emotion, in the proportion appropriate to each individual; all experience a *catharsis* and pleasurable relief.   (*Politics* 1342a4–15)

Aristotle here observes that people who are morbidly prone to 'enthusiasm' (that is, ecstatic frenzy of the kind associated with orgiastic religious cults like that of Dionysus), can be relieved of their symptoms by the same kind of music as that which induces their frenzy. In other words, *catharsis* is a kind of homeopathic therapy that can be used in the treatment of neurotics. But what connection does this passage have with the *Poetics* and what does Aristotle mean by *catharsis* in the context of tragedy? This is probably a question to which we shall never know the answer, but it has generated endless debate.

An interpretation widely favoured by modern commentators derives from that put forward by Jacob Bernays (whose niece was married to Sigmund Freud) in a highly influential essay published in 1857. Emphasizing the importance of the *Politics* passage, Bernays argued for a quasi-medical interpretation of *catharsis*, according to which tragedy provides us with a harmless outlet for pent-up emotions: just as music can induce frenzy in those susceptible to it and thereby relieve them of their disturbance, so tragedy, by arousing our pity and fear, purges us of these undesirable feelings. But the problem with such a theory is that it assumes that the emotions of pity and fear are bad in themselves. It also implies that an audience who would most benefit from a perform-ance of tragedy would consist of emotionally disturbed people. Another line of interpretation, advanced in various forms by different scholars, is to think of *catharsis* as a kind of purification of the emotions of pity and fear. For Aristotle the emotions have an important part to play in our ethical lives, and it is important that we learn to have correct emotional responses. As he explains in the *Nicomachean Ethics*, we can feel fear, anger, desire, pity and so on, either too much or too little: for example, too much fear makes us cowards, whereas too little makes us foolhardy. What we need to do is to feel our emotions appropriately, that is, at the right time, in response to the right things, towards the right people, for the right reason and in the right way (1106b18–23). Perhaps tragedy helps us to achieve this state by encouraging us to feel the right amount of pity and fear in relation to the events that we witness on stage. On this view tragedy offers us the opportunity to develop our emotional responses correctly, without our having to undergo the sufferings that tragic drama represents. And *catharsis* is, in some unexplained way, the mechanism whereby we feel the appropriate amount of pity and fear.

Interpretations such as these are bound to be speculative, but whatever Aristotle did mean by *catharsis* (and we shall probably never be sure), it is clear that, unlike Plato, he attaches considerable value to the emotional appeal of tragedy, and the pleasure which we derive from it. That pleasure stems directly from the pity and fear which tragedy arouses, for, as he says in chapter 14, we should not demand every kind of pleasure from tragedy, but only that which is proper to it: the tragic poet's aim is to produce by means of his representation 'the tragic pleasure that is associated with pity and fear'. A large part of Aristotle's discussion (chapters 7–14) is concerned with plot, 'the ordered arrangement of the incidents', since he regards plot as the single most important element in tragedy. It takes precedence over character because, as he explains in chapter 6: 'tragedy is a representation, not of people, but of action and life, of happiness and unhappiness – and happiness and unhappiness are bound up with action. The purpose of living is an end which is a kind of activity, not a quality; it is their characters, indeed, that make people what they are, but it is by reason of their actions that they are happy or the reverse.'

Aristotle considers several possible types of plot and concludes that the best, that is, the best at arousing pity and fear, will represent a man who is neither a paragon of virtue, nor utterly worthless, but somewhere in between these two extremes, who falls from prosperity into misfortune through some error (*hamartia*). By *hamartia* he does not mean a fatal flaw in the hero's character such as we see depicted in, for example, Shakespeare's *Othello*, whose tragic fall is brought about by his own obsessive jealousy. *Hamartia* is, rather, a mistake or error which the hero commits in ignorance of what he is doing. The classic case is Sophocles' *Oedipus the King*, a play which Aristotle takes as the model Greek tragedy. Oedipus kills his father and marries his mother in ignorance of the fact that they are his parents, not because he is morally flawed. Indeed, he does everything that is humanly possible to avoid the terrible fate predicted for him, and it is because his sufferings are so undeserved that we feel such pity for him. Yet his punishment is not accidental because it results from his own actions, actions that are well intentioned, but misguided.

Aristotle places suffering and the mutability of all things human at the heart of his conception of tragedy, yet the *Poetics* is notoriously reticent about the religious explanations of human suffering which are integral to the genre. His neglect of the gods, together with his apparent lack of interest in the social and political implications of tragedy, have been severely criticized by modern scholars. But these omissions are symptomatic of Aristotle's essentially formalist approach. The *Poetics* does not set out to provide a comprehensive account of tragedy; rather, it aims to discover for each kind of poetry the form that will best bring about its characteristic effects. In the case of tragedy that is the form that will most successfully produce the tragic pleasure associated with pity and fear, through the representation of pitiable and fearful events.

The *Poetics* has been enormously influential in the history of literary criticism, but it seems to have been little known in antiquity. It was only in the Renaissance, after its rediscovery by Italian humanists in the sixteenth century AD, that it became a canonical text, and was thereafter disseminated throughout Europe, notably in England and France. Renaissance critics tended to read the treatise as if it were a set of rules for composition (a misconception which is still to some extent current), and many theories were ascribed to Aristotle which are not actually in the *Poetics*. The most well known of these is the law of the three unities of action, time and place. In fact, this law was invented by the Italian critic Castelvetro, who published an annotated translation of the *Poetics* in 1570, on the basis of Aristotle's observation in chapter 5 that 'tragedy tries as far as possible to keep within a single revolution of the sun . . . whereas the epic observes no limits in its time of action'. The so-called Aristotelian doctrine of the unities became a fundamental tenet of Neo-classical criticism, which established a rigid framework of rules for the various genres of poetry. This process reached its zenith in seventeenth-century France, where the impact of the *Poetics* was evident not only amongst the critics, but also in the production of new tragedies in the theatre, as we can see most clearly from the plays of Corneille and Racine. From the sixteenth to the eighteenth centuries, Aristotle's *Poetics* dominated literary theory in Europe. Thereafter, with the rise of Romanticism, its influence waned, but it has nevertheless retained its status as the fundamental work of theoretical criticism to emerge from antiquity.

6. *The Alexandrians*

Despite its subsequent reputation, Aristotle's treatise made little direct impact on ancient literary criticism. In the Hellenistic period (the third to the first centuries BC) poetry and poetic criticism were carried on in the new environment of the royal court at Alexandria, where the Ptolemies who ruled Egypt after its conquest by Alexander the Great, eager to enhance the prestige of the new capital city, founded the famous museum and library, which became the centre of culture and scholarship in the Greek-speaking world. Here scholars and poets, handsomely paid and freed from worldly cares, were able to devote their time to study and research, living 'like fatted fowls in a coop', as a contemporary satirist remarked, in what must have been the original ivory tower. Their task was to collect, edit, interpret and preserve the great literature of the past, at a time when the old world which had produced that literature had completely disappeared. Dedicated to establishing the authenticity of texts, these scholars were not only editors, but critics in the original sense of the word, judging, selecting and discriminating between authors and works, and deciding which should be particularly admired. This process of evaluation led to the establishment of a classical canon of authors, at first in relation to poetry, but later extended to oratory, which remained substantially unchanged for the rest of antiquity; although new authors were added from time to time, contemporary works were always excluded from the list. This veneration for the tradition accounts in part for the importance attached to the imitation of previous authors, one of the most distinctive features of later Greek and Latin literature, and a hallmark of classicism in subsequent eras. And the very notion of a canon has had a profound influence on the history of Western literature, which continues to be hotly debated today.

In the Alexandrian context, reverence for the old masters and nostalgia for the past did not stifle the literature of the present; indeed, the question of what the relationship of contemporary poetry should be to the tradition was one of the crucial factors in the revival of poetry. The problem was not simply the trivial one of which poets to imitate, but rather that of defining the function of poetry in a post-philosophical age (in Bruno Snell's phrase). The fourth century BC, the great age of philosophical prose, had seen the demise of the city-state, and though the great public genres of epic, tragedy and comedy continued to be performed before vast audiences in Hellenistic cities, poets no longer commanded the status and moral authority that had once been theirs.

In the changed circumstances of the Hellenistic world it was inevitable that poets should reflect on the purposes of their art.

Callimachus (c. 305–c. 240 BC), whose learned, allusive and self-conscious poetry typifies the Alexandrian spirit in literature, was the most polemical and the most influential of the scholar poets of the period, and seems to have been a key figure in the development of new approaches to poetry. He rejected the traditional genres of poetry and their hackneyed themes, clearly stating his preference for shorter, discontinuous poems, for 'slim' poetry rather than 'thick', for poetry that travelled along untrodden pathways and came, like pure drops of water, from a sacred spring. Poetry was no longer to be judged by the epic criteria of the past, but by new standards of subtlety, allusiveness and wit, a view which is summed up in Apollo's words to the poet in Callimachus' *Prologue to the Aetia*: 'Learn to judge poetic skill by art (*techne*).' The audience was no longer to be the public at large ('I detest all common things', as Callimachus says in one of his epigrams), but an elite circle of highly cultured and sophisticated scholars. Art for art's sake was born precisely at a time when poetry turned in upon itself and became the playful preserve of the learned few.

The union of poetry, criticism and scholarship is one distinctive feature of the literary culture of the Hellenistic period. But another development which significantly affected the history of criticism was the merging of poetics and rhetoric. Plato had been as hostile to rhetoric as he was to poetry, both being seen by him as rivals to the one true discipline of philosophy. In the *Gorgias* (462ff.) he contemptuously dismisses rhetoric as nothing but a knack for gratifying and pleasing an audience, an activity on a level with cookery and beauty culture, which cannot be classified as an art (a *techne*) because it is unable to give a rational account of what it has to offer. In a later dialogue, the *Phaedrus*, he remains equally sceptical about rhetoric as it is currently practised, and suggests that if rhetoric were truly a *techne*, it would need to be based on a proper understanding of the human soul, such as only the philosopher can possess. That suggestion is taken up by Aristotle in the *Rhetoric*, a treatise which, like the *Poetics*, is at least in part a response to Plato's challenge. Aristotle argues that rhetoric is indeed a *techne*, which he defines not simply as the art of persuasion, but as 'the faculty of discovering the available means of persuasion in any particular case' (*Rhetoric* 1.2.1). Whereas earlier rhetorical handbooks had apparently consisted largely of lists of oratorical tricks and devices derived from experience, Aristotle approached the subject as a philosopher, and for the first time provided a firm theoretical framework for the study of rhetoric, which was based on rational principles. His treatise covers three major areas: the logical arguments that the orator can use; audience psychology and arguments based on knowledge of human emotions and character; and style, including the virtues of clarity and appropriateness.

For Aristotle the art of rhetoric was to be clearly distinguished from the art of poetry, the one being a practical skill, dedicated to persuading an audience, the other an imitative art whose purpose is to produce the particular pleasure that is appropriate to it. But since the medium of both is language, there is inevitably the possibility of some overlap between the two. In the area of stylistic analysis in particular, much rhetorical theory might equally well be applied to poetry as to prose, and it is not altogether surprising that, despite Aristotle's insistence on the distinction between the stylistic virtues of poetry and prose, that distinction was largely forgotten by his successors. After Aristotle the main focus of criticism was on the analysis of style and the practical application of techniques to be derived from the study of literature of all kinds, whether poetry or prose. And as rhetoric came more and more to dominate secondary education in the Hellenistic Greek world (a process which had begun with the sophists in the late fifth century BC), so literary criticism itself became increasingly absorbed into the teaching of rhetoric. Henceforward the major developments in criticism centred on the stylistic analysis of discourse rather than on literary theory and the larger philosophical questions that the subject of literature raises.

7. *Horace*

Horace's *Art of Poetry*, though a work specifically devoted to poetry, nevertheless shows the influence of this rhetorical approach, both in its prescriptive tone and in its concern for poetry's effect on an audience.

Cast in the form of a verse epistle, it gives advice to its addressees, the young Piso brothers, on how to compose a successful tragedy, whilst at the same time ranging over a number of more general topics related to the art of poetry. Whether the Piso brothers really were writing a tragedy, or whether this is merely a convenient fiction on Horace's part, is a matter of debate. But the choice of tragedy as the focus of Horace's poem clearly indicates the influence of Aristotle's followers in the Peripatetic school (though there is no indication that Horace knew the *Poetics* itself), since tragedy was not the major genre in Augustan Rome that it had been in classical Greece. But the poem does not slavishly reflect the views of one particular school; rather it draws freely on a number of different sources, both poetic and rhetorical, to produce its own particular blend of traditional theories, adapted for a Roman audience.

Horace's tone is discursive and informal, and his poem appears to have little structure, leaping from theme to theme in a seemingly chaotic fashion. But we should not be deceived by his casual epistolary manner or his apparent lack of method. This is no systematic treatise, but a poetic presentation of a vast and various field, whose unity derives from the highlighting and repetition of certain key themes. Principal amongst these is the notion of decorum, which runs as a leitmotif throughout the poem. This doctrine of fitness, or literary propriety, had been discussed by Aristotle in both the *Poetics* and the *Rhetoric*, and Cicero made much of it in his rhetorical theory; but for Horace it constitutes a guiding principle. He stresses the need for organic unity in any work of art, emphasizing that every part and every aspect of that work must be appropriate to the nature of the work as a whole: the choice of subject in relation to the chosen genre, the characterization, the form, the expression, the metre, the style, and tone; the poet must avoid the mixing of genres, the creation of characters who lack verisimilitude, and so on. Horace insists that dramatic characters should be true to life, a theme which is elaborated in the memorable description of the various ages of man (155–78), and in his discussion of the differing qualities that are appropriate to the portrayal of particular types of character (310–18). Both of these passages reflect the view, so central to the theories of Plato and Aristotle, that poetry is an imitative art, and Horace explicitly alludes to this idea when he declares that 'the skilled imitator should look to human life and character for his models, and from there derive a language that is true to life' (317–18). The worst possible fault, in Horace's view, is incongruity, whether it be in characterization, subject matter or diction, and, as if to stress the importance of this principle, he begins his poem with a picture of inappropriateness: 'Supposing a painter chose to put a human head on a horse's neck, or to spread feathers of various colours over the limbs of several different creatures, or to make what in the upper part is a beautiful woman tail off into a hideous fish, could you help laughing when he showed you his efforts?' A poem that lacks unity and decorum will be like such a picture.

Another prominent theme in the poem is that of the skill, craftsmanship and sheer hard work involved in the composition of poetry. Horace takes it for granted that the poet needs natural talent (*ingenium*), but talent is nothing without training and labour. The early Roman poets, Ennius, Accius, Plautus and so on, are much beloved by the public, but in Horace's view their work lacks the sophistication, refinement and artistry which the best poetry needs. If Rome is to have a literature to rival that of the Greeks, the younger generation of poets must be prepared to take infinite pains over their work, revising, correcting and, above all, responding to the advice of the experienced critic. As Gerald Else has put it, Horace's advice to aspiring writers is to 'polish, polish, polish, rather than to publish, publish, publish'. But, as it is, Roman poets 'one and all, shrink from the tedious task of polishing their work' (290–91). This is as true of the great figures of early Roman poetry as it is of the scribblers one meets everywhere in Rome today. Poetry, for Horace, is above all a skilled craft, not some amateur activity to be pursued by gentlemen of leisure in their spare time, or by those who think that they can be poets merely by looking the part. Inspiration is all very well, he says, but Rome nowadays is full of bearded, long-haired would-be geniuses with uncut fingernails, seeking solitary places and avoiding the baths (295–303). The caricature of the mad poet, spouting his verses as he falls into a well (453–76), similarly satirizes the notion of poetic inspiration, and brings the poem to a riotous conclusion, effectively underlining the need for an alternative approach to the writing of poetry, which Horace himself has supplied.

The new poetics which Horace advocates for his contemporaries in Augustan Rome looks back to the Hellenistic aesthetic of Callimachus, with its emphasis on *ars* (skill or craftsmanship) as the essential criterion of value in poetry. Horace also shares with the Hellenistic poets a keen awareness of the need for the new poets of his day to define themselves in relation to the great literature of the past. And it is the Alexandrian canon of classical Greek authors, rather than the early Roman poets, whom Horace prescribes as models. 'You must give your days and nights to the study of Greek literature', he says (268–9); and in mentioning only Homer and the Attic tragic playwrights he makes it clear that he is thinking especially of the great writers of the classical period of Greek literature. The imitation of previous authors was a well-established technique in the training of orators, which Horace here extends to the composition of poetry. An awareness of tradition was endemic in ancient literature as a whole, and allusion to earlier practitioners of one's chosen genre (what we now call intertextuality) was a striking feature of Greek and Latin poetry almost from the start. But in advocating the study and imitation of canonical models as the principal means of revitalizing Latin poetry, Horace articulates a theory of classicism which clearly reflects his own poetic practice (as, for example, in the *Odes*), and that of Virgil and his other Augustan compatriots. A parallel development can be seen in rhetoric, where Horace's contemporary, Dionysius of Halicarnassus, as part of his crusade to restore stylistic standards, was promoting the great Attic writers of the past as the best models for imitation by budding orators in Augustan Rome. This doctrine of imitation of the ancients was also a key feature of classicism in Renaissance thinking about poetry and eloquence, and was, of course, the *raison d'être* of Neoclassical literature.

For all Horace's emphasis on the technical aspects of the poet's craft, being a good poet is not merely a matter of technical expertise, for the poet will need to have a knowledge of moral philosophy and of life if he is to create convincing characters, and improve his audience in the process. 'The foundation and fountain-head of good composition is wisdom', as he says (309), and by this he means primarily a knowledge derived from the study of ethics, which will enable the poet to set appropriate examples of human behaviour before his audience. This emphasis on the exemplary role of poetry is well illustrated in another of Horace's *Epistles* (1.2), in which he speaks of the moral benefits to be derived from reading Homer: the *Iliad* depicts models of human folly and vice, the *Odyssey* teaches wisdom and virtue through the example of Odysseus, and in general Homer will be found to be a better teacher of ethics than the professional philosophers. For Horace (in marked contrast with Aristotle) character takes precedence over plot, and the moral function of poetry is paramount.

The poet must combine Callimachean standards of artistry with the moral responsibility traditionally accorded to his role, a theme which Horace reinforces by elaborating the *topos* (first encountered in Aristophanes' *Frogs*) of the benefits that poets have conferred on society. Since time immemorial poets have played a vital part in the development of civilization (391–407), and Rome no less than Greece needs its poets to continue that tradition. As far as the function of poetry is concerned, Horace sums up centuries of debate when he says that poets should aim to benefit or to please (333), or, best of all, to do both (343–4), a doctrine which was endlessly echoed and developed by Renaissance critics.

The emotional impact of poetry, a key theme in all ancient discussions of poetry, is treated by Horace in the passage beginning at line 99: 'It is not enough that poems should have beauty; if they are to carry the audience with them, they must have charm as well.' What Horace says here is not new: already in Plato's *Ion* (535b–e) Socrates describes how the rhapsode inspires his audience with the emotions which he himself feels; and in the *Poetics* (chapter 17) Aristotle states that emotions will be most vividly depicted by poets who are moved themselves. In the field of rhetoric too it became a commonplace that the speaker must feel the emotions he wishes to communicate in order to be convincing. But this idea receives its classic expression in Horace's famous words: '*Si vis me flere, dolendum est primum ipsi tibi*' ('If you want to move me to tears, you must first feel grief yourself').

In general the importance of the *Art of Poetry* lies not so much in the originality of its ideas as in its memorable expressions, its vivid images and vignettes, and in its evocation of the lived experience of poets at work in the Rome of Horace's day. Behind the poem lie the abstractions of literary theory, but Horace writes as a poet, drawing eclectically from the complex tradition of Graeco-Roman theory to produce his own idiosyncratic picture of the poet's vocation. By placing himself in the roles of both poet and critic, Horace adapted and transformed that tradition to produce a poem on poetics which is unique in the history of criticism, and which was of major importance in the transmission of classical views of poetry to later ages.

8. *Longinus*

Horace's poem was known and widely read throughout the Middle Ages; Longinus, by contrast, was a shadowy figure, of uncertain date and identity, whose treatise, *On the Sublime*, survived antiquity in a single, incomplete manuscript. Even after its rediscovery in the Renaissance, the work made little impact on the history of criticism until the latter part of the seventeenth century, when Boileau's famous translation (1674) marks a turning point in its fortunes. Thereafter acquaintance with Longinus fast became essential for educated readers, as Swift's satirical comment shows:

> A forward critic often dupes us
> With sham quotations *Peri Hupsous* [*On the Sublime*]
> And if we have not read Longinus,
> Will magisterially outshine us.
> Then, lest with Greek he overrun ye,
> Procure the book for love or money,
> Translated from Boileau's translation,
> And quote quotation on quotation.
> *On Poetry: a Rhapsody* (271–8) (1733)

Longinus' influence was central to the literary criticism of the eighteenth century; but it was also the starting point for a wide-ranging debate on 'the Sublime' in nature, literature and art, which was developed by aestheticians and philosophers of the period in ways which go far beyond Longinus' text.

Longinus' treatise is quite unlike any other work of criticism that has come down to us from antiquity, but the tradition from which it emerges is that of the rhetorical schools. From the Hellenistic period onwards higher education in the Graeco-Roman world was based on rhetoric, which included the art of writing as well as the art of speaking. We know little of the details of rhetorical teaching in Hellenistic times, but it was during this period that the well-known classification of the three styles of oratory – grand for rousing the emotions, plain for setting out arguments and intermediate for giving pleasure – became firmly established. Poetry and prose were studied together from a formal point of view, the emphasis being placed primarily on the techniques of style rather than on content or general meaning. The study of literature continued to be an important part of the curriculum in the training of the orator throughout antiquity, and the purpose of such study was to enable the student to acquire verbal facility.

This rhetorical approach to literature is very clearly exemplified in Quintilian's well-known survey of Greek and Latin authors in the tenth book of his *Education of the Orator* (c. AD 95), the fullest account that we have of the educational system that prevailed in the Roman imperial period. Quintilian is here concerned with the development of the orator's skills through the reading and imitation of the best writers, and for this purpose he draws up a reading list, together with brief comments on the 'special virtue' of each author mentioned. In Greek poetry Homer is seen, in the traditional manner, as the model and inspiration for every department of eloquence; after Homer, Old Comedy is the most suitable genre for orators to read; in tragedy Aeschylus is lofty and impressive, but often uncouth and inharmonious (a view which goes back to Aristophanes' *Frogs*); Sophocles and Euripides are equally good, but Euripides will be most useful to those preparing to speak in court because his style is nearer to the oratorical type. These examples show something of the flavour of Quintilian's discussion, which ranges over poetry, history, philosophy and oratory, and includes both Greek and Latin authors. If at times the judgements seem somewhat bizarre (in philosophy, for example, Cicero is seen as a rival to Plato), that is because Quintilian's critique is written from the point of view of the needs of the orator, and authors are evaluated primarily on the basis of what they can contribute to the formation of oratorical style.

This rhetorical tradition provides the background to Longinus' treat-ise *On the Sublime*. Its subject is what he calls *hupsos* ('height', 'grandeur' or 'sublimity'). This is not so much a style relating to the standard division of oratory into the three styles, already mentioned, of grand, plain and middle, but rather a particular quality of writing which he describes as the hallmark of great literature. Sublimity is characterized by its ability to amaze and transport an audience, overwhelming them with its irresistible power. In contrast with Plato, Aristotle and Horace, Longinus makes no distinction between poetry and prose: in his work rhetoric and poetics merge to produce a notion of criticism which embraces literature as a whole. The quality of sublimity, 'from which the greatest poets and prose-writers have acquired . . . an eternity of fame', is to be found in such diverse authors as Homer, Demosthenes, Plato, Sappho, and even the book of Genesis; it manifests itself in individual passages and single phrases as much as in whole works, indeed, no writer can be expected to maintain an unbroken level of sublimity; even the godlike Homer and Plato have their lapses, and many other writers cannot long sustain the sublimity to which they are capable of rising. However, the writer who can occasionally flash into sublimity is superior to the one who, like the orator Hyperides, does everything well, but never quite achieves the sublime. True sublimity stands up to repeated examination by the educated reader, and withstands the test of time, appealing to all people of all ages. As to the question of whether there is such a thing as an art of the sublime, Longinus' answer recalls what we have already heard from Horace and other earlier critics: sublimity, he says, is innate, an inborn gift, but it must be cultivated; art is necessary if the natural ability is to be used to the best effect. Longinus is unusual amongst ancient critics, however, in the importance which he attaches to the instinctive elements from which great writing derives.

The main body of his treatise is concerned with the discussion and illustration of five sources of sublimity. Of these, three are the product of art, but the two principal sources are largely innate. The first and most important (chapters 8–15) is grandeur of thought, the ability to form grand conceptions, which is a characteristic of natural greatness;

excellence in literature depends upon the mental powers of the author, for 'sublimity is the echo of a noble mind' (chapter 9). Sublimity may also arise from the author's capacity to choose the most striking details to describe a situation and to fuse them into a whole, a point which Longinus illustrates by an analysis of a famous poem by Sappho, known to us only through his quotation of it. Although greatness of mind is a natural capacity, the sublimity that results from it can be inspired by the imitation or emulation of previous writers who have shown themselves capable of achieving sublimity. Longinus uses the term imitation in a far broader sense than any of his predecessors, comparing the influence of the great men of the past on aspiring writers to the divine inspiration which empowers the priestess at Delphi to deliver her oracles (chapter 13). Longinus' application of Platonic metaphors of inspiration to the rhetorical concept of *mimesis* suggests that the imitation of past models should not be regarded merely as a mechanical technique or skill, but rather as a creative and even mysterious process.

Another way of cultivating this capacity for sublimity is through *phantasia*, or visualization, when the speaker imagines the scene he describes so vividly that he can bring it before the eyes of his audience. Here Longinus does distinguish between poetry and oratory: whereas the poet aims to astonish us by the depiction of scenes which can exceed the bounds of credibility, the orator's goal is vividness and realistic description; but in both cases the effect is to overwhelm the audience with emotion. Powerful and inspired emotion, the second source of sublimity, is discussed only briefly here (a separate study of this topic, which is promised right at the end of the present treatise, does not survive), but Longinus leaves us in no doubt as to its importance: 'I would confidently maintain,' he says, 'that nothing contributes so decisively to grandeur as noble emotion in the right setting.' (Chapter 8.)

The third source of the sublime, reflecting standard rhetorical doctrine, is the effective use of stylistic and rhetorical figures as a means of increasing the emotional impact of literature (chapters 16–29); and Longinus observes that a figure is best used when the fact that it is a figure escapes attention. The fourth source is to be found in noble diction and phrasing (chapters 30–38); this includes the skilful use of metaphors and other figures of speech. Finally (chapters 39–40) comes dignified and elevated composition, that is, an insistence on the most effective arrangement of words, and the now well-established conception of organic unity.

Longinus writes as a rhetorician whose work is intended to be of some use to men in public life. But despite its textbook structure and its concern with the formal analysis of literature, Longinus' treatise is far from being a practical handbook on the art of public speaking. Longinus is interested above all in questions of value which go well beyond the analysis of style, for the sublimity on which great literature depends is not simply a stylistic quality, but an expression of the author's mind and character. As he says in chapter 9: 'It is not possible for those whose thoughts and habits are mean and servile throughout their lives to produce anything that is remarkable or worthy of immortal fame; no, greatness of speech is the province of those whose thoughts are deep, and this is why lofty expressions come naturally to the most high-minded of men.' For all Longinus' discussion of the techniques for producing sublimity, what his treatise highlights is the importance of the personality of the author in the genesis of great writing. This, together with his frequent use of the language of enthusiasm and inspiration (in which Plato's influence is strongly evident), makes him unique in the ancient world as a precursor of that complex of ideas associated with genius, inspiration and emotion, which fascinated the eighteenth century, and which led ultimately to the birth of Romanticism.

Longinus combines the philosophical and rhetorical traditions of ancient literary criticism to create a work that is remarkable both for the passion with which it is written, and for the quality of its critical analyses of individual passages of literature. Famous amongst these are his praise of 'the lawgiver of the Jews, no ordinary person, [who] having formed a worthy conception of the power of the Divine Being, gave expression to it when at the very beginning of his *Laws* he wrote: "God said – what? 'Let there be light', and there was light; 'Let there be land', and there was land"' (chapter 9). Equally well known are his reflections on Homer in the same chapter, and particularly his comparison between the *Iliad* and the *Odyssey*. Aristotle had already commented on the general differences between the two, the one being essentially simple in structure and centring on suffering, the other complex and full of character (*Poetics*, chapter 24); but Longinus breathes new spirit into these judgements. The *Iliad*, he says, was written in the prime of life, and is therefore dramatic and vivid, whereas the *Odyssey* is dominated by narrative, the characteristic of old age: 'Thus in the *Odyssey* Homer may be likened to the setting sun: the grandeur remains, but without the force . . . In saying this I have not forgotten the storms in the *Odyssey* and the episode of the Cyclops and other things of the kind. I am speaking of old age, but it is, after all, the old age of Homer.' Longinus communicates a love of literature which speaks across the centuries, as Edward Gibbon observed in his *Journal* (3 September 1762):

The ninth chapter is one of the finest monuments of antiquity. Till now I was acquainted only with two ways of criticising a beautiful passage: the one, to shew by an exact anatomy of it the distinct beauties of it and whence they sprung; the other, an idle exclamation or a general encomium which leaves nothing behind it. Longinus has shown me that there is a third. He tells me his own feelings upon reading it, and tells them with such energy that he communicates them.

Significantly Gibbon traces the power of Longinus' criticism to his ability to inspire the reader with the emotion which great writing evokes in him. As Pope put it in his famous tribute:

> Thee, bold Longinus, all the Nine inspire,
> And bless their critic with a poet's fire.
> An ardent judge, who, zealous in his trust,
> With warmth gives sentence, yet is always just;
> Whose own example strengthens all his laws,
> And is himself the great Sublime he draws.
>
> *Essay on Criticism* (1709)

Epilogue

The story of ancient literary criticism is a difficult one to write, not least because of the open-endedness of the term 'literary criticism'. There is certainly no one genre of ancient literature to which we could apply the label, but rather a vast range of different types of writing which could be said to fall within its province. Broadly speaking, however, we can distinguish between two types of approach, one philosophical, the other rhetorical, both of which were in place by the end of the fifth century BC. In time it was the rhetorical tradition which predominated, and, because of the way in which education developed in the Graeco-Roman world, the history of criticism became intimately bound up with the history of education and of rhetoric.

The present volume does not intend to provide a comprehensive account of the entire subject of ancient literary criticism, not least for reasons of space. Such an account would need to include the major works of rhetorical theory – Aristotle, Cicero, Tacitus and Quintilian – as well as examples of the more technical treatises on rhetoric and style. Rather than selecting examples from all the various types of writing which could be said to constitute the discourse of criticism in the ancient world, this book concentrates on the canonical texts and the background from which they emerge. The works which have had the greatest influence on the course of European criticism are those of Aristotle, Horace and Longinus, and behind them stands the towering figure of Plato. It is often said that ancient literary criticism is something of a disappointment, being fundamentally inferior to the literature it is criticizing. Whilst this may be true of literary criticism, narrowly conceived as the activity of analysing the minutiae of style, the same cannot be said of the philosophical tradition in ancient criticism, which has its beginning in the speculations of the earliest Greek poets and culminates in the remarkable treatise of Longinus. For it is here that the ancient critics have made a lasting contribution to the study of literature as a human activity. In his celebrated essay 'Why Read the Classics?' the writer Italo Calvino suggests that 'a classic is a book that has never finished saying what it has to say', and further, that 'the classics are the books that come down to us bearing the traces of readings previous to ours, and bringing in their wake the traces they themselves have left on the culture or cultures they have passed through'.[6] In both these senses the texts which follow are the classic works of ancient literary criticism.

NOTES

1. T. S. Eliot, *The Use of Poetry and the Use of Criticism* (London, 1933), p. 141.

2. T. Todorov, *Introduction to Poetics*, trans. R. Howard (Brighton, 1981), p. xxiii.

3. Aristophanes, *Thesmophoriazusae* (or *The Poet and the Women*), trans. D. Barrett (London, 1964), lines 146–67. I have used the same translation for extracts quoted from the *Frogs*.

4. This formulation is taken from E. Belfiore, *Tragic Pleasures: Aristotle on Plot and Emotion* (Princeton, 1992), p. 48.

5. A. D. Nuttall, *Why Does Tragedy Give Pleasure?* (Oxford, 1996), p. 38.

6. Italo Calvino, 'Why Read the Classics?' in *The Literature Machine*, trans. P. Creagh (London, 1987), pp. 125–34.

FURTHER READING

The suggestions which follow are intended to provide a preliminary guide to the vast bibliography on ancient literary criticism in so far as it relates to the issues and texts presented in this volume. I have not included items in languages other than English.

I. GENERAL WORKS ON CLASSICAL
LITERARY CRITICISM

Many of the principal texts are collected together and translated in D. Russell and M. Winterbottom (eds), *Ancient Literary Criticism* (Oxford, 1982).

The following general works can also be recommended:

Else, G., 'Classical Poetics' in *The Princeton Encyclopedia of Poetry and Poetics* (Princeton, 1974), pp. 128–34.

Ford, A., *The Origins of Criticism: Literary Culture and Poetic Theory in Classical Greece* (Princeton, 2002).

Grube, G., *The Greek and Roman Critics* (London, 1965).

Halliwell, S., *The Aesthetics of Mimesis: Ancient Texts and Modern Problems* (Princeton, 2002).

Harriott, R., *Poetry and Criticism before Plato* (London, 1969).

Kennedy, G. (ed.), *The Cambridge History of Literary Criticism, vol. 1: Classical Criticism* (Cambridge, 1988). This contains extensive bibliographies.

McKeon, R., 'Literary Criticism and the Concept of Imitation in Antiquity', in R. Crane (ed.), *Critics and Criticism: Ancient and Modern* (Chicago, 1952), pp. 147–75.

Murray, P., 'Poetic Inspiration in Early Greece', *Journal of Hellenic Studies* 101 (1981), pp. 87–100.

Russell, D., *Criticism in Antiquity* (London, 1981).

Schaper, E., *Prelude to Aesthetics* (London, 1968).

Too, Y. L., *The Idea of Ancient Literary Criticism* (Oxford, 1998).

Verdenius, W., 'The Principles of Greek Literary Criticism', *Mnemosyne* 36 (1983), pp. 14–59.

There is also much that is relevant in the following studies:

Finkelberg, M., *The Birth of Literary Fiction in Ancient Greece* (Oxford, 1998).

Gill, C. and Wiseman, T. P. (eds), *Lies and Fiction in the Ancient World* (Exeter, 1993).

Pratt, L., *Lying and Poetry from Homer to Pindar* (Michigan, 1993).

On the influence of classical literary criticism I recommend the following general studies:

Abrams, M. H., *The Mirror and the Lamp: Romantic Theory and the Critical Tradition* (Oxford, 1953).

Curtius, E. R., *European Literature and the Latin Middle Ages*, trans. W. R. Trask (Princeton, 1953); reprinted with a new epilogue by P. Godman (Princeton, 1990).

Nisbet, H. B. and Rawson, C. (eds), *The Cambridge History of Literary Criticism, vol. 4: The Eighteenth Century* (Cambridge, 1997).

2. PLATO

Ion

Translations which may be compared with mine include those by D. Russell in D. Russell and M. Winterbottom (see section 1 above), and by T. J. Saunders in *Plato: Early Socratic Dialogues* (Penguin Books, London, 1987).

There is a full commentary on the *Ion* with introduction and notes in P. Murray (ed.), *Plato on Poetry* (Cambridge, 1996).

Republic

Amongst the numerous translations of this dialogue I recommend those by D. Lee (2nd edn, Penguin Books, London, 1974) and by P. Shorey in the Loeb edition (Cambridge, Mass. and London, 1930).

For the relevant sections of books 2, 3 and 10, *see also* the translation by D. Russell in D. Russell and M. Winterbottom (section 1 above).

J. Annas, *An Introduction to Plato's Republic* (Oxford, 1981) is an excellent general study which sets Plato's discussions of art within the context of the dialogue as a whole.

There is a complete commentary by J. Adam, *The Republic of Plato* (2nd ed., Cambridge, 1963). Murray, *Plato on Poetry* (as above on the *Ion*), provides a commentary on the sections of the dialogue translated in this volume, and there is a translation and commentary on *Republic*, book 10, by S. Halliwell (Warminster, 1988).

For discussion of Plato's views on literature and the arts *see* in particular the following studies:

Burnyeat, M., 'Culture and Society in Plato's *Republic*', *The Tanner Lectures on Human Values* 20 (1999).

Else, G., *Plato and Aristotle on Poetry* (Chapel Hill and London, 1986).

Ferrari, G., 'Plato and Poetry', in G. Kennedy (see section 1 above), pp. 92–148.

Havelock, E., *Preface to Plato* (Oxford, 1963).

Janaway, C., *Images of Excellence: Plato's Critique of the Arts* (Oxford, 1995).

Murdoch, I., *The Fire and the Sun: Why Plato Banished the Artists* (Oxford, 1977).

Nehamas, A., 'Plato and the Mass Media', *The Monist* 71 (1988), pp. 214–34; reprinted in A. Nehamas, *Virtues of Authenticity: Essays on Plato and Socrates* (Princeton, 1999), pp. 279–99.

Rutherford, R., *The Art of Plato* (London, 1995). This is primarily a literary study of Plato's work, but it contains much that is relevant to Plato's views on art.

Tigerstedt, E., *Plato's Idea of Poetical Inspiration* (Helsinki, 1969).

On the Platonic legacy in relation to literary criticism, *see* the following:

Baldwin, A. and Hutton, S. (eds), *Platonism and the English Imagination* (Cambridge, 1994).

Hankins, J., *Plato in the Italian Renaissance*, 2 vols (Leiden, 1990).

Weinberg, B., *A History of Literary Criticism in the Renaissance*, 2 vols (Chicago, 1961).

3. ARISTOTLE

Poetics

Translations which can be recommended include the following:

Halliwell, S., *The Poetics of Aristotle: translation and commentary* (London, 1987); the commentary takes the form of a continuous exposition, chapter by chapter.

Halliwell, S., *Aristotle, Poetics* (Loeb edition, Cambridge, Mass. and London, 1995). This is different from the 1987 version, and rather more literal.

Heath, M., *Aristotle, Poetics* (Penguin Books, London, 1996).

Hubbard, M., *Aristotle, Poetics*, in D. Russell and M. Winterbottom (see section 1 above).

Janko, R., *Aristotle, Poetics* (Indianapolis and Cambridge, 1987). This translation 'attempts to follow the original Greek closely, with minimal alterations for the sake of natural English', and has extensive notes on the detailed interpretation of the text.

The standard commentary on the Greek text is that by D. W. Lucas, *Aristotle, Poetics* (Oxford, 1968).

As far as general studies are concerned, the *Poetics* 'has destroyed forests', in the words of an eminent ancient philosopher. Bibliography on the treatise is comprehensively listed and clearly set out in Schrier, O., *The Poetics of Aristotle and the Tractatus Coislinianus: a Bibliography from about 900 till 1996* (Leiden, 1998). There are helpful indices including an index of passages and an index of subjects (e.g. *catharsis, hamartia, mimesis*), which make this a very useful bibliographical resource.

From the welter of material I recommend the following as a starting point:

Belfiore, E., *Tragic Pleasures: Aristotle on Plot and Emotion* (Princeton, 1992).

Else, G., *Plato and Aristotle on Poetry* (Chapel Hill and London, 1986).

Halliwell, S., *Aristotle's Poetics* (London, 1986). Chapter 10 of this book provides a useful account of the influence of the *Poetics* on the history of criticism.

Jones, J., *On Aristotle and Greek Tragedy* (London, 1962).

Nuttall, A., *Why does Tragedy Give Pleasure?* (Oxford, 1996).

Rorty, O. (ed.), *Essays on Aristotle's Poetics* (Princeton, 1992).

4. HORACE

The Art of Poetry

The present translation can be compared with that by D. Russell in Russell and Winterbottom (see section 1 above).

There is a detailed and comprehensive commentary on the poem, with bibliography, by C. O. Brink, *Horace on Poetry vol. 1: Prolegomena to the Literary Epistles* (Cambridge, 1963); *vol. 2: The Ars Poetica* (Cambridge, 1971); this is a major work of scholarship, but somewhat daunting for the non-specialist. A shorter and more accessible commentary is provided by N. Rudd, *Horace, Epistles Book II and Epistle to the Pisones (Ars Poetica)* (Cambridge, 1989).

For general discussions of the poem, *see* G. Grube (section 1 above), pp. 238–52, and the chapter on 'Augustan Critics' by D. C. Innes in G. Kennedy (ed.), as in section 1 above. Also useful is the chapter by D. Russell, '*Ars poetica*', in *Horace*, ed. C. Costa (London, 1973), pp. 113–34, which includes a brief account of the history of the poem's influence.

On this topic see also:

Herrick, M., *The Fusion of Horatian and Aristotelian Literary Criticism, 1531–1555* (New York, 1946).

Weinberg, B., as above in section 2.

5. LONGINUS

On the Sublime

Translations of this text include those by D. Russell in D. Russell and M. Winterbottom (see section 1 above) and by W. H. Fyfe, revised by D. Russell in the Loeb edition (Cambridge, Mass. and London, 1995). There is a full commentary, with bibliography, by D. Russell (Oxford, 1964).

Useful discussions of the treatise include those by G. Grube, and by D. Russell in G. Kennedy (both in section 1 above). *See also* D. Russell, 'Longinus Revisited', *Mnemosyne* 34 (1981), pp. 72–86.

On the influence of Longinus *see* the following:
Abrams (section 1 above), pp. 72–8.
Brody, J., *Boileau and Longinus* (Geneva, 1958).
Henn, T., *Longinus and English Criticism* (Cambridge, 1934).
Lamb, J., 'The Sublime', in H. B. Nisbet and C. Rawson (as in section 1 above).
Monk, S. H., *The Sublime* (New York, 1935; 2nd edn, 1960).

NOTE ON THE TEXT

The extracts from Plato have been newly translated for this volume, and are based on the Oxford Classical Text of Plato by J. Burnet. The translations of Aristotle, Horace and Longinus are revised versions of those by T. S. Dorsch (Penguin Books, 1965), and are based on the Oxford Classical Text of R. Kassel (ed.), Aristotle's *Poetics* (Oxford, 1965); C. O. Brink's text of Horace's *Ars Poetica* (Cambridge, 1971); and for Longinus the text of D. Russell (Oxford, 1964).

LITERARY CHRONOLOGY

The dates given are those when authors were active. Authors whose names appear in italic are discussed in the Introduction.

HISTORICAL EVENTS | AUTHORS

BC

c. 1600–1200 Mycenaean
Civilization
c. 1270 The destruction of Troy VI,
perhaps the Troy of legend
c. 1250–900 The Dark Age and the
period of Migrations
c. 800–650 The Age of Colonization
776 First Olympic Games

c. 750–700 *Homer* and *Hesiod*

Archaic Period
Lyric poetry and the beginnings of philosophy

c. 650–550 Tyrannies established in
many Greek cities

c. 650 Archilochus

c. 600 Sappho and Alcaeus

594 Solon's reforms of Athens

HISTORICAL EVENTS	AUTHORS
	c. 585 Thales of Miletus; the first of the 'Presocratic' philosophers
	c. 570–475 Lifetime of *Xenophanes*
560–510 Tyranny of Pisistratus and his sons at Athens	
	c. 530 Beginnings of Attic tragedy
	c. 530 Pythagoras active in south Italy as philosopher
508 Reforms of Cleisthenes at Athens	

Classical Period: The Fifth Century
Lyric poetry, tragedy, comedy, history, the beginnings of rhetoric

	499–458 *Aeschylus*
	498–446 *Pindar*
490 First Persian invasion of Greece: Battle of Marathon	
480 Second Persian invasion of Greece: Battles of Thermopylae and Salamis	
479 Defeat of Persians at Plataea: withdrawal of Persians from Greece	
478–429 Domination of the Aegean by Athens	
	c. 468–406 *Sophocles*
	c. 460–430 Herodotus
	c. 455–408 *Euripides*
c. 450–429 Periclean Age in Athens	c. 450–400 The Age of Sophists
431–404 Peloponnesian War between Athens and Sparta	c. 431–400 Thucydides

HISTORICAL EVENTS

AUTHORS

c. 430 Socrates active
c. 429 Birth of *Plato*
427 *Gorgias* visits Athens; the formal
art of rhetoric begins
c. 427–388 *Aristophanes*

415–413 Disastrous Athenian
expedition to Sicily
404 Athens surrenders to Sparta

Classical Period: the Fourth Century
Philosophy, rhetoric and prose in general

404–371 Supremacy of Sparta

399 Trial and execution of Socrates
397–338 Isocrates
390–354 Xenophon
c. 387 *Plato* founds the Academy
384 Birth of *Aristotle*

371–362 Supremacy of Thebes
359–336 Philip II is King of
Macedon

355 Literary and political career of
the orator Demosthenes begins
347 Death of *Plato*
343–342 *Aristotle* in Macedonia as
tutor to Alexander

338 Philip defeats Athens and Sparta
at Chaeronea
336 Alexander the Great becomes
King of Macedon

335 *Aristotle* founds the Lyceum
(Peripatetic school)

331 Foundation of Alexandria

HISTORICAL EVENTS	AUTHORS
	c. 324–292 Menander, poet of New Comedy
323 Death of Alexander	
	322 Death of *Aristotle*

Hellenistic Period
Court poetry, philosophy, literary scholarship

323–31 Egypt ruled by the Ptolemies	
	c. 310 Zeno (335–263) establishes Stoic school at Athens
	c. 307 Epicurus (341–270) founds his school at Athens
c. 300 Ptolemy I Soter founds Museum and Library at Alexandria	
283 Ptolemy I dies; Ptolemy II Philadelphus succeeds	
	270s *Callimachus* and Theocritus working at Alexandrian court
	c. 270–245 Apollonius of Rhodes writes *Argonautica*

Rome
The beginnings of the literary influence of Greece on Rome

264–241 First Carthaginian War	
218–202 Second Carthaginian War: Hannibal defeated	
	c. 205–184 Career of Plautus
	c. 204–160 Ennius

HISTORICAL EVENTS   AUTHORS

200—146 Rome victorious in wars
against Macedon, Syria and
Carthage. Carthage destroyed 146

166—60 Plays of Terence

The Late Republic
The Golden Age of Latin Literature I

107—100 Marius consul six times
88—82 Civil war between Marius
and Sulla
88—63 Rome victorious in three
wars against Mithridates of Pontus

c. 81—43 *Cicero*
70 Birth of Virgil
65 Birth of *Horace*

60 First triumvirate: Caesar,
Pompey, Crassus

59—54 Catullus

58—51 Caesar's campaigns in Gaul
55—54 Caesar's invasions of Britain

55 Death of Lucretius; his poem
published posthumously

49 Caesar crosses the Rubicon: civil
war
48 Caesar defeats Pompey at
Pharsalus
44 Caesar murdered on the Ides of
March
42 Republicans under Brutus and
Cassius defeated at Philippi

c. 42—43 Sallust

c. 38 Virgil, *Eclogues*
37—30 *Horace, Satires*; patronage of
Maecenas

HISTORICAL EVENTS	AUTHORS
31 Octavian defeats Antony and Cleopatra at Actium	
	30 *Horace, Epodes*
	c. 30–16 Propertius
	29 Virgil, *Georgics*

The Augustan Age
The Golden Age of Latin Literature II

27 Octavian takes the name of Augustus	*c.* 27–19 Tibullus
	c. 25 – AD 17 Ovid
	24–23 *Horace, Odes* 1–3
Extensive conquests (Gaul, Spain, Germany, Austria, the Balkans)	20 *Horace, Epistles* 1
	19 Death of Virgil; *Aeneid* published posthumously
	12 *Horace, Epistles* 2.1 to Augustus
	?10 *Horace, Art of Poetry*
	8 Deaths of *Horace* and Maecenas
Birth of Christ	

AD

The Julio-Claudian Dynasty
The Silver Age of Latin Literature 1

14–37 Tiberius
c. 30 The crucifixion of Christ
37–41 Caligula
41–54 Claudius
43 Invasion of Britain
54–68 Nero

HISTORICAL EVENTS   AUTHORS

64 Nero's persecution of the
Christians

                                  65 Suicides of Seneca and Lucan
66–73 Jewish Revolt   66 Suicide of Petronius

The Flavian Dynasty
The Silver Age of Latin Literature II

69 The year of the four emperors:
Galba, Otho, Vitellius and Vespasian
struggle for power
69–79 Vespasian
70 Destruction of the Temple at
Jerusalem; Diaspora
79–81 Titus
79 Eruption of Vesuvius; destruction
of Pompeii and Herculaneum
81–96 Domitian

                                  88–94 Quintilian
                                  ? *Longinus*

The Age of the Antonines

96–98 Nerva   *c.* 98–110 Pliny
98–117 Trajan   *c.* 98 – *c.* 120 Tacitus
117–138 Hadrian

                                  120s Suetonius and Juvenal active

PLATO

Ion

[530] 'Ion, greetings! Where have you come from to visit us here? From your home in Ephesus?'

'No, Socrates. I've come from the festival of Asclepius at Epidaurus.'[1]

'Do you mean to say that the people of Epidaurus have a competition for rhapsodes too in honour of the god?'

'They do indeed, and for all the musical arts.'

'Well, did you compete? How did you get on?'

'We won first prize, Socrates.'

'Congratulations! Let's hope we win at the Panathenaea too.'[2]

'So we shall, god willing.'

'I've often envied you rhapsodes your profession, Ion. Your art requires you to dress up in fine clothes and look as splendid as possible, and also compels you to occupy yourself with the works of many excellent poets, especially those of Homer, the best and most divine of all. And you have to understand his thought, not only his words – an enviable lot indeed. For a rhapsode would never be any good if he didn't understand what the poet says. He has to be an interpreter of the poet's meaning for his audience, and it's impossible for anyone who doesn't understand what the poet says to do this well. All this is well worth envying.'

'You're right, Socrates. At any rate this is the aspect of my profession which has given me most trouble, and I think I'm better at speaking on Homer than anyone. Neither Metrodorus of Lampsacus nor Stesimbrotus of Thasos, nor Glaucon[3] nor anyone else who has ever lived has had so many fine thoughts about Homer to express as I have.'

'Bravo, Ion. Obviously you won't grudge me a display.'

'Indeed it's worth hearing how well I have embellished Homer. I think I deserve to be crowned with a golden crown by the Homeridae.'[4]

'Indeed, I'll make time to hear you, but for the moment just [531] answer me this. Are you good at speaking about Homer alone, or are you good at Hesiod and Archilochus too?'

'No, only about Homer. I think that's enough.'

'Is there any subject about which Homer and Hesiod say the same?'

'I should think there are many.'

'Would you explain better what Homer says about these things or what Hesiod says?'

'I'd explain both equally well, when they are saying the same things about the same subjects.'

'What about the subjects on which they don't say the same thing? For example, both Homer and Hesiod have something to say about divination.'

'Yes.'

'Well, who would explain better the similarities and differences between what these poets say about divination, you, or one of the good prophets?'

'One of the prophets.'

'If you were a prophet, wouldn't you be able to explain the things about which they differ, if you could explain the things about which they agree?'

'Clearly.'

'Then why ever are you good at Homer and not at Hesiod or any of the other poets? Does Homer speak about different things from all the other poets? Doesn't he for the most part talk about war and men's dealings with one another, good and bad, laymen and professionals? About the gods and how they associate with each other and with mortals, what goes on in the heavens and in Hades, the genealogies of gods and heroes? Aren't these the subjects of Homer's poetry?'

'They are, Socrates.'

'Well, then, don't the other poets speak about these same things?'

'Yes, Socrates, but not in the same way as Homer.'

'Worse?'

'Much worse.'

'Homer's better?'

'Much better, by Zeus.'

'Ion, my dear chap, when a lot of people are talking about arithmetic and one of them speaks best, someone, I suppose, will be able to pick out the good speaker?'

'Yes.'

'Will he be the same person as one who knows who the bad speakers are, or a different person?'

'The same.'

'Won't this person be one who is skilled in arithmetic?'

'Yes.'

'Well, then, when a lot of people are talking about what sorts of food are healthy and one of them speaks best, will one person know who is the best speaker and who is the worse, or will the same person know both?'

'The same, clearly.'

'Who is this? What is he called?'

'A doctor.'

'So, to sum it up, we're saying that when a group of people are discussing the same subject, it will always be the same [532] person who knows who is speaking well and who is speaking badly. If he can't tell the bad speaker, clearly he can't tell the good speaker either, at any rate when the subject is the same.'

'Yes.'

'So the same person will be skilled in both?'

'Yes.'

'Now, you say that Homer and the other poets, including Hesiod and Archilochus, speak about the same things, but not in the same way, Homer speaking well, the others less well?'

'Yes, and I'm right.'

'So if you recognize the good speaker, you will also recognize the inferiority of the bad speakers.'

'So it would seem.'

'So, my excellent fellow, we shall not go wrong in saying that Ion is equally skilled in Homer and in the other poets, since you your-self agree that the same person will be an adequate judge of all who

3

speak on the same subjects, and almost all poets deal with the same themes.'

'Then why on earth is it, Socrates, that whenever someone talks about any other poet I don't pay attention and can't contribute anything of any value, but simply doze off, but whenever anyone mentions Homer I wake up immediately and pay attention and have lots to say?'

'That's not difficult to guess, my friend. It's clear to anyone that you're incapable of speaking about Homer with skill and knowledge. For if you were, you would be able to speak about all the other poets as well; the whole thing is poetry, isn't it?'

'Yes.'

'And when one takes any skill whatsoever as a whole, there will be the same method of inquiry in the case of every one of them. Do you want to hear what I mean by this, Ion?'

'Indeed, by Zeus, I do, Socrates. I love listening to you clever people.'

'If only you were right there, Ion. But you rhapsodes and actors and those whose poems you recite are the clever ones; I only speak the truth, as a simple layman. Take the question I asked you just now: look at how commonplace and simple it is. Anyone can understand my point, that when one takes any skill as a whole the method of inquiry will be the same. Let's take an example: is there an art of painting as a whole?'

'Yes.'

'And there are and have been many painters both good and bad?'

'Certainly.'

'And have you ever seen anyone who is good at explaining the merits and defects in the paintings of Polygnotus, son of Aglaophon,[5] but who is incapable of doing the same for other [533] painters? Someone who, when the works of other painters are displayed, dozes off and is at a loss and has nothing to contribute, but, when he is required to express an opinion on Polygnotus or any other individual painter you choose, wakes up and pays attention and has a lot to say?'

'No, by Zeus, I haven't.'

'Or again, in sculpture, have you ever seen anyone who is good at explaining the merits of the work of Daedalus, son of Metion, or Epeius, son of Panopeus, or Theodorus of Samos[6] or any other individual sculptor, but is at a loss and dozes off and has nothing to say when it comes to the works of other sculptors?'

'No, by Zeus, I haven't seen anyone like that either.'

'Indeed, when it comes to pipe playing or lyre playing, or singing to the lyre or being a rhapsode, I don't suppose that you have ever seen a man who is good at expounding the work of Olympus or Thamyras or Orpheus, or Phemius the rhapsode from Ithaca,[7] but is at a loss and has nothing to say about the merits and defects of the recitations of Ion of Ephesus.'

'I can't contradict you on that one, Socrates. But I *know* that I'm the finest speaker of all on Homer, and have plenty to say, and everyone says that I speak well about him – though not about the other poets. You explain it if you can.'

'I can, and I'm going to tell you what I think it is. This ability of yours to speak well about Homer is not a skill, as I was saying just now. It is a divine power which moves you, like the power in the stone which Euripides calls a magnet, but which most people call the "Heraclean stone". This stone not only attracts iron rings, it also confers on them the power to do the same, that is, to attract other rings, so that sometimes a long chain of rings and pieces of iron, suspended one from another, is formed, the power of all of them depending on the stone. In the same way the Muse herself inspires people, and from these inspired people a chain of others is strung out, all inspired with the same enthusiasm. For all good poets utter all those fine poems of theirs not through skill, but when inspired and possessed, and good lyric poets do the same. Just as Corybantic [534] worshippers[8] are not in their right minds when they dance, so too lyric poets compose those fine poems of theirs when they are not in their right minds; when they embark on melody and rhythm they become frenzied and possessed like Bacchic women who draw milk and honey from rivers when possessed and out of their minds; the souls of lyric poets undergo the same experience, as they themselves say. For they tell us, you see, that they bring us their songs from honey-flowing springs in groves and gardens of the Muses, gathering them as bees gather honey; and they too are on the wing. And they are right. For a poet is a light and winged and sacred thing, and is unable to compose until he is inspired and out of his mind and his reason is no longer in him. So long as he has his reason, no man can compose or prophesy. Since, then, it's not skill, but divine dispensation that enables them to compose poetry and say many fine things about the deeds of men, as you do about Homer, the only thing that each individual poet is able to compose well is what the Muse has stirred him to do – one dithyrambs, one encomia, one dancing songs, one epic, one iambics.[9] Each of them is no good at anything else. For it's not skill that makes them utter these fine things, but a divine force; since if they knew how to speak well about one topic through skill, they would be able to speak about all the others too. This is why god takes away their reason and uses them as servants, as he uses prophets and divine seers, so that we who hear them may know that it is not these people, whose reason has left them, who are uttering such valuable words, but that it is god himself who speaks and addresses us through them. The strongest proof of this is Tynnichus the Chalcidian, who never composed anything worth mentioning except the paean[10] which everyone sings, probably the finest of all lyrics, literally 'an invention of the Muses', as he himself says. In this case especially god seems to have shown us, lest we should doubt it, that these fine poems are not mortal and of human beings, but divine and of the gods, and poets are nothing but interpreters of the gods, each possessed by his own possessing god. To show us this, god deliberately sang the finest lyric through the mouth of [**535**] the worst poet. Or don't you think I'm right, Ion?'

'Yes, by Zeus, I do. For your words somehow touch my soul, Socrates, and I do believe that good poets interpret these utterances from the gods for us by divine dispensation.'

'And you rhapsodes in turn interpret the utterances of the poets?'

'You're right there, too.'

'So you are interpreters of interpreters?'

'Exactly.'

'Well now, tell me this, Ion, and don't conceal anything from me. When you give a good recital and especially stun your audience – when you sing of Odysseus leaping on to the threshold, revealing himself to the suitors and pouring forth arrows at his feet, or of Achilles rushing at Hector, or one of the pitiful passages about Andromache or Hecuba or Priam[11] – are you then in your right mind or are you beside yourself?

6

And does your soul, in its enthusiasm, imagine that it is present at those events which you describe, whether in Ithaca or in Troy or wherever the epic sets the scene?'

'How vividly you make your point, Socrates, and I'll tell you without concealment. When I recite something pitiful my eyes fill with tears; when it's something terrifying or dreadful my hair stands on end in terror and my heart thumps.'

'Well now, Ion, when a man, dressed in fine robes and a golden crown, bursts into tears at a sacrifice or festival, although he has lost none of his finery, or feels afraid when he is standing amongst more than twenty thousand friendly people, none of whom is trying to rob him or do him any harm – are we to say that such a man is in his right mind?'

'No, by Zeus, not at all, Socrates, to tell you the truth.'

'And are you aware that you people produce the same effects on most of your audience?'

'Yes, very much so. For I look down on them every time from the platform and see them weeping and looking at me with awestruck gaze, amazed at my story. And it's very important that I pay attention to them; since if I make them cry, I shall be laughing at the money I'll make, but if I make them laugh, I'll be the one crying because of the money I'll lose.'

'Do you realize, then, that your spectator is the last of the rings which I said derived their power from each other, under the influence of the Heraclean stone? The middle one is you, the [536] rhapsode and actor, and the poet himself is the first. Through all these, the god draws the souls of men wherever he wants, making the power of one depend upon the other. And, just as from that stone, a huge chain of choral performers and trainers and assistant trainers is suspended, attached sideways to the rings that hang from the Muses. Different poets depend on different Muses – we call that being "possessed" which is more or less right, since the poet is indeed "held". From these first rings – that is, the poets – others in turn are suspended and inspired, some by Orpheus, some by Musaeus, but the majority are possessed and held by Homer. And you, Ion, are one of these: you are possessed by Homer. When anyone performs the work of another poet, you doze off and are at a loss for words, but when any strain of Homer is uttered you immediately wake up, and your soul dances and you have lots to say. For it's not through skill and knowledge that you say what you do about Homer, but through divine dispensation and possession. Just as Corybantic dancers are only sensitive to the melody which belongs to the particular god by whom they are possessed, and have plenty of gestures and words to suit that melody, though they take no notice of others, so you, Ion, are full of words whenever anyone mentions Homer, but are at a loss when it comes to others. This is the reason, to answer your question, why you are fluent about Homer, but not about others, because it is not skill, but divine dispensation that makes you such a formidable praiser of Homer.'

'You're a good speaker, Socrates; but I should be surprised if you could speak well enough to persuade me that I am possessed and mad when I praise Homer. I don't think you would believe it yourself if you heard me speaking about Homer.'

'Indeed, I'd like to hear you, but not before you have answered me this: on which of the subjects that Homer talks about do you speak well? It can't be all of them, surely?'

'On every single one of them, Socrates, I assure you.'

'But surely not on those subjects which Homer speaks of, and which you know nothing about?'

'And what subjects does Homer speak of that I know nothing about?'

[537] 'Doesn't Homer talk a lot about skills of different sorts? For example, chariot driving. If I can remember the words, I'll quote them to you.'

'No, I will: I can remember them.'

'Tell me, then, what Nestor says to his son, Antilochus, advising him to be careful at the turning-post in the horse race in honour of Patroclus.'

> Lean over yourself in your polished chariot
> Slightly to the left; goad the right-hand horse,
> Shouting, and slacken his reins in your hands.
> At the post let the left-hand horse swerve close,
> So that the hub of your well-wrought wheel
> Seems to touch the edge; but avoid hitting the stone.[12]

'Stop. Now, Ion, who would know better whether Homer is right or not in these lines, a doctor or a charioteer?'

'A charioteer, of course.'

'Because he has this particular skill, or for some other reason?'

'No, because he has this skill.'

'So has the god given to each skill the ability to understand a particular activity? For I assume that what we know through the pilot's skill, we don't also know through medicine.'

'Indeed not.'

'And what we know through medicine, we cannot know through carpentry?'

'Indeed not.'

'Isn't it so in the case of all skills, that what we know through one skill we shall not know through another? But answer me this first: do you say that skills are different from one another?'

'Yes.'

'Do you judge as I do and differentiate between skills when their knowledge is of different objects?'

'Yes.'

'For if there were some field of knowledge which dealt with the same subject matter, how could we say that there were two different skills involved, when both could give us the same knowledge? For example, I know that these fingers are five in number, and you know the same about them as I do. And if I were to ask you whether you and I know this same thing by the same skill, that is by arithmetic, or by a different one, you would say, no doubt, by the same.'

'Yes.'

[538] 'Tell me now what I was just going to ask you. Do you think that in the case of all skills we must know the same things by the same skill and different things by a different skill, and that if the skill is different then the things we know by it must be different?'

'Yes, I do, Socrates.'

'So anyone who does not have a particular skill will be incapable of knowing properly the words or actions which belong to that skill?'

'True.'

'So in the case of the words you quoted, would you or a charioteer know better whether Homer is right or not?'

'A charioteer.'

'Because you are a rhapsode and not a charioteer?'

'Yes.'

'And the rhapsode's skill is different from that of the charioteer?'

'Yes.'

'Then if it is different, it is also a knowledge of different things.'

'Yes.'

'Now what about when Homer says that Hecamede, Nestor's concubine, gives a potion to the wounded Machaon to drink. He says something like this:

> . . . with Pramnian wine; over it she grated goat's cheese
> With a bronze grater; with it an onion as relish.[13]

Is it for the doctor's skill or for the rhapsode's to decide whether Homer speaks correctly here or not?'

'The doctor's.'

'Well, then, what about when Homer says:

> She went to the bottom like a plummet
> Which, set on the horn of an ox of the field,
> Goes to bring pain to the ravenous fish.[14]

Are we to say that it is for the fisherman's skill or for the rhapsode's to judge what he says here, and whether he says it well or not?'

'The fisherman's, obviously, Socrates.'

'Look, then, if you were questioning me and were to ask me: "Socrates, since you are finding passages in Homer which it is appropriate for each of these skills to judge, come on now, and find something relating to the prophet and his skill. What sorts of passages will it be appropriate for him to judge for their correctness?" – look at how easily I can give you an answer. For Homer talks a lot about such matters in the *Odyssey*, as, for example, when Theoclymenus, the seer descended from Melampus' line, says to the suitors:

[539] Wretched men, what evil is this you suffer?
Your heads and faces and limbs are shrouded in night,
Wailing blazes up and your cheeks are wet with tears;
The porch and hall are full of ghosts
Hastening to hell beneath the gloom; the sun
Has gone from the sky, and an evil mist is spread about.[15]

And there is a lot in the *Iliad* too, as, for example, in the battle at the
wall where he says:

A bird came upon them as they were eager to cross,
An eagle that flies aloft, pressing the host on the left,
Carrying a blood-red monstrous snake in its claws,
Alive, still struggling; nor yet had it forgotten its fight.
For it struck its captor on the breast by the neck
Bending back, and the bird, racked with pain,
Dropped it on the ground in the midst of the host;
And with a loud cry he flew off with the wind.[16]

I should say that this and passages like it are appropriate for the prophet
to consider and judge.'

'You're right, Socrates.'

'And you're right too, Ion. So come now and do as I did for you
when I picked out from the *Odyssey* and the *Iliad* the sorts of things
that concern the seer and the doctor and the fisherman; you now pick
out for me, since you are much more knowledgeable about the works
of Homer than I am, the sorts of things that concern the rhapsode's
skills, Ion – things which it's appropriate for the rhapsode to consider
and judge better than other people.'

'My answer to that is, everything, Socrates.'

'You don't really mean everything, Ion. Or are you so forgetful? It
ill becomes a rhapsode to be forgetful.'

[540] 'What am I forgetting then?'

'Don't you remember that you said that the rhapsode's skill is different
from that of the charioteer?'

'I remember.'

'And you agreed that since it was different it would know different things?'

'Yes.'

'Then by your own account the rhapsode's skill will not know everything, nor will the rhapsode himself.'

'Well, everything except things like that, Socrates.'

'By "things like that" you mean more or less the things that belong to other skills. But what sorts of things will he know, since he doesn't know everything?'

'The sorts of things, I think, that it is appropriate for a man to say, what a woman should say, what a slave or a freeman or a subject or a ruler should say.'

'Are you saying, then, that a rhapsode will know better than a pilot the sorts of things that a captain should say when his ship is in a storm at sea?'

'No, a pilot would know that.'

'Will a rhapsode know better than a doctor what someone in charge of a sick person should say?'

'No, not that either.'

'Do you mean that he knows what a slave should say?'

'Yes.'

'Do you mean that in the case of a slave who is, for example, a cowherd, a rhapsode will know better than a cowherd what he should say to quieten his cattle down when they are excited?'

'Not at all.'

'Will he know what a spinning-woman should say about working wool?'

'No.'

'Then will he know what a general should say when he is exhorting his soldiers?'

'Yes, a rhapsode will know that sort of thing.'

'So is the rhapsode's skill the same as the general's?'

'Well, I should certainly know the sort of things that a general ought to say.'

'Perhaps because you're good at generalship too, Ion. And if you were good at horsemanship as well as playing the lyre you would know when horses were handled well or badly. But if I asked you, "By which skill do you know that horses are well handled, by that which makes you a horseman, or by the one which makes you a lyre player?", what would you answer me?'

'By my skill as a horseman, I should say.'

'And if you recognized good lyre playing, you would agree that you did so by the skill which makes you a lyre player, not by the one which makes you a horseman.'

'Yes.'

'Now since you understand military matters, is that because you understand generalship or because you are a good rhapsode?'

'There's no difference, in my opinion.'

[541] 'What? No difference? Are you saying that the skill of the rhapsode and the skill of the general is one skill or two?'

'One, in my opinion.'

'So anyone who is a good rhapsode is also, in fact, a good general?'

'Certainly, Socrates.'

'And anyone who is a good general is also a good rhapsode?'

'No, that's not so.'

'But you do think that anyone who is a good rhapsode is also a good general?'

'Yes.'

'And you are the best rhapsode in Greece?'

'Much the best, Socrates.'

'And are you the best general in Greece too, Ion?'

'Certainly, Socrates, and I've learned these things from Homer.'

'Then if you are the best general in Greece and the best rhapsode, why in heaven's name do you go around Greece performing as a rhapsode and not as a general? Or do you think that Greece really needs a rhapsode crowned with a golden crown and doesn't need a general?'

'My city,[17] Socrates, is ruled by you Athenians and is under your command, and doesn't need a general; besides, neither you nor Sparta would elect me as general because you think you're good enough yourselves.'

'Ion, my dear chap, don't you know Apollodorus of Cyzicus?'

'And who is he?'

'A man whom the Athenians have often elected as their general, even though he is a foreigner. And there is Phanosthenes of Andros and Heraclides of Clazomenae whom this city appoints to generalships and other offices, despite being foreigners, because they have shown themselves to be men of worth. So won't it elect Ion of Ephesus as general and honour him if he seems to be a man of worth? And anyway, aren't you Ephesians Athenians in origin, and isn't Ephesus a city that is second to none? The fact is, Ion, that if you are right in saying that it is skill and knowledge which enable you to praise Homer, you are being unfair: for you professed to know many fine things about Homer and promised to give me a display, but you're deceiving me and are nowhere near giving a display. Indeed, you won't even tell me what it is that you're good at, despite my insistence. Like a real Proteus you turn yourself into all manner of things, twisting this way and that, until finally you escape me in the shape of a general, [542] so as to avoid displaying your amazing wisdom about Homer. So, as I said just now, if you do have skill and are deceiving me in your promise to give a display about Homer, you are being unfair; but if you are not skilled, and are possessed by Homer, and say many fine things about him by divine dispensation, but without any knowledge, as I suggested, then you are not being unfair. So choose which you prefer: do you want us to think you unfair or divine?'

'There's a great difference, Socrates. It's a much finer thing to be thought divine.'

'Well then, Ion, as far as I'm concerned, this finer alternative will do: you are not a skilled praiser of Homer, but divine.'

PLATO

Republic 2

'What education shall we give them, then? Isn't it difficult to improve on the time-honoured system, that is, gymnastics for the body and music[1] for the soul?'

'It is.'

'Then shall we begin our education with music before gymnastics?'

'Of course.'

'Under music do you include stories or not?'

'I do.'

'And there are two kinds of stories, one true, the other false?'

'Yes.'

[377] 'Should children be educated in both or only in the false ones?'

'I don't understand what you mean.'

'Don't you understand that we tell myths to children first of all? And myth is in general false, but also contains some truth. And we tell children myths before we give them physical training.'

'That's so.'

'This is what I meant by saying that we should start with music before gymnastics.'

'That's right.'

'And, as you know, the beginning is the most important part of every task, especially when dealing with anything young and tender; for then it is most easily moulded and takes on any impression which one wishes to stamp on it.'

'Certainly.'

'Shall we then carelessly allow the children to listen to any myths made up by anyone, and to absorb into their souls opinions which are for the most part the opposite of those we think they should have when they grow up?'

'No, we certainly shan't allow that.'

'So first of all we must supervise the making of myths, and accept the good ones, but reject the bad. And we shall persuade nurses and mothers to tell the accepted ones to children, and to mould their souls with myths much more than they mould their bodies with their hands. Most of those we now tell will have to be rejected.'

'Which ones?'

'If we take the greater myths as examples, we shall see in them the pattern of the lesser ones too, for both must be cast in the same mould and have the same effect, don't you think?'

'I do; but I don't understand what you mean by the greater myths.'

'Those that Hesiod and Homer and the other poets have told us. For they composed false myths and told them to people, and still do.'

'What sort of myths, and what fault do you find in them?'

'The worst possible fault, especially if someone tells a lie that is ugly.'

'What is that?'

'When someone makes a bad verbal likeness of gods and heroes, like a painter whose painting bears no resemblance to the things he wants to portray.'

'It's certainly right to find fault with that kind of thing. But which ones are we talking about?'

'First of all there is the biggest lie about the most important matters – the ugly lie that Ouranos[2] did what Hesiod [378] says he did, and that Kronos took vengeance on him. The story of what Kronos did and what he suffered at the hands of *his* son should not be lightly repeated to the young and foolish, even if it were true. If possible it should be passed over in silence, but if it had to be told, it should be done in secrecy before the smallest possible audience, and after the sacrifice, not of a pig,[3] but of some large and inaccessible victim, so that very few would hear the story.'

'Indeed these are difficult stories.'

'And they must not be told in our city, Adeimantus. Nor should we allow a young person to hear that, if he committed the worst crimes, or did his utmost to punish an unjust father, he would be doing nothing out of the ordinary, but merely doing what the first and the greatest of the gods have done.'

'No indeed, I don't think these stories are suitable.'

'And stories about the gods making war and plotting and fighting against each other will be absolutely forbidden, for they are not true. If we want our future guardians to believe that hating one another is the worst evil, they must not be told tales about the battles of giants or have them embroidered on robes,[4] nor must they hear about the various other quarrels of gods and heroes with their kinsmen and friends. If somehow we are to persuade them that no citizen has ever quarrelled with any other, and that it is wrong to do so, we must make old men and women tell children stories to that effect from the start, and poets must be compelled to tell them similar stories when they grow up. Stories of Hera being tied up by her son, or of Hephaestus being thrown out by his father for trying to defend his mother from a beating, and all those battles of the gods in Homer must not be allowed in our city, whether they were composed allegorically or not. For a child cannot distinguish between what is allegorical and what is not, and opinions formed at that age tend to become permanent and indelible. For these reasons everything must be done to ensure that the first stories they hear are as suitable as possible for the encouragement of virtue.'

'Yes, indeed, that's reasonable. But if someone were to ask us what stories we had in mind, what would we say?'

'Adeimantus, you and I are not poets at the moment, but [379] founders of a city; and founders need to know the patterns on which poets are to compose their stories, and from which they must not be allowed to deviate, but they don't need to compose the stories themselves.'

'True, but what *are* the patterns for stories about the gods?'

'Something like this: god must surely always be represented as he really is, whether in epic or lyric or tragedy.'

'He must.'

'And in reality god is good and must be so described.'

'Of course.'

'And nothing that is good is harmful, is it?'

'No.'

'And can what is not harmful cause harm?'

'Not at all.'

'And can what does no harm do any evil?'

'No again.'

'And what does no evil is the cause of no evil?'

'How could it be?'

'Now then, is the good useful?'

'Yes.'

'Therefore the cause of well-being?'

'Yes.'

'So the good is not the cause of everything, but only of what is good; it is not the cause of evil.'

'Quite so.'

'So, since god is good he is not responsible for everything that happens to human beings, as most people say, but only for a few things; there is much for which he is not responsible. For the good things in human life are far fewer than the evils, and whilst god alone must be the cause of the good, we must find the cause of evils elsewhere.'

'I think that's perfectly true.'

'So we cannot allow Homer or any other poet to make this foolish mistake about the gods when he says that

> Two urns stand at Zeus' door
> Full of fates, one of good, one of evil,

and that the man to whom Zeus gives a mixture of both

> Now meets with evil, now with good,

but as for the man to whom he gives unmixed evil,

> Dread hunger drives him over the earth.[5]

Nor can we allow that Zeus is "dispenser of good and evil". Nor shall we approve of anyone who says that Pandarus' breaking of the treaty and the oath was prompted by Athena and Zeus,[6] or that [380] Themis and Zeus caused strife and dissension among the gods. And we must not allow the young to hear the words of Aeschylus, when he says that

> God implants a fault in mortals
> When he wants to destroy a house utterly.

But if anyone does write about the sufferings of Niobe (the subject of the play in which these lines occur), or the house of Pelops, or the Trojan war, or anything else like that, either he must not be allowed to say that they are the work of god, or, if they are, he must find some account such as we are now seeking: he must say that what god did was just and good, and that the sufferers benefited from being punished. But the poet must not be allowed to say that those who were punished were miserable, and that it was god who made them so. What he can say, however, is that the wicked were miserable because they needed punishment, and that they benefited from being punished by god. But we must resist at all costs the notion that god, who is good, is the cause of evil; no one must be allowed to say this in our city if it is to be well governed, and no one, young or old, is to hear stories of this kind either in verse or in prose. To say such things would be unholy, unprofitable and self-contradictory.'

'I shall vote with you for this law. I approve of it.'

'This then will be one of the laws and patterns which poets and speakers will have to observe: god is not the cause of everything, but only of good.'

'I am quite satisfied with that.'

'Well, then, what about this for the second one?'

'Do you think that god is a magician and deliberately appears in different forms at different times, sometimes turning himself into different shapes and changing his form, sometimes deceiving us and making us think such things about himself? Or is he single in nature and of all things least likely to depart from his own form?'

'I can't say at the moment.'

'Well, if something departs from its own form, mustn't it be changed either by itself or by something else?'

'Yes.'

'And aren't things that are in the best condition least affected by change from outside? For example, take the effects of food and drink and exercise on the body, or those of sun and wind and other such things on plants: the healthiest and strongest are [381] least subject to change, aren't they?'

'Of course.'

'And isn't the bravest and wisest soul least disturbed and affected by external influence?'

'Yes.'

'And the same principle applies to all manufactured things – furniture, houses, clothes: those that are well made and in good condition are least affected by time and other influences.'

'That's so.'

'So anything that is in good condition, whether by nature or art or both, is least subject to change from outside.'

'So it seems.'

'But god and what belongs to god is surely perfect in every way?'

'Of course.'

'So god would be least likely to take on many shapes through external influence.'

'Yes, least of all.'

'But would he change and alter himself?'

'Clearly, if he changes at all.'

'Well then, does he change himself for the better or for the worse?'

'Necessarily for the worst; for we certainly can't say that god is deficient in beauty or goodness.'

'You're absolutely right. And this being so, Adeimantus, do you think that anyone, human or divine, would willingly change himself for the worse in any way?'

'That's impossible.'

'Then it's also impossible for a god to want to change himself; rather, every god, being perfectly beautiful and good, remains simple, always in his own shape.'

'Necessarily so.'

'So, my friend, none of the poets must tell us that

The gods in the guise of strangers from afar
Assume all shapes and visit cities.[7]

Nor must anyone tell false tales against Proteus and Thetis, or bring
Hera into tragedy or any other poetry in the guise of a priestess collecting
alms

For the life-giving children of Inachus, river of Argos.[8]

And there are many other lies like this which must be forbidden.
Mothers must not be persuaded by the poets into terrifying children
with wicked stories of how the gods prowl around at night taking on
all sorts of strange shapes: we don't want them blaspheming the gods
or making cowards of their children.'

'No indeed.'

'But can we suppose that, though the gods themselves do not change,
they make us think that they appear in different forms, deceiving and
bewitching us?'

'Perhaps.'

[382] 'What? Would a god want to deceive us by his words or actions,
and present us with an apparition?'

'I don't know.'

'Don't you know that all gods and mortals hate true falsehood, if I
can use that expression?'

'What do you mean?'

'I mean that no one willingly wants to be deceived in the most
important part of himself about the most important things, but is
particularly afraid of being deceived there.'

'I still don't understand.'

'That's because you think I'm saying something mysterious. But I
only mean that the last thing anyone wants is to be deceived in his soul
about reality, and to be the victim of ignorance and falsehood there.
Everyone hates that.'

'Indeed.'

'But, as I was saying, it is ignorance in the soul of the deceived that is rightly called true falsehood. For spoken falsehood is a representation of the state of the soul, a subsequent image, not pure unmixed falsehood. Isn't that so?'

'Certainly.'

'So real falsehood is hated by gods and human beings alike?'

'Yes.'

'What about spoken falsehood? Isn't it sometimes useful and not to be despised? Isn't it useful against enemies, or as a kind of preventive medicine for our friends if they try to do something bad through madness or folly? Again, in the case of the myths we were talking about just now, since we don't know the truth about the past we have to make our falsehood as like the truth as possible, and thus make it useful.'

'That's quite right.'

'Well, then, in which of these cases would falsehood be useful to god? Would he lie because he doesn't know the truth about the past?'

'That would be ridiculous.'

'So there is no false poet in god.'

'No.'

'Would he lie through fear of his enemies?'

'Certainly not.'

'Or because of the foolishness or madness of his friends?'

'No fool or madman is god's friend.'

'So there's no reason why god should lie.'

'No.'

'So the spiritual and the divine are totally free from falsehood.'

'Totally.'

'God, then, is simple and true in deed and word. He does not change himself, nor does he deceive others, awake or asleep, through visions or words or the sending of signs.'

[383] 'I agree with what you say.'

'Do you agree, then, that this is the second pattern concerning the gods to which storytellers and poets must conform, that they are neither magicians who transform themselves, nor do they mislead us with lies in word or deed?'

'I do.'

'So, though there is much to praise in Homer, we shall not approve

of the dream sent by Zeus[9] to Agamemnon; nor shall we praise the
passage in Aeschylus where Thetis says that Apollo sang at her wedding
in celebration of her future offspring, telling of their long and happy
life:

> . . . he sang of my good fortune,
> Blessed by the gods, cheering my heart.
> And I thought the divine mouth of Phoebus,
> Full of prophetic skill, could speak no falsehood.
> But he who sang the hymn, he who was present at the feast,
> He who said these things, is the one who killed
> My child.[10]

When someone speaks like this about the gods, we shall be angry and
not allow his play to be produced, nor shall we allow teachers to use
such poetry in educating the young, if our guardians are going to be
god-fearing and divine, in so far as that is possible for human beings.'

'I altogether agree with these patterns, and I would treat them as
laws.'

PLATO

Republic 3

[386] 'These, then, are the sorts of things which people should and should not hear about the gods from their earliest childhood, if they are to honour the gods and their parents, and to value their friendship with each other.'

'Yes, and I think we are right.'

'And what if they are to be brave? Shouldn't they be told stories of a kind that will make them least likely to fear death? Or do you think a man can be brave if he has this fear in him?'

'No, I don't.'

'Well, then, do you think that anyone who believes in the existence of Hades and its terrors will be fearless in the face of death, and choose death in battle rather than defeat and slavery?'

'No.'

'It seems, then, that we must supervise the telling of these myths too, and require poets not to speak ill of Hades unthinkingly, as they do now – for, if they do, they won't be saying anything true or useful to future warriors – but rather to praise it.'

'We must, indeed.'

'So we shall cut out all such passages, beginning with these lines:

> I would rather live on earth as a serf
> To a landless man, whose livelihood was small,
> Than rule over all the perished dead;[11]

and this:

> And his house be seen by mortals and immortals,
> Dreadful, dank and hated by the gods;

and:

> Ah me! even in Hades' house there is
> A phantom soul, but with no mind at all;

and:

> He alone can think, but the rest are flitting shadows;

and:

> His soul from his limbs to Hades flew,
> Lamenting his fate, leaving manhood and youth behind;

and:

[387]
> His soul from the earth like smoke
> Went gibbering away;

and:

> As when bats in the corner of a wondrous cave
> Flit about gibbering, when one of the colony
> Falls from the rock, and the others hold on above
> So these souls went gibbering together.

We shall ask Homer and the other poets not to be angry if we cut out all such passages. It's not that they are not poetic or pleasurable for the general public to hear; indeed the more poetic they are the less they should be heard by boys and men who must be free and fear slavery more than death.'

'Certainly.'

'And we must also ban all the horrible and terrifying names that are used in this connection like "Cocytus" and "Styx",[12] "infernal ones" and "withered dead", and all other names of this sort which make people shudder just to hear them. They may be good for some purposes, but we are afraid that such shuddering may make our guardians feverish and softer than they should be.'

'And we're right to be afraid.'

'Shall we remove them then?'

'Yes.'

'And stories and poems must conform to the opposite pattern?'

'Clearly.'

'Then shall we also cut out the weepings and wailings of famous men?'

'We shall have to, if we are to be consistent.'

'Well, consider whether we're right to cut them out or not. We say, don't we, that a good man will not think death a terrible thing for another good man whose friend he is.'

'We do.'

'So he wouldn't mourn for his friend's sake, as though something terrible had happened to him?'

'No.'

'Moreover we also say that such a man is especially self-sufficient for living a good life and, of all men, is least dependent on others.'

'True.'

'So he would be the last person to think it a terrible thing to lose a son or a brother, or possessions or anything else of that sort.'

'Yes.'

'So he laments least and bears it most calmly when any such misfortune overtakes him.'

'Certainly.'

'So we would be right to remove the lamentations of famous [388] men and give them to women – but not to the serious ones – and to the inferior men, so that those whom we claim to be educating as guardians of the country will be ashamed to act like this.'

'Quite right.'

'Then, again, we shall ask Homer and the other poets not to describe Achilles, the son of a goddess, as

> Lying now on his side, now
> On his back, and now face down,[13]

then standing up and wandering distraught by the shore of the restless sea; nor as taking up the dark dust in both his hands and pouring it over his head, nor weeping and lamenting in the way Homer has made him. Nor do we want Priam, a descendant of the gods, imploring and

> grovelling in dung,
> Calling on each man by name.

But even more than this we shall ask them not to make the gods lament and say:

> Alas, poor me, unhappy mother of the noblest son.

If they do show the gods lamenting, at least they should not dare to misrepresent the greatest of the gods and make him say:

> Ah me, dear is the man I see with my eyes
> Pursued around the city, and my heart grieves;

and:

> Alas, Sarpedon the dearest of men to me
> Is destined to die by Patroclus' hand.

For, dear Adeimantus, if our young men were to listen seriously to such unworthy utterances instead of laughing at them, it would be difficult for them, being mere mortals, to think themselves above such behaviour, and to rebuke themselves if it occurred to them to speak or act in this way; without shame or restraint they would break out into dirges and laments at the slightest occurrence.'

'Very true.'

'But they mustn't do this, as our argument has just indicated – and we should be persuaded by it until someone persuades us with a better one.'

'No, indeed, they mustn't.'

'Again, they mustn't be fond of laughter either. For whenever anyone gives way to violent laughter it tends to provoke a violent change.'

'I agree.'

'So we must reject any descriptions of reputable people [389] being overcome by laughter, let alone gods.'

'Certainly.'

'So, according to your argument, we shall reject the sort of thing that Homer says about the gods in the lines:

> Unquenchable laughter rose among the blessed gods
> When they saw Hephaestus bustling through the hall.'[14]

'You can call it my argument if you want; but this sort of thing must be rejected.'

'Again, truth must be highly valued. If we were right in saying just now that falsehood is of no use to the gods, but useful to human beings as a kind of medicine, clearly it must be administered by doctors and not touched by laymen.'

'Clearly.'

'So it's appropriate for the rulers of the state, if anyone, to tell lies involving enemies or fellow citizens for the benefit of the state, but no one else must do so. We shall say that, if a private person deceives these rulers, it's the same kind of mistake, but on a larger scale, as for a sick person to deceive a doctor about his physical condition, or an athlete his trainer, or for a sailor to lie to his captain about the ship and its crew, or about his own condition and that of his fellow sailors.'

'Very true.'

'But if the ruler catches anyone in the state lying,

> Anyone of those who are craftsmen,
> Whether seer, healer of ills, or joiner of timbers[15]

he will punish him for introducing a practice as subversive and destructive of a state as it would be of a ship.'

'Yes, if he is as good as his word.'

'Well now, won't our young men need self-control?'

'Of course.'

'For the mass of men aren't the main points of self-control these — obeying their rulers, and ruling their own pleasures in relation to drink and sex and food?'

'I think so.'

'So we shall approve, I think, of the sort of thing that Diomedes says in Homer:

> Friend, stay quiet and obey my word,[16]

and the words which are connected with these:

> The Achaeans moved forward, breathing might
> In silence, fearing their commanders,

and all other such things.'

'Yes indeed.'

'But what about lines like this —

> Drunkard with the eyes of a dog and the heart of a deer.[17]

[390] — can we approve of this and what comes after it, and all the other insolent things, either in prose or in poetry, that private individuals have said to their rulers?'

'No.'

'I don't think they will encourage self-control in young men who hear them, but if they give some other pleasure it's not surprising. What do you think?'

'I agree.'

'Well, what about making the wisest man say that what he likes best of all is when

> . . . the tables are full
> Of bread and meat, and the cup-bearer, drawing wine
> From the bowl, carries it round and pours it into their cups.[18]

– do you think that this will encourage self-restraint in a young man who hears it? Or this:

> Most pitiful it is to meet one's doom and die of hunger;

And what about the story of how Zeus[19] stayed awake alone, when all the other gods and men were asleep, making plans, but quickly forgot them all through his desire for sex? So smitten was he on seeing Hera that he wanted to lie with her right there on the ground without going into the house, saying that he had not felt such desire even when they slept together for the first time, "without the knowledge of their dear parents". And there's the story of how Hephaestus trapped Ares and Aphrodite[20] for similar reasons.'

'No, by Zeus, I don't think they are at all suitable.'

'But any speeches and deeds of endurance against all odds by famous men must be seen and heard, as for example:

> He struck his chest and rebuked his heart, saying,
> "Endure, my heart; you have endured worse before." '[21]

'Certainly.'

'But we mustn't allow our men to be money-lovers or to take bribes.'

'Not at all.'

'Nor must they hear that

> Gifts persuade the gods and reverend kings.[22]

Nor must Phoenix,[23] Achilles' tutor, be praised for speaking reasonably when he advises Achilles to help the Achaeans if they give him gifts, but not to give up his anger without gifts. Nor shall we think it right or agree that Achilles himself was so mercenary that he took gifts from

Agamemnon, and released the [391] corpse in return for a ransom,[24] but was otherwise unwilling to do so.'

'It wouldn't be right to praise such things.'

'I hesitate to say it out of regard for Homer, but it is impious to say these things of Achilles or to believe them when others say them; and, again, that he said to Apollo:

> You have wronged me, far-shooter, deadliest of gods.
> And I would avenge myself on you, had I the power;[25]

and that he refused to obey the river-god[26] and was ready to fight him, or that he said of the lock of his hair which was dedicated to another river, Spercheius: "I give this lock to the hero Patroclus to carry away", although he was dead.[27] We must not believe that he did this. As for the dragging of Hector's body round the tomb of Patroclus and the slaughter of the prisoners at the pyre, we shall say that this whole story is untrue; nor shall we allow our people to believe that Achilles, the son of a goddess and of Peleus, a most self-controlled man and a grandson of Zeus, Achilles, who was reared by Cheiron the wise, was so full of turmoil that he had in him two contradictory diseases, mean avarice on the one hand, and contempt for gods and men on the other.'

'You're right.'

'We should not believe or allow people to say that Theseus, son of Poseidon, and Peirithous, son of Zeus,[28] attempted such terrible rapes, or that any other hero or son of a god dared to do the kind of dreadful and impious deeds which are now falsely attributed to them. We should compel our poets to say, either that they did not do such things, or that they were not the children of gods, but they must not say both these things; nor must they try to persuade our young men that the gods are the source of evil, or that heroes are no better than ordinary human beings. As we said before, this is neither holy nor true, for we showed that it is impossible for evil to come from the gods.'

'Of course.'

'Moreover, these stories are harmful to those who hear them. For everyone will excuse his own wickedness if he believes that such things are done and have been done by

> . . . close kin of the gods
> Near to Zeus, to whom belongs the ancestral altar
> On Mount Ida in the heavens,
> In whom the blood of divinities still flows fresh.[29]

That's why such stories must be stopped, to prevent them from [**392**] breeding in our young men a complete indifference to wickedness.'

'Quite so.'

'Well, then, what class of story is left for us in our attempt to define what should and should not be told? For we have discussed the kinds of things that should be said about gods, demi-gods, heroes and Hades.'

'Yes.'

'So we're left with stories about human beings?'

'Obviously.'

'But it's impossible for us to sort that out at present, my friend.'

'Why?'

'Because we shall say, I think, that poets and prose writers are wrong about the most important matters in human life, when they say that there are many unjust men who are happy, and just men who are miserable, that wrongdoing pays if you can get away with it, and that justice is another person's good, but your own loss. We shall forbid them to say such things and order them to compose poems and stories which are quite the opposite. Don't you think so?'

'I'm certain of it.'

'If you admit that I'm right, then, shall I say that you have now admitted the point[30] we were trying to establish all along?'

'Yes, quite right.'

'So we shall be in a position to agree that these are the kinds of stories that should be told about human beings only when we have discovered what justice actually is, and how it naturally benefits the one who possesses it, whether he seems to be just or not.'

'Very true.'

'So much, then, for the content of stories. I think we must now look at the question of expression, and then we shall have thoroughly considered both *what* should be said and *how* it should be said.'

'I don't understand what you mean.'

'Well, I shall have to make you. Perhaps you'll understand better if I put it like this: isn't everything related by storytellers and poets a narration of things past, present or future?'

'Of course.'

'And they do this by using either pure narrative, or narrative conveyed through imitation or both.'

'I still need clarification on this.'

'I must be a ridiculously obscure teacher. I'll do what poor speakers do and try and show you by taking an example, rather than the subject as a whole. Tell me, you know the beginning of the *Iliad*, where the poet says that Chryses asks Agamemnon to release [393] his daughter, Agamemnon is angry, and Chryses, when he fails in his request, calls down the god's curses on the Achaeans.'

'I do.'

'And you know that up until these lines

> . . . he entreated all the Achaeans,
> And especially the two Atreidae, leaders of the people,[31]

the poet speaks in his own person, and doesn't try to make us think that the speaker is anyone other than himself. But after this he speaks as though he were Chryses and tries as hard as possible to make us think that it is not Homer speaking, but the old priest. And he has composed almost all the narrative of the events in Troy, and in Ithaca, and in the whole of the *Odyssey* in the same way.'

'Yes, indeed.'

'So the narrative consists both of the various speeches that are made and of the passages in between?'

'Yes.'

'But whenever he makes a speech as if he were someone else, shall we not say that he then assimilates his style of speech as far as possible to that of the person he has introduced as speaker?'

'Yes, we shall.'

'And to make oneself like someone else either in voice or in gesture is to imitate that person?'

'Yes.'

'In such cases it seems, then, that Homer and the other poets compose their narrative by means of imitation.'

'Indeed.'

'But if the poet never concealed himself, all his poetry and his narrative would be composed without imitation. Before you say that you don't understand again, I'll tell you how this would happen. If Homer, having said that Chryses went with ransom for his daughter and made supplication to the Achaeans, and especially to the kings, had gone on speaking not as if he were Chryses, but still as Homer, that would not have been imitation, but pure narrative. It would have been something like this – I'll do it without metre, since I'm no poet: "The priest came and prayed that the gods might grant them to capture Troy and return home safely, and begged them to accept his ransom and return his daughter out of respect for the gods. When he had said this, the others respected his words and agreed, but Agamemnon was angry and ordered him to go away immediately and not to come back again, otherwise his sceptre and the garlands of the god might not protect him. Before his daughter was released, she would grow old with him in Argos, he said, and he ordered him to go away and not to provoke him, if he wanted to get home safe. Hearing this the [394] old man was afraid and went away in silence; but when he had left the camp he prayed many times to Apollo, calling on the god by his titles, reminding him of and begging recompense for any of his gifts that had found favour, either in the building of temples or in the sacrifice of victims; in return for these things he prayed that the Achaeans might pay for his tears with the god's arrows." That, my friend, is pure narrative without imitation.'

'I understand.'

'Understand, then, that the opposite happens when one removes the poet's words between speeches and leaves only dialogue.'

'I understand that too; that's what happens in tragedies.'

'Exactly. And I think I can now make clear to you what I couldn't before, that one kind of poetry and storytelling consists wholly of imitation, like tragedy and comedy, as you say; another consists of the poet's own report – you would find this especially in dithyrambs;[32]

another, again, consists of both, as in epic poetry and in many other places, if you understand my meaning.'

'Yes, now I understand what you were trying to say earlier.'

'And remember that before that, we said that we had discussed *what* should be said, but we needed to consider *how* it should be said.'

'I remember.'

'This is what I meant, then, that we must decide whether we shall allow our poets to use imitation in the composition of their narratives, or whether they should use it in parts, and, if so, what parts, or whether they should not imitate at all.'

'I surmise that you are considering whether we should allow tragedy and comedy into the city or not.'

'Perhaps, but perhaps more than that. I don't know yet – we must go wherever the wind of the argument blows.'

'You're right.'

'Well, then, Adeimantus, consider whether our guardians should be imitative or not. Perhaps the answer follows from what we said before, that each individual can do one job well, but not many; if he tries his hand at a lot of things, he will fail to be distinguished in any of them.'

'Certainly.'

'Doesn't the same argument hold for imitation: the same person can't imitate many things as well as he can imitate one?'

'No, he can't.'

[395] 'So he will hardly be able to practise any worthwhile occupation and at the same time imitate many things and be imitative. Even in the case of two forms of imitation which seem to be closely related to each other, like tragedy and comedy, the same person can't successfully compose both. You did just call them imitations, didn't you?'

'I did. And you're right that the same person can't do both.'

'Nor can the same people be both rhapsodes and actors.'

'True.'

'Or even actors in comedy as well as in tragedy. But all these are imitations, aren't they?'

'Yes, they are imitations.'

'It seems to me, Adeimantus, that human nature is even more specialized than these examples suggest: it is incapable of imitating many things well, or of doing well those things of which the imitations are likenesses.'

'Very true.'

'So if we are going to abide by the first argument – that our guardians must be released from all other crafts and be expert craftsmen of freedom in the city and must do nothing that is not conducive to that end – they must not do or imitate anything else. But if they do imitate, they should imitate what is appropriate to them from childhood onwards: men who are brave, self-controlled, pious, free and so on. They must not do anything mean or otherwise disgraceful, nor must they be good at imitating such things, in case as a result of the imitation they are infected with the reality. Haven't you noticed that imitations, if continued from childhood onwards, become established into habits of body, voice and mind, which are second nature?'

'Yes, indeed.'

'So, since we profess to care for our guardians and want them to become good men, we won't allow them, being men, to imitate a woman young or old, whether she is quarrelling with her husband, or reviling the gods or boasting of her supposed happiness, or overwhelmed by misfortune, grief and tears. Far less shall we allow them to imitate a woman who is sick or in love or in labour.'[33]

'Certainly not.'

'Nor slaves, male or female, performing servile tasks.'

'No.'

'Nor bad men or cowards or men whose behaviour is the opposite of what we just described, men who revile and ridicule and abuse each other, whether drunk or sober, or who speak and [396] behave in ways that are offensive to themselves and to others, as such people do. Nor must they form the habit of likening themselves to madmen either in their words or in their actions; they must be able to recognize mad and bad men and women, but they must not do or imitate any of these things.'

'Very true.'

'Well then, shall we allow them to imitate smiths or any other craftsmen at work, or men who row triremes or call time for the oarsmen, or anything else of this sort?'

'How could they, since they won't be allowed even to think of such things?'

'What about horses neighing, bulls bellowing, rivers rushing, seas roaring, thunder, and so on?[34] Will they imitate this sort of thing?'

'No. They have been prohibited from being mad or from making themselves like madmen.'

'If I understand what you mean, there is one style of narrative which the really good man will use whenever he has to speak, and another different kind which a man of the opposite nature and education will always use for his narratives.'

'What are these?'

'It seems to me that a decent man, when he comes in his narrative to the speech or action of a good man, will want to speak as if he were himself that man, and will not be ashamed of imitation of this kind. He will be especially keen to imitate the good man behaving reliably and sensibly, but to a lesser extent when he's brought low by illness or love or drunkenness or any other misfortune. When he comes to an unworthy man, he won't want seriously to liken himself to his inferior, except perhaps on the few occasions when he does something good, but he'll be ashamed. He won't have had any practice in imitating such people, and he will be disgusted at modelling himself on inferior people and conforming to their patterns of behaviour, a thing which he despises in his mind, unless it's simply for fun.'

'That seems likely.'

'So he will use the style of narrative we described earlier in connection with Homer's epic; his expression will include both imitation and pure narrative, but the proportion of imitation will be small. Or am I talking nonsense?'

'No, that must be the pattern for such a speaker.'

[397] 'But in the case of the other kind of speaker, the worse he is the more he will include everything in his narrative, and think nothing beneath him, so that he will be eager to imitate all the things we were talking about just now, seriously and in front of a lot of people – thunder and the noise of wind and hail, of axle and pulley, the sound of trumpets, oboes and pipes and all kinds of instruments, and even the cries of dogs and sheep and birds. His expression will consist entirely

of imitation, in voice and gesture, or it will have a small narrative element.'

'That must be so.'

'These, then, are the two kinds of expression I was talking about.'

'They are indeed.'

'And so one of them involves small variations, and if the appropriate musical mode and rhythm is added to the expression, a correct speaker will speak in more or less the same mode and in one mode – for the variations are small – and in more or less the same rhythm.'[35]

'Quite right.'

'What about the other kind? Doesn't it need the opposite – all modes and all rhythms – if it's going to be appropriately delivered, because of the manifold forms of its variations?'

'Yes, indeed.'

'Don't all poets and speakers hit upon one or other or these patterns of expression, or on one that results from a combination of the two?'

'Necessarily.'

'What shall we do then? Shall we admit all these patterns of expression into the city, or one or other of the unmixed, or the mixed?'

'If my vote prevails, it will be the unmixed imitator of the good man.'

'But, Adeimantus, the mixed form of expression does give pleasure; and the one that gives most pleasure to children and their attendants and to the general public is the opposite of the one you have chosen.'

'Yes, it does give the greatest pleasure.'

'But perhaps you will say that it doesn't fit in with our political system, because no man in our city has two roles or a multiplicity of roles, since each person does one job.'

'No, it doesn't fit.'

'And isn't this the reason why ours is the only city where we shall find a cobbler who is a cobbler and not a ship's pilot as well, a farmer who is a farmer and not a juryman as well, a soldier who is a soldier and not a money-maker as well, and so on?'

'It is.'

[398] 'Well, then, if a man arrived in our city, who could turn himself into anything by his skill and imitate everything, wanting to show

himself off together with his poems, we would fall down and worship him as a sacred and wondrous pleasure-giver, but we would say that there is no place for such a man in our city, nor is it right that there should be; we would send him away to another city, anointing his head with myrrh and garlanding him with wool. But we ourselves, for our own good, would employ the more austere and less pleasing poet and storyteller, who would imitate the expression of the good man and tell stories according to the patterns we laid down at the beginning, when we undertook the task of educating our soldiers.'

'Indeed we would do that, if it were in our power.'

'Now, my friend, it looks as though we have completely finished with the branch of music which is concerned with myths and stories. We have discussed both what should be said and how it should be said.'

PLATO

Republic 10

[595] 'I think we have certainly founded our city along the right lines in many respects, and especially in relation to poetry.'

'In what way?'

'In our refusal to allow poetry which is imitative. For I think it's even more obvious that we shouldn't allow it now that we have distinguished between the different parts of the soul.'[1]

'What do you mean?'

'Just between ourselves, and please don't denounce me to the tragic poets and all the other imitators – all such things damage the minds of those who hear them, unless they have knowledge of what they are really like as an antidote.'

'What do you have in mind when you say this?'

'I must speak out, even though the love and respect I have had for Homer since I was a boy inhibits me, for he is the original master and leader of all those fine tragic poets. Still, a man mustn't be honoured before the truth, so, as I say, I must speak out.'

'Indeed.'

'Listen, then, or rather, answer.'

'Ask away.'

'Can you tell me what imitation in general is? For I don't quite understand what it means.'

'Well, how do you expect me to understand it?'

'It wouldn't be surprising if you did, since duller eyes [596] often see before sharp ones.'

'That's so. But if anything did occur to me I wouldn't want to talk about it in front of you. So you do the looking.'

'Shall we begin, then, with our customary method? As you know, we are in the habit of assuming a Form[2] – one in each case – in relation to each group of particulars to which we apply the same name. Or don't you understand?'

'I do.'

'So now let's take any set of particulars you like. For example, if you want, there are many couches and tables.'

'Of course.'

'But there are only two Forms of these items of furniture, I suppose, one of couch and one of table.'

'Yes.'

'And we're accustomed to saying that the craftsman looks to the Form as he makes each piece of furniture that we use, whether it's a table or a couch or anything else of that kind. For surely no craftsman makes the Form itself?'

'Of course not.'

'Well, consider what you would call the craftsman I'm going to describe.'

'What craftsman?'

'One who makes everything that each individual craftsman makes.'

'You're talking about a wonderfully clever man.'

'Wait a minute, and you'll be even more impressed. For, besides making all artefacts, this same craftsman can also create everything that grows out of the earth and all living creatures, including himself; besides, he makes the earth, the sky, the gods and everything in the heavens and in Hades beneath the earth.'

'A wonderful sophist indeed.'

'Don't you believe me? Tell me, do you think that no such craftsman could possibly exist, or might there be a person who could make all these things, at least in some sense? Don't you realize that there's a way in which you yourself could do all this?'

'How?'

'It's not difficult; indeed, there are many quick ways of doing this, but the quickest is to take a mirror and carry it around everywhere. You'll soon create the sun and stars and the earth, yourself and all living creatures and artefacts and plants, and all the other things we mentioned just now.'

'Yes, but only in appearance, not, I think, as they are in reality.'

'Well said, you're giving my argument the help it needs. For the painter too, I suppose, is a craftsman of this sort, isn't he?'

'Yes.'

'But you'll say, I think, that what he makes isn't real, though in a way a painter also makes a couch, doesn't he?'

'Yes, the appearance of a couch.'

[597] 'What about the couch-maker? Didn't you say just now that he doesn't make the Form, which we call the real couch, but a particular couch?'

'I did.'

'So if he doesn't make the real couch, he makes something like the real thing, but which is distinct from it. And anyone who says that the product of a couch-maker or any other craftsman is completely real is unlikely to be telling the truth.'

'Not, at any rate, in the opinion of those who are familiar with such arguments.'

'So we shouldn't be surprised if the couch-maker's product seems somewhat shadowy in relation to the true couch.'

'No.'

'Shall we use these examples to discover what the imitator actually is?'

'If you want.'

'Well, then, there are these three couches: one exists in nature, and we could say, I suppose, that god makes it. Who else could?'

'No one.'

'There's one which the carpenter makes.'

'Yes.'

'And one which the painter makes.'

'Let's grant that.'

'So, painter, couch-maker, god: these three preside over the three kinds of couch.'

'Yes.'

'Now god made only one real couch, whether because he so chose, or because he was under some necessity not to make more than one couch in nature. But two or more such couches never were produced by god, and never will be.'

'How so?'

'Because if god were to make only two such couches, another one would appear whose Form the other two would possess, and that one, not the two, would be the real couch.'

'Right.'

'So god, I think, knew this, and, since he wanted to be the real maker of a real couch, not a particular maker of a particular couch, he created one in its essential nature.'

'That seems likely.'

'Shall we call him, then, the nature-maker of this couch, or something of the sort?'

'That would be appropriate, since he has made this and everything else that exists in nature.'

'What about the craftsman? Is he the manufacturer of the bed?'

'Yes.'

'And is the painter also the manufacturer and maker of it?'

'Certainly not.'

'Then what will you say he is in relation to the couch?'

'I think it would be fairest to call him the imitator of what the other two make.'

'Well, then, do you use the term "imitator" for one whose product is at third remove from nature?'

'Certainly.'

'So the tragic poet too, since he's an imitator, will be, as it were, at third remove from the throne of truth, and the same goes for all other imitators.'

'It looks like it.'

'Then we have agreed about the imitator. Now tell me this [598] about the painter: do you think that he tries to imitate each thing as it really is in nature, or the products of the craftsman?'

'Those of the craftsman.'

'As they are or as they appear to be? For you still have this distinction to make.'

'What do you mean?'

'This: if you look at a couch from the side or from the front or from any other angle, the couch remains the same, but it *looks* different, doesn't it? And it's the same with other objects?'

'Yes, it appears to be different, but it isn't.'

'Consider this, then: in the case of any given object, does painting aim to imitate the real thing as it is, or the appearance of it as it looks? Is it an imitation of an appearance or of truth?'

'Of an appearance.'

'The art of imitation, therefore, is far removed from truth, and the reason why it produces everything, so it seems, is that it grasps only a small part of any object, and only an image at that. The painter, for example, will paint a cobbler for us, or a carpenter, or any other craftsman, without understanding any of their crafts; but nevertheless, if he is a good painter, he may paint a carpenter and show it from a distance, and deceive children and stupid men into thinking it is a real carpenter.'

'No doubt.'

'But, my friend, what we need to bear in mind about all such things, I think, is this: whenever someone tells us that he has met a man who is a master of all crafts and understands everything more accurately than any individual expert, we must reply that he is a fool: having met with a wizard and imitator, he has been deceived, it seems, into thinking him all wise because of his own inability to distinguish between knowledge, lack of knowledge, and imitation.'

'Very true.'

'Next, then, we must consider tragedy and its leader, Homer, since some people claim that these poets understand all kinds of skills, and everything about human conduct, good and bad, and even things divine. For the good poet, they say, must understand the subjects he's writing about if he's going to compose fine poetry, otherwise he won't be able to compose. So we need to consider whether these people have met with a group of imitators and been deceived by them, not realizing that the productions of theirs which they see [599] are at third remove from reality and easy to make without knowledge of the truth – for what they make are appearances, not reality. Or is there something in

44

what they say, and do good poets really understand the subjects on which most people think they speak so well?'

'That must certainly be investigated.'

'Well, do you think that if a man could make both the object of imitation and the image, he would seriously give himself up to the manufacture of images and make this the most important thing in his life, as though it were the best thing he had?'

'No, I don't.'

'But, I suppose, if he really understood the things which he imitates, he would devote himself to deeds rather than their imitations; he would try to leave behind many fine deeds as his memorials, and would be more eager to be praised than to praise.'

'I should think so; for he'd gain greater honour and do more good.'

'There are certain things, then, that we need not ask Homer or any other poet about. We won't ask, for example, even supposing one of them were a doctor, and not just an imitator of medical language, whether any poet, ancient or modern, has ever cured anyone, as Asclepius did, or left behind pupils in medicine, as Asclepius left his sons.[3] We won't ask about skills such as these. But it *is* fair for us to question Homer about the finest and most important subjects on which he tries to speak – warfare, strategy, the government of cities and the education of man. "Dear Homer," we shall say, "if you are not at third remove from truth in relation to virtue, an image-maker, or an imitator as we have defined it, but at second remove, and you really do know what pursuits make people better and worse in public and private life, tell us what city has been better governed because of you, as Sparta was because of Lycurgus, and many other cities, great and small, because of many other legislators? Does any city claim you as a good lawgiver and benefactor? Italy and Sicily claim Charondas, and we claim Solon, but who claims you?" Will he be able to name one?'

'I don't think so. Even the Homeridae[4] themselves don't make such claims.'

[**600**] 'Well, then, is there any record of a war in Homer's time, which was successfully fought under his command or on his advice?'

'No.'

'Do we hear of ingenious ideas and technical inventions and other activities, which would show him to be a man of practical ability, like Thales of Miletus and Anacharsis[5] the Scythian?'

'No, there is nothing of that kind.'

'Well, then, if there is nothing in public life, what about the private sphere? Do we hear that Homer was the leader of a group of disciples who took pleasure in associating with him during his lifetime, and who passed on a Homeric way of life to their successors, like Pythagoras, who was especially revered in this way? Even now his followers speak of a Pythagorean way of life, and seem to be quite different from other people.'

'No, we don't hear of anything like that either. Indeed, Socrates, perhaps Homer's companion, Creophylus,[6] would appear an even more ridiculous example of education than his name suggests, if the stories about Homer are true. For it's said that he was completely neglected by him in his lifetime.'

'So they say. But, Glaucon, if Homer had really been able to educate men and make them better – if he'd been capable of knowing about these things and not merely imitating them – don't you think he would have made many friends and been honoured and loved by them? Why, Protagoras of Abdera and Prodicus[7] of Ceos and many others are able to persuade their contemporaries in private conversation that they won't be able to run either household or city unless *they* are in charge of their education, and they are so loved for this wisdom that their followers almost carry them about shoulder-high. But as for Homer, if he really had been able to help mankind acquire virtue, would his contemporaries have allowed him, or Hesiod, to go round reciting poetry? Wouldn't they have held on to them rather than to their gold, and forced them to stay at home with them, or, if they couldn't persuade them, wouldn't they have danced attendance on them wherever they went, until they had learnt all they could from their teaching?'

'I think what you say is perfectly true, Socrates.'

'Shall we agree, then, that all poets from Homer onwards are imitators of images of virtue, and all the other subjects which they write about, and have no grasp on truth? As we were saying just now, the painter will produce something that looks like a cobbler, even though [**601**] he knows nothing about cobbling; and the people who look at it are equally ignorant, judging simply by colours and shapes.'

'Certainly.'

'In the same way, I think, we shall say that the poet, too, applies the colours of every art with his words and phrases, though he understands nothing other than how to imitate; but the result is that other people like himself, who judge only by the words, think that, if someone speaks about cobbling or strategy or anything else in metre, rhythm and mode, he has spoken very well. These things by their very nature possess such great magical power. For when the works of the poets are stripped of the colours of music and spoken alone and on their own I think you know what they look like – you must have seen.'

'I have indeed.'

'They are like the faces of people in the bloom of youth, but who aren't beautiful, as one can see when the bloom deserts them.'

'Exactly.'

'Well, then, consider this. The maker of an image, the imitator, we say, knows nothing about the reality, but only about the appearance. Isn't that so?'

'Yes.'

'But that's only half the story. Let's look at it more thoroughly.'

'Go on then.'

'The painter, we say, will paint reins and a bit.'

'Yes.'

'But the saddler and the smith will make them.'

'Certainly.'

'Now does the painter know what the reins and the bit should be like? Or is this something that not even the maker – the smith and the saddler – knows? Isn't this something that only the horseman knows, because he understands their use?'

'Very true.'

'Then shall we say the same about everything?'

'What do you mean?'

'In relation to any object there are three arts, those of the user, the maker and the imitator.'

'Yes.'

'And we judge the excellence, beauty and rightness of any implement or creature or action in relation to the use for which it was made, by man or nature?'

'Yes.'

'So the user of each thing must inevitably have the most experience of it, and must tell the maker the good and bad points about the instrument which he uses. For example, the pipe-player informs the pipe-maker about the pipes which would serve him best in his playing, and will instruct him about what sort he ought to make, and the pipe-maker will do what he says.'

'Of course.'

'So the one pronounces on the merits and defects of pipes because he knows about them, whilst the other, believing him, will make them?'

'Yes.'

'In relation to any implement, then, the maker will have correct belief about its goodness and badness because he associates with one who has knowledge, and is obliged to [602] listen to him; but the user will have knowledge.'

'Certainly.'

'Now, will the imitator have knowledge, derived from use, of whether the things which he depicts are good and right or not? Or will he have correct belief, because he has been obliged to associate with one who knows, and received instructions from him about what he ought to depict?'

'Neither.'

'So the imitator will have neither knowledge nor correct belief about the goodness and badness of the things which he imitates.'

'It seems not.'

'The poetic imitator will certainly be in a fine position as regards wisdom on the subjects of his poetry!'

'Far from it.'

'None the less, he will still go on imitating, although he doesn't know in what way any given thing is good or bad. But presumably what he will imitate is the sort of thing that appears to be good to the ignorant masses.'

'Of course.'

'It seems, then, that we have pretty well agreed that the imitative person knows nothing to speak of about the subjects which he imitates; that imitation is a form of play and not serious; and that all those who compose tragic poetry, whether in iambic or epic verse,[8] are imitators in the highest degree possible.'

'Yes, indeed.'

'So, by Zeus, this imitating is concerned with something at third remove from the truth, isn't it?'

'Yes.'

'And on what element in a human being does it exercise its power?'

'What sort of thing are you talking about?'

'Something like this: an object doesn't look the same size when seen from close up as it does from a distance.'

'No.'

'And the same things can look bent or straight depending on whether they are seen in water or out of it; or both concave and convex, because our vision can be distorted by colours. Clearly our souls are susceptible to all kinds of confusion of this sort; and it's by exploiting this natural weakness that perspective painting and conjuring and many other such tricks work their magic.'

'True.'

'And haven't measuring and counting and weighing proved to be the best means of counteracting these effects, preventing what is apparently larger or smaller or more numerous or heavier from prevailing in us, and giving control to the element which has counted or measured or weighed?'

'Of course.'

'And this will be the task of the reasoning element in the soul.'

'It will.'

'But even when it has measured and shown that some things are bigger or smaller than others or are equal, appearances may still contradict it.'

'Yes.'

'Now we said, didn't we, that the same thing cannot have different opinions at the same time about the same object?'

'Yes, and rightly so.'

[603] 'So the part of the soul which contradicts the measurements will not be the same as the part which agrees with them.'

'No.'

'But that which relies on measurement and calculation will be the best part of the soul.'

'Of course.'

'So that which opposes it will be one of the inferior elements in us.'

'Necessarily.'

'This, then, is what I wanted us to agree when I said that painting and imitative art in general produces work which is far removed from the truth, and associates with that element in us which is far removed from wisdom, and is its companion and friend for no healthy or true purpose.'

'Absolutely.'

'Imitative art, then, is an inferior thing which associates with an inferior element in us and produces inferior offspring.'

'It seems so.'

'Does this apply only to visual imitation or to aural imitation as well – what we call poetry?'

'It probably applies to that too.'

'Well, let's not simply rely on the analogy from painting, but let's approach directly that part of the mind with which poetic imitation consorts, to see whether it is inferior or serious.'

'Yes, we must.'

'Let's put it like this: imitative art imitates people performing voluntary or involuntary actions, and thinking that they have been successful or unsuccessful as a result of those actions, and feeling pain or pleasure throughout. Have I left anything out?'

'No.'

'Now in all these circumstances does a person remain at one with himself? Or is he in a state of conflict and at war with himself in his actions too, just as he was in relation to sight, when he held contrary opinions in himself about the same things at the same time? But, as I recall, we needn't agree on this now, because we've already agreed in our earlier discussion that our souls are full of countless contradictions of this sort arising simultaneously.'

'And we were right.'

'Indeed we were. But we left something out then which I think we need to go into now.'

'What's that?'

'We said, didn't we, that a good man who meets with misfortune, such as losing a son or anything else which he values very highly, will bear it more easily than other people?'

'Indeed.'

'Now let's consider this: will he feel no pain, or is that impossible, and will it be the case, rather, that he observes due measure in his grief?'

'The latter is nearer the truth.'

[604] 'Now tell me this about him: do you think that he will be more likely to fight against his grief and resist it when he is seen by his peers, or when he is alone by himself in solitude?'

'He'll bear it much better when others can see him.'

'When he's on his own, I imagine, he won't be afraid of saying many things which he would be ashamed to let anyone hear, and he'll do many things which he wouldn't allow anyone to see him doing.'

'That's so.'

'Now that which urges him to resist is reason and custom, but that which pulls him towards his sorrows is the experience itself.'

'True.'

'And since there are contrary impulses in the man concerning the same thing at the same time, we say that there must be two elements in him.'

'Of course.'

'And one is ready to obey custom, and follow wherever it leads?'

'What do you mean?'

'Custom dictates, surely, that it is best to remain as calm as possible in misfortunes and not to display grief. For we cannot know what is really good and bad in such matters, and taking them badly brings no advantage; nothing in human affairs is worth taking very seriously, and grieving prevents us from attaining the very thing that we need as quickly as possible in these circumstances.'

'And what's that?'

'The ability to reflect on the event and to regulate one's affairs in relation to the fall of the dice, as it were, in the way that reason decides is best. We mustn't spend our time wailing and holding the place where it hurts, like children who have bumped themselves, but accustom the soul to attend as quickly as it can to curing the hurt and raising up what has fallen, banishing lamentation with healing.'

'That is certainly the right way to deal with misfortune.'

'So the best element in us, we're saying, wants to follow this reasoning.'

'Clearly.'

'But shall we say that the element which drives us towards the recollection of suffering and towards lamentation, and which can never have enough of these things, is irrational and lazy and inclined to cowardice?'

'We shall indeed.'

'Now the irascible element lends itself to much and varied imitation; but the prudent and calm character, always at one with itself, is not easy to imitate, nor, when it is imitated, is it easy to understand, especially at a festival when all kinds of people are crowded together into the theatre. For the imitation is of an experience which is foreign to them.'

[605] 'Indeed.'

'So clearly the imitative poet is not by nature inclined towards this element in the soul – and his wisdom is not set on pleasing it if he wants to win popularity – but towards the irascible and varied character, because it is easy to imitate.'

'Clearly.'

'So we can justly take hold of the poet and set him down as the counterpart of the painter. For he is like him in making things that are inferior in relation to the truth, and also because he associates with an inferior part of the soul, and not with the best part. So we shall now be justified in refusing to admit him into a city which is going to be well governed, because he arouses and nourishes this part of the soul, and, by strengthening it, destroys the rational part. It's just as in a city when someone gives power to bad men and hands the city over to them, and destroys the better men. In the same way, we shall say, the imitative poet sets up a bad constitution in the soul of each individual, gratifying the foolish part which cannot distinguish between greater and lesser, but thinks the same things are sometimes large and sometimes small; he is a maker of images and very far removed from truth.'

'Certainly.'

'But we haven't yet laid the greatest charge against poetry. For its power to corrupt even good men, except for a very few, is surely a terrible thing.'

'It is, indeed, if it really can do that.'

'Listen and consider. When we hear Homer or some other tragic poet imitating one of the heroes in a state of grief, delivering a long speech of lamentation, or chanting and beating his breast with the chorus, you know that even the best of us enjoy it and give ourselves up to it. We follow in genuine sympathy, and praise as an excellent poet the one who most affects us in this way.'

'Yes, I know.'

'But when the sorrow is our own, you notice that we pride ourselves on just the opposite, that is, on our ability to keep calm and be strong, because this is manly behaviour, whereas that which we admired in the theatre is womanish.'

'Yes, I notice that.'

'Is this praise right? Is it right not to be disgusted, but to enjoy it and give praise, when you see the sort of man you would despise and be ashamed to be yourself?'

'No, by Zeus, it doesn't seem reasonable.'

[606] 'That's right, especially if you look at it in this way.'

'How?'

'If you reflect that the part which is forcibly kept in check in our own misfortunes, which hungers after tears and having its fill of lamentation, since it naturally desires these things, is the very part which the poets satisfy and please. But that part which is by nature best in us, not being adequately trained by reason or habit, relaxes its guard over this mournful element, because it is looking at another man's sufferings; and there is no disgrace in praising and pitying someone else who claims to be a good man, and abandons himself to excessive grief; rather, we think the pleasure we get is a positive gain, and wouldn't consent to being deprived of it by despising the poem altogether. Few people, I think, are capable of reasoning that the enjoyment we derive from other people's experiences inevitably affects our own; for it's not easy to restrain pity in our own sufferings when we have nurtured it and made it strong on those of others.'

'Very true.'

'Well, doesn't the same argument apply to the ridiculous too? If there are jokes which you are ashamed to make yourself, but which you very much enjoy hearing in comedy, or in private, and don't despise as being morally bad, aren't you doing the same thing as in the cases involving pity? For you are releasing that part of yourself which your reason used to restrain when you wanted to play the fool, being afraid of a reputation for buffoonery; but having made it vigorous at the theatre, you don't notice that you have often been carried away in your private life and become a comedian.'

'Indeed.'

'And poetic imitation has the same effect on us with regard to sex and anger and all the other desires and feelings of pain and pleasure, which, in our view, accompany all our actions. For it nourishes and waters them when they ought to be dried up, and puts them in control of us when they should themselves be controlled, if we are to become better and happier people rather than worse and more miserable.'

'I can't say otherwise.'

'So, Glaucon, whenever you meet admirers of Homer, who say that this poet has educated Greece and that his works should be studied for the management of human conduct and culture, and that one should live one's whole life in accordance with his views, you must treat these people kindly, [607] for they are good men in so far as they can be; you can agree that Homer is the most poetic and the first of the tragedians, but you must know that the only poetry which will be admitted into our city are hymns to the gods and encomia[9] to good men. But if you allow the sweetened Muse of lyric or epic, pleasure and pain will rule in the city instead of custom and the rational principle which in any given instance seems best in the opinion of the community.'

'Very true.'

'So, since we have returned to the subject of poetry, let this be our defence: given its nature, we were right to banish it from our city before. It stands to reason. But let us say to her, in case she condemns us of being harsh and boorish, that there is an ancient quarrel between philosophy and poetry. There are countless examples of this old antagonism: remarks such as that "yapping bitch barking at her master", and "great in the empty talk of fools", and "the crowd of know-alls holding sway", and "the subtle thinkers" who after all "starve"[10] and so on. Nevertheless, let it be said that if poetic imitation designed for pleasure has any arguments to show that she should have a place in a well-governed city, we would gladly receive her back from exile, for we are very conscious of her spell. But it would be impious to betray what we believe to be the truth. Aren't you too enchanted by the magic of poetry, my friend, especially when you see her through the medium of Homer?'

'Very much so.'

'So it would be right for poetry to return from exile if she could defend herself in lyric or in some other metre?'

'Certainly.'

'And we might allow her patrons, who are not poets themselves, but lovers of poetry, to speak on her behalf in prose to show that she is not only a source of pleasure, but also a benefit to societies and human life. And we shall listen favourably, since it will be our gain if she turns out to be not only pleasing, but also useful.'

'It will certainly be our gain.'

'But if not, my dear friend, we must be like men who have fallen in love, who realize that their passion is doing them no good and force themselves to turn away against their will. We too, because of the passion for such poetry engendered and nurtured in us by our fine societies, [608] shall be glad if poetry can be shown to be good and true; but so long as she is unable to defend herself, we shall, as we listen to her, chant to ourselves this argument of ours as a spell, to prevent us from falling back into that childish passion beloved of so many. Our chant will be that such poetry must not be taken seriously, as though it had a serious grasp of truth, but that anyone who hears it must be careful, fearing for the constitution of his soul, and that what we have said about poetry must be believed.'

'I entirely agree.'

'For the contest is great, my dear Glaucon, far greater than it seems, whether a person becomes good or bad; so we shouldn't be tempted by honour or wealth or power, or even by poetry, into neglecting justice and the rest of virtue.'

'I agree with you after everything we've said, and I think anyone else would too.'

ARISTOTLE

Poetics

INTRODUCTION

Poetry as Imitation

[**1447a**] Under the general heading of the art of poetry, I propose not only to speak about this art itself, but also to discuss the various kinds of poetry and their characteristic effects, the types of plot structure that are required if a composition is to succeed, the number and nature of its constituent parts, and similarly any other matters that may be relevant to a study of this kind. I shall begin in the natural way, that is, by going back to first principles.

Epic and tragic poetry, comedy too, dithyrambic poetry[1] and most music composed for the pipe and the lyre, can all be described in general terms as forms of imitation or representation. However, they differ from one another in three respects: either in using different media for the representation, or in representing different things, or in representing them in entirely different ways.

CHAPTER I

The Media of Poetic Imitation

Some people, whether by art or by practice, can represent things by imitating their shapes and colours, and others do so by the use of the voice;[2] in all the arts mentioned above the imitation is produced by means of rhythm, language, and melody, these being used either separately or in combination. Thus the art of the pipe and of the lyre consists only in melody and rhythm, as does any other of the same type, such as that of the pan-pipes. The imitative medium of dancers is rhythm alone, without melody, for it is by the manner in which they arrange the rhythms of their movements that they represent characters and emotions and actions.

The art that uses language alone, whether in prose or [1447b] verse, and verse either in a mixture of metres or in one particular kind, has up to the present been without a name. For we have no common name that we can apply to the prose mimes of Sophron and Xenarchus[3] and the Socratic dialogues, or to compositions employing iambic trimeters or elegiac couplets or any other metres of these types. We can say only that people associate poetry with the metre employed, and speak, for example, of elegiac poets and epic poets; they call them poets, however, not from the fact that they are making imitations, but indiscriminately from the fact that they are writing in metre. For it is customary to describe as poets even those who produce medical and scientific works in verse. Yet Homer and Empedocles[4] have nothing in common except their metre, and therefore, while it is right to call the one a poet, the other should rather be called a natural philosopher than a poet. In the same way, an author composing his imitation in a mixture of all the metres, as Chaeremon[5] did in his *Centaur*, a recitation piece employing just such a mixture, would also have to be called a poet. Such are the distinctions I would make.

Again, there are some arts which make use of all the media I have mentioned, that is, rhythm, song, and metre; such are dithyrambic and nomic poetry,[6] tragedy and comedy. They differ, however, in that the first two use all these media together, while the last two use them separately, one after another.

These, then, are what I mean by the differences between the arts as far as the media of representation are concerned.

CHAPTER 2

The Objects of Poetic Imitation

[**1448a**] Since imitative artists represent men in action, and men who are necessarily either of good or of bad character (for as all people differ in their moral nature according to the degree of their goodness or badness, characters almost always fall into one or other of these types), these men must be represented either as better than we are, or worse, or as the same kind of people as ourselves. Thus among the painters Polygnotus[7] represented his subjects as better, and Pauson as worse, while Dionysius painted them just as they were. It is clear that each of the kinds of imitation I have referred to will admit of these variations, and they will differ in this way according to the differences in the objects they represent. Such diversities may occur even in dancing, and in music for the pipe and the lyre; they occur also in the art that is based on language, whether it uses prose or verse unaccompanied by music. Homer, for example, depicts the better types of people, and Cleophon those like ourselves, while Hegemon of Thasos, the first writer of parodies, and Nicochares, the author of the *Deiliad*,[8] those who are worse. The same thing happens in dithyrambic and nomic poetry; for instance, the Cyclops might be represented in different ways, as was done by Timotheus and Philoxenus.[9] This is the difference that marks the distinction between comedy and tragedy; for comedy aims at representing people as worse than they are nowadays, tragedy as better.

CHAPTER 3

The Manner of Poetic Imitation

There remains the third point of difference in these arts, that is, the manner in which each kind of subject may be represented. For it is possible, using the same medium, to represent the same subjects in a variety of ways. It may be done partly by narration and partly by the assumption of a character other than one's own, which is Homer's way; or by speaking in one's own person without any such change; or by representing the characters as performing all the actions dramatically.

These, then, as I pointed out at the beginning, are the three factors by which the imitative arts are differentiated: their media, the objects they represent, and their manner of representation. Thus in one sense Sophocles might be called an imitator of the same kind as Homer, for they both represent good people; in another sense he is like Aristophanes, in that they both represent people in action. And this, some say, is why their works are called dramas, from the fact that they represent people doing things. For this reason too the Dorians claim the invention of both tragedy and comedy. Comedy is claimed by the Megarians, both by those here in Greece on the grounds that it came into being when they became a democracy, and by those in Sicily because the poet Epicharmus, who was much earlier than Chionides and Magnes,[10] came from there; certain Dorians of the Peloponnese lay claim also to tragedy. They regard the names as proof of their belief, pointing out that, whereas the Athenians call outlying villages *demoi*, they themselves call them *komai*; so that comedians take their name, not from *komazein*, ('to revel'), but from their touring in the *komai* when lack of appreciation drove them from the city. Furthermore, their word [**1448b**] for 'to do' is *dran*, whereas the Athenian word is *prattein*.

So much then for the number and character of the different kinds of imitation.

CHAPTER 4

The Origins and Development of Poetry

The creation of poetry generally is due to two causes, both rooted in human nature. The instinct for imitation is inherent in human beings from our earliest days; we differ from other animals in that we are the most imitative of creatures, and learn our earliest lessons by imitation. Also inborn in all of us is the instinct to enjoy works of imitation. What happens in actual experience is evidence of this; for we enjoy looking at the most accurate representations of things which in themselves we find painful to see, such as the forms of the lowest animals and of corpses. The reason for this is that learning is a very great pleasure, not only for philosophers, but for other people as well, though their capacity for it may be limited. They enjoy seeing images because they learn as they look at them, and reason out what each thing is (for instance, that 'this is a picture of so and so'); for if by any chance the thing depicted has not been seen before, it will not be the fact that it is an imitation of something that gives the pleasure, but the execution or the colouring or some other such cause.

Imitation, then, is natural to us, and so too are melody and rhythm (and metres are obviously detached sections of rhythms). From the beginning those with special natural aptitudes for these things gradually made improvements and created poetry from their improvisations. However, poetry soon branched into two channels, according to the characters of individual poets. The more serious-minded among them represented noble actions and the doings of noble persons, while the more trivial represented the actions of inferior people; thus while the one type composed hymns and panegyrics, these others began by composing invectives. We know of no poems of this kind by any poet earlier than Homer, though it is likely enough that many poets composed them; but from Homer onwards examples may be found, his own *Margites*,[11] for instance, and poems of the same type. It was in such poems that the iambic metre was brought into use because of its appropriateness for the purpose, and it is still called iambic today, from being the metre in which they wrote 'iambs', or lampoons, against one another.

In this way it came about that some of our early poets became composers of heroic, and some of iambic, verse. But just as Homer was the supreme poet in the serious style, standing alone both in excellence of composition and in the dramatic quality of his representations, so also, in the dramatic character that he imparted, not to invective, but to his treatment of the ridiculous, he was the first to indicate the form of comedy; for his *Margites* bears the same relationship to comedy as his [**1449a**] *Iliad* and *Odyssey* bear to tragedy. When tragedy and comedy appeared, those whose natural aptitude inclined them towards the one kind of poetry composed comedies instead of lampoons, and those who were drawn to the other composed tragedies instead of epics; for these new forms were both grander and more highly regarded than the earlier.

It is beyond my scope here to consider whether or not tragedy is now developed as far as it can be in its various forms, and to decide this both absolutely and in relation to theatrical performances.

Both tragedy and comedy had their first beginnings in improvisation. The one originated with those who led the dithyramb,[12] the other with the leaders of the phallic songs which still survive today as traditional institutions in many of our cities. Little by little tragedy advanced, as poets developed whatever potential they saw in it, until after many changes it attained its natural form and came to a standstill. Aeschylus was the first to increase the number of actors from one to two; he cut down the part of the chorus, and gave speech the leading role. Sophocles introduced three actors and scene painting. As for the grandeur of tragedy, it was not until late that it acquired its characteristic dignity, when, changing from the satyric style,[13] it discarded slight plots and comic diction, and its metre changed from the trochaic tetrameter to the iambic. At first the poets had used the tetrameter because they were composing satyr-poetry, which was more closely related to the dance; but once spoken dialogue had been introduced, by its very nature it hit upon the right measure, for the iambic is of all measures the one best suited to speech. This is shown by the fact that we most usually drop into iambics in our conversation with one another, whereas we seldom talk in hexameters, and then only when we depart from the normal tone of conversation. Another change was the increased number of episodes. We must pass over other features of tragedy and the ways in which each is said to have been elaborated, for it would probably be a long business to go into them in any detail.

CHAPTER 5

The Rise of Comedy: Epic Compared with Tragedy

As I have remarked, comedy represents the worse types of people; worse, however, not in the sense that it embraces any and every kind of badness, but in the sense that the ridiculous is a species of ugliness or badness. For the ridiculous consists in some form of error or ugliness that is not painful or injurious; the comic mask, for example, is distorted and ugly, but causes no pain.

Now we know something of the successive stages by which tragedy developed, and of those who were responsible for them; the early history of comedy, however, is obscure, because it was [**1449b**] not taken seriously. It was a long time before the archon granted a chorus[14] to comedies; until then the performers were volunteers. Comedy had already acquired certain clear-cut forms before there is any mention of those who are named as its poets. Nor is it known who introduced masks, or prologues, or a plurality of actors, and other things of that kind. The composition of plots originated in Sicily; of Athenian poets Crates[15] was the first to discard the lampoon pattern and to construct stories and plots of a more general nature.

Epic poetry corresponds to tragedy to the extent that it is a representation, in metrical language, of serious people. They differ, however, in that epic keeps to a single metre and is in narrative form. Another point of difference is their length: tragedy tries as far as possible to keep within a single revolution of the sun, or only slightly to exceed it, whereas the epic observes no limits in its time of action – although at first the practice in this respect was the same in tragedies as in epics. Of the constituent parts, some are common to both kinds, and some are peculiar to tragedy. Thus anyone who can discriminate between what is good and what is bad in tragedy can do the same with epic; for all the elements of epic are found in tragedy, though not everything that belongs to tragedy is to be found in epic.

CHAPTER 6

A Description of Tragedy

I shall speak later about the form of imitation that uses hexameters and about comedy,[16] but for the moment I propose to discuss tragedy, first drawing together the definition of its essential character from what has already been said.

Tragedy, then, is a representation of an action that is serious, complete, and of some magnitude; in language that is pleasurably embellished, the different forms of embellishment occurring in separate parts; presented in the form of action, not narration; by means of pity and fear bringing about the *catharsis*[17] of such emotions. By 'language that is pleasurably embellished' I refer to language possessing rhythm and melody; and by 'the different forms of embellishment occurring in separate parts' I mean that some parts are composed in verse alone, and others again make use of song.

Now since the representation is carried out by people performing actions, it follows, in the first place, that spectacle will necessarily be a part of tragedy and, secondly, that there must be song and diction, these being the medium of representation. By diction I mean here the arrangement of the verses; song is a term whose sense is obvious to everyone.

In tragedy it is action that is imitated, and this action is brought about by agents who necessarily display certain distinctive qualities both of character and of thought, according [1450a] to which we also define the nature of the actions; and it is on their actions that all men depend for success or failure. The representation of the action is the plot of the tragedy; for the ordered arrangement of the incidents is what I mean by plot. Character, on the other hand, is that which enables us to define the nature of the participants, and thought comes out in what they say when they are proving a point or expressing an opinion.

Necessarily, then, tragedy as a whole has six constituents, which determine its quality. They are plot, character, diction, thought, spectacle, and song. Of these, two represent the media in which the action is represented, one involves the manner of representation, and three are connected with the objects of the representation; there are no others. These, it may be said, are the dramatic elements that have been used by practically all playwrights; for all plays alike possess spectacle, character, plot, diction, song, and thought.[18]

Of these elements the most important is the plot, the ordering of the incidents; for tragedy is a representation, not of people, but of action and life, of happiness and unhappiness – and happiness and unhappiness are bound up with action. The purpose of living is an end which is a kind of activity, not a quality; it is their characters, indeed, that make people what they are, but it is by reason of their actions that they are happy or the reverse. Tragedies are not performed, therefore, in order to represent character, although character is involved for the sake of the action. Thus the incidents and the plot are the end aimed at in tragedy, and as always, the end is everything. Furthermore, there could not be a tragedy without action, but there could be without character; indeed, the tragedies of most of our recent playwrights fail to present character, and the same might be said of many playwrights of other periods. A similar contrast could be drawn between Zeuxis and Polygnotus as painters,[19] for Polygnotus represents character well, whereas Zeuxis is not concerned with it in his painting. Again, if someone writes a series of speeches expressive of character, and well composed as far as thought and diction are concerned, he will still not achieve the proper effect of tragedy; this will be done much better by a tragedy which is less successful in its use of these elements, but which has a plot giving an ordered combination of incidents. Another point to note is that the two most important means by which tragedy plays on our feelings, that is, 'reversals' and 'recognitions', are both constituents of the plot. A further proof is that beginners can achieve accuracy in diction and the portrayal of character before they can construct a plot out of the incidents, and this could be said of almost all the earliest dramatic poets.

The plot, then, is the first essential of tragedy; its soul, so to speak, and character takes the second place. It is much the [1450b] same in painting; for if an artist were to daub his canvas with the most beautiful colours laid on at random, he would not give the same pleasure as he would by drawing a recognizable image in black and white. Tragedy is the representation of an action, and it is chiefly on account of the action that it is also a representation of persons.

The third property of tragedy is thought. This is the ability to say what is possible and appropriate in any given circumstances, which in prose speeches is the function of the arts of politics and of rhetoric. The older dramatic poets made their characters talk like citizens, whereas those of today make them talk like rhetoricians. Character is that which reveals personal choice; thus there is no revelation of character in speeches in which the speaker shows no preferences or aversions whatever. Thought, on the other hand, is present in speeches where something is being shown to be true or untrue, or where some general opinion is being expressed.

Fourth comes diction. By diction I mean, as I have already explained, the expressive use of words, and this has the same effect in verse and in prose.

Of the remaining elements, song is the most important of the pleasurable embellishments. Spectacle, or stage effect, is an attraction, of course, but it has the least to do with the playwright's craft or with the art of poetry. For the power of tragedy is independent both of performance and of actors, and besides, the production of spectacular effects is more the province of the property man than of the playwright.

CHAPTER 7

The Scope of the Plot

Now that these definitions have been established, I must go on to discuss the arrangement of the incidents, for this is of the first importance in tragedy. I have already laid down that tragedy is the representation of an action that is complete and whole and of a certain magnitude – for a thing may be whole and yet lack magnitude. Now a whole is that which has a beginning, a middle, and an end. A beginning is that which does not necessarily come after something else, although something else exists or comes about after it. An end, on the contrary, is that which naturally follows something else either as a necessary or as a usual consequence, and is not itself followed by anything. A middle is that which follows something else, and is itself followed by something. Thus well-constructed plots must neither begin nor end in a haphazard way, but must conform to the pattern I have been describing.

Furthermore, whatever is beautiful, whether it be a living creature or an object made up of various parts, must necessarily not only have its parts properly ordered, but also be of an appropriate size, for beauty is bound up with size and order. A minutely small creature, therefore, would not be beautiful, for it would take almost no time to see it and our perception of it would be blurred; nor would an extremely large one, for it could not be taken in all at once, and its unity and wholeness would be [1451a] lost to the view of the beholder – if, for example, there were a creature a thousand miles long.

Now in just the same way as inanimate bodies and living organisms must be of a reasonable size, so that they can be easily taken in by the eye, so too must plots be of a reasonable length, so that they may be easily held in the memory. The limits in length to be observed, in as far as they concern performance on the stage, have nothing to do with dramatic art; for if a hundred tragedies had to be performed in the dramatic contests, they would be regulated in length by the water-clock, as indeed it is said they were on another occasion.[20] With regard to the limit set by the nature of the action, the larger the plot is, the more beautiful it will be, provided that it is quite clear. To give a simple definition, a length that, as a matter either of probability or of necessity, allows of a change from misery to happiness or from happiness to misery is the proper limit of length to be observed.

CHAPTER 8

Unity of Plot

A plot does not possess unity, as some people suppose, merely because it is about one man. Many things, countless things indeed, may happen to one man, and some of them will not contribute to any kind of unity;

and similarly he may carry out many actions from which no single unified action will emerge. It seems, therefore, that all those poets have been on the wrong track who have composed a *Heracleid*, or a *Theseid*, or some other poem of this kind, in the belief that, Heracles being a single person, his story must necessarily possess unity. Homer, exceptional in this as in all other respects, seems, whether by art or by nature, to have been well aware of what was required. In composing his *Odyssey*, he did not put in everything that happened to Odysseus – that he was wounded on Mount Parnassus, for example, or that he feigned madness at the time of the call to arms, for it was not a matter of necessity or probability that either of these incidents should have led to the other; on the contrary, he constructed the *Odyssey* round a single action of the kind I have spoken of, and he did this with the *Iliad* too. Thus, just as in the other imitative arts each individual representation is the representation of a single object, so too the plot of a play, being the representation of an action, must present it as a unified whole; and its various incidents must be so arranged that if any one of them is differently placed or taken away the effect of wholeness will be seriously disrupted. For if the presence or absence of something makes no apparent difference, it is no real part of the whole.

CHAPTER 9

Poetry and History

It will be clear from what I have said that it is not the poet's function to describe what has actually happened, but the kinds of thing that might happen, that is, that could happen because they are, in the circumstances, either probable or necessary. The difference between the historian and the poet is [**1451b**] not that the one writes in prose and the other in verse; the work of Herodotus might be put into verse, and in this metrical form it would be no less a kind of history than it is without metre. The difference is that the one tells of what has happened, the other of the kinds of things that might happen. For this reason poetry is something more philosophical and more worthy of serious attention than history; for poetry speaks more of universals, history of particulars.

By 'universals' I mean the kinds of thing a certain type of person will probably or necessarily say or do in a given situation; and this is the aim of poetry, although it gives individual names to its characters. 'Particulars' are what, say, Alcibiades did, or what happened to him. By now this distinction has become clear where comedy is concerned, for comic poets build up their plots out of probable occurrences, and then add any names that occur to them; they do not, like the iambic poets, write about actual people.[21] In tragedy, on the other hand, the authors keep to the actual names, the reason being that what is possible is credible. Whereas we cannot be certain of the possibility of something that has not happened, what has happened is obviously possible, for it would not have happened if this had not been so. Nevertheless, even in some tragedies only one or two of the names are well known, and the rest are made up; and indeed there are some in which nothing is familiar, Agathon's *Antheus*,[22] for example, in which both the incidents and the names are made up, yet the play gives no less pleasure for that. It is not necessary, therefore, to keep entirely to the traditional stories which form the subjects of our tragedies. Indeed, it would be absurd to do so, since even the familiar stories are familiar only to a few, and yet they please everybody.

What I have said makes it obvious that the poet must be a maker of plots rather than of verses, since he is a poet by virtue of his representation, and what he represents is actions. And even if he deals with things that have actually happened, that does not make him any the less a poet, for there is nothing to prevent some of the things that have happened from being the kind of thing that may happen according to probability, and thus he will be a poet in writing about them.

Of simple plots and actions those that are episodic are the worst. By an episodic plot I mean one in which the sequence of the episodes is neither probable nor necessary. Plays of this kind are composed by bad poets because they cannot help it, and by good poets because of the actors; writing for the dramatic competitions, they often strain a plot beyond the bounds of [1452a] possibility, and are thus obliged to dislocate the continuity of events.

However, tragedy is the representation not only of a complete action, but also of incidents that awaken fear and pity, and effects of this kind are heightened when things happen unexpectedly but because of each other, for then they will be more remarkable than if they seem merely mechanical or accidental. Indeed, even chance occurrences seem most remarkable when they have the appearance of having been brought about by design – when, for example, the statue of Mitys at Argos killed the man who had caused Mitys' death by falling down on him as he looked at it. Things like this do not seem mere chance occurrences. Thus plots of this type are necessarily better than others.

CHAPTER 10

Simple and Complex Plots

Some plots are simple, and some complex, for the obvious reason that the actions of which they are representations are of one or other of these kinds. By a simple action I refer to one which is single and continuous in the sense of my earlier definition, and in which the change of fortune comes about without a reversal or a recognition. A complex action is one in which the change is accompanied by a recognition or a reversal, or both. These should develop out of the very structure of the plot, so that they are the inevitable or probable consequence of what has gone before; for there is a big difference between what happens as a result of something else and what merely happens after it.

CHAPTER 11

Reversal, Recognition, and Suffering

As has already been noted, a reversal is a change from one state of affairs to its opposite, one which conforms, as I have said, to probability or necessity. In *Oedipus*, for example, the Messenger who came to cheer

Oedipus and relieve him of his fear about his mother, did the very opposite by revealing to him who he was.[23] In the *Lynceus*,[24] again, Lynceus is being led off to execution, followed by Danaus who is to kill him, when, as a result of events that occurred earlier, it comes about that he is saved and it is Danaus who is put to death.

As the word itself indicates, a recognition is a change from ignorance to knowledge, and it leads either to love or to hatred between persons destined for good or ill fortune. The most effective form of discovery is that which is accompanied by a reversal, like the one in *Oedipus*. There are of course other forms of recognition, for what I have described may happen in relation to inanimate and trifling objects, and moreover it is possible to recognize whether a person has done something or not. But the form of recognition most essentially related to the plot and action of the play is the one described above, for a recognition of this kind in combination with a reversal will carry with it [**1452b**] either pity or fear, and it is actions such as these that, according to my definition, tragedy represents; and further, such a combination is likely to lead to good or bad fortune.

Since recognition is a recognition between people, it may be that only one person's identity is revealed to another, that of the second being already known. Sometimes, however, a recognition of two parties is necessary, as for example, when Iphigenia[25] was recognized by Orestes through the sending of the letter, and a second recognition was required to make him known to Iphigenia.

These, then, are two elements of the plot, reversal and recognition. A third is suffering. Of these three, reversal and recognition have already been defined. Suffering is an action of a destructive or painful nature, such as deaths openly represented, physical agonies, woundings, and the like.

CHAPTER 12

The Main Parts of Tragedy

I spoke earlier of the various elements that are to be employed as the constituents of tragedy. The separate sections into which the work is divided are as follows: prologue, episode, *exodos*, and choral song, the last being subdivided into *parodos* and *stasimon*. These are common to all tragedies; songs from the actors and *kommoi*, however, are a characteristic only of some tragedies.

The prologue is the whole of that part of a tragedy that precedes the *parodos*, or first entry of the Chorus. An episode is the whole of that part of a tragedy that comes between choral songs. The *exodos* is the whole of that part of a tragedy which is not followed by a song of the Chorus. In the choral sections the *parodos* is the whole of the first utterance of the Chorus, and a *stasimon* is a choral song without anapaests or trochees.[26] A *kommos* is a passage of lament in which both Chorus and actors take part.

These then are the separate sections into which the body of the tragedy is to be divided; I mentioned earlier the elements of which it must be composed.

CHAPTER 13

Tragic Action

Following upon the points I have already made, I must go on to say what is to be aimed at and what guarded against in the construction of plots, and what are the sources of the tragic effect.

We saw that the structure of tragedy at its best should be complex, not simple, and that it should represent actions capable of awakening fear and pity – for this is a characteristic function of representations of this type. It follows in the first place that good men should not be shown passing from prosperity to misery, for this does not inspire fear or pity, it merely disgusts us. Nor should evil men be shown progressing from misery to prosperity. This is the most untragic of all plots, for it has none of the requisites of tragedy; it does not appeal to our [**1453a**] humanity, or awaken pity or fear in us. Nor again should an utterly worthless man be seen falling from prosperity into misery. Such a course might indeed play upon our humane feelings, but it would not arouse either pity or fear; for our pity is awakened by undeserved misfortune, and our fear by that of someone just like ourselves – pity for the undeserving sufferer and fear for the man like ourselves – so that the situation in question would have nothing in it either pitiful or fearful.

There remains a mean between these extremes. This is the sort of man who is not conspicuous for virtue and justice, and whose fall into misery is not due to vice and depravity, but rather to some error, a man who enjoys prosperity and a high reputation, like Oedipus and Thyestes and other famous members of families like theirs.

Inevitably, then, the well-conceived plot will have a single interest, and not, as some say, a double. The change in fortune will be, not from misery to prosperity, but the reverse, from prosperity to misery, and it will be due, not to depravity, but to some great error either in such a man as I have described or in one better than this, but not worse. This is borne out by existing practice. For at first the poets treated any stories that came to hand, but nowadays the best tragedies are written about a handful of families, those of Alcmaeon, for example, and Oedipus and Orestes and Meleager and Thyestes and Telephus,[27] and others whom it has befallen to suffer or inflict terrible experiences.

The best tragedies in the technical sense are constructed in this way. Those critics are on the wrong tack, therefore, who criticize Euripides for following such a procedure in his tragedies, and complain that many of them end in misfortune; for, as I have said, this is the right ending. The strongest evidence of this is that on the stage and in the dramatic competitions plays of this kind, when properly worked out, are the most tragic of all, and Euripides, faulty as is his management of other points, is nevertheless regarded as the most tragic of our dramatic poets.

The next best type of structure, ranked first by some critics, is that which, like the *Odyssey*, has a double structure, and ends in opposite ways for the good and the bad characters. It is considered the best only because of the feeble judgement of the audience, for the poets pander to the taste of the spectators. But this is not the pleasure that is proper to tragedy. It belongs rather to comedy, where those who have been the bitterest of enemies in the story – Orestes and Aegisthus, for example – go off at the end as friends, and nobody is killed by anybody.

CHAPTER 14

Fear and Pity

[1453b] Fear and pity may be excited by means of spectacle; but they can also take their rise from the very structure of the incidents, which is the preferable method and the mark of a better poet. For the plot should be so ordered that, even without seeing it performed, anyone merely hearing about the incidents will shudder with fear and pity as a result of what is happening – as indeed would be the experience of anyone hearing the plot of *Oedipus*. To produce this effect by means of stage spectacle is less artistic, and requires the cooperation of the producer. Those who employ spectacle to produce an effect, not of fear, but of something merely monstrous, have nothing to do with tragedy, for not every kind of pleasure should be demanded of tragedy, but only that which is proper to it; and since the poet has by means of his representation to produce the tragic pleasure that is associated with pity and fear, this clearly ought to be bound up with the events of the plot.

Let us now consider what kinds of incident are to be regarded as fearful or pitiable. Deeds that fit this description must of course involve people who are either friends to one another, or enemies, or neither. Now if a man injures his enemy, there is nothing pitiable either in his act or in his intention, except in so far as suffering itself is concerned; nor is there if they are indifferent to each other. But when the sufferings involve those who are near and dear to one another, when for example brother kills brother, son father, mother son, or son mother, or if such a deed is contemplated, or something else of the kind is actually done, then we have a situation of the kind to be aimed at. Thus it will not do to tamper with the traditional stories, the murder of Clytemnestra by Orestes, for instance, and that of Eriphyle by Alcmaeon; on the other hand, the poet must be inventive and handle the traditional material effectively.

I must explain more clearly what I mean by 'effectively'. The deed may be done by characters acting consciously and in full knowledge of the facts, as was the way of the early dramatic poets, when, for instance, Euripides made Medea kill her children. Or they may do it without realizing the horror of the deed until later, when they discover the relationship; this is what Sophocles did with Oedipus. Here, indeed, the relevant incident occurs outside the action of the play; but it may be a part of the tragedy, as with Alcmaeon in Astydamas' play, or Telegonus in The Wounded Odysseus.[28] A third alternative is for someone who is about to do a terrible deed in ignorance of the relationship to discover the truth before he does it. These are the only possibilities, for the deed must either be done or not done, and by someone either with or without knowledge of the facts.

The least acceptable of these alternatives is when someone in possession of the facts is on the point of acting but fails to do so, for this merely shocks us, and, since no suffering is involved, it is not tragic. Hence nobody is allowed to behave [1454a] like this, or only seldom, as when Haemon fails to kill Creon in the Antigone.[29] Next in order of effectiveness is when the deed is actually done, and here it is better that the character should act in ignorance and only recognize the truth afterwards, for there is nothing in this to outrage our feelings, and the recognition comes as a surprise. However, the best method is the last, when, for example, in the Cresphontes Merope intends to kill her son, but recognizes him and does not do so; or when the same thing happens with brother and sister in Iphigenia in Tauris; or when, in the Helle,[30] the son recognizes his mother when he is just about to betray her.

This, then, is the reason why, as I said before, our tragedies keep to a few families. For in their search for dramatic material it was by chance, rather than by technical knowledge, that the poets discovered how to gain tragic effects in their plots. And they are still obliged to have recourse to those families in which sufferings of the kind I have described have been experienced.

I have said enough now about the arrangement of the incidents in tragedy and the types of plot it ought to have.

CHAPTER 15

The Characters of Tragedy

Regarding character, there are four things to aim at. First and foremost, the characters should be good. Now character will be displayed, as I have pointed out, if some preference is revealed in speech or action, and if it is a preference for what is good the character will be good. There can be goodness in every class of person; for instance, a woman or a slave may be good, though the one is possibly an inferior being and the other in general an insignificant one.

In the second place the portrayal should be appropriate. For example, a character may possess manly qualities, but it is not appropriate that a female character should be given manliness[31] or cleverness in this way.

Thirdly, the characters should be lifelike. This is not the same thing as making them good, or appropriate in the sense in which I have used the word.

And, fourthly, they should be consistent. Even if the person who is being represented is inconsistent, and this trait is the basis of his character, he must nevertheless be portrayed as consistently inconsistent.

As an example of unnecessary badness of character, there is Menelaus in the *Orestes*.[32] The character who behaves in an unsuitable and inappropriate way is exemplified in Odysseus' lament in the *Scylla*,[33] and in Melanippe's speech.[34] An inconsistent character is shown in *Iphigenia at Aulis*,[35] for Iphigenia as a suppliant is quite unlike what she is later.

As in the arrangement of the incidents, so too in characterization one must always look for what will be either necessary or probable; in other words, it should be necessary or probable that such and such a person should say or do such and such a thing, and similarly that this particular incident should follow on that.

Furthermore, it is obvious that the unravelling of the plot should arise from the circumstances of the plot itself, and not [**1454b**] be brought about *ex machina*,[36] as is done in the *Medea* and in the episode of the embarkation in the *Iliad*. The *deus ex machina* should be used only for matters outside the play proper, either for things that happened before it which a human being could not know, or for things that are yet to come and that require to be foretold prophetically – for we allow to the gods the power to see all things. However, there should be nothing irrational in the events, or if there must be, it should be kept outside the tragedy, as in Sophocles' *Oedipus*.

Since tragedy is a representation of people who are better than ourselves, we must emulate the good portrait painters. These, while reproducing the distinctive appearance of their subjects and making likenesses, paint them better-looking than they are. In the same way the poet, in portraying men who are hot-tempered, or lazy or who have other defects of character, must bring out these qualities in them, and at the same time show them as decent people: Homer, for instance, portrayed Achilles as a good man, but also made him an example of harshness.[37]

These points must be carefully watched, as too must those arising from the perceptions which are necessarily dependent on the poet's art; for here too it is often possible to make mistakes.[38] However, enough has been said about these matters in my published work.

CHAPTER 16

The Different Kinds of Recognition

I have already explained what I mean by recognition. Of the different kinds of recognition, the first is the least artistic, and is mostly used from sheer lack of invention; this is recognition by means of visible signs or tokens. These may be congenital marks, like 'the spearhead that the Earthborn bear',[39] or 'stars', such as those that Carcinus uses in his *Thyestes*;[40] or they may be acquired, whether marks on the body such as scars, or external objects such as necklaces – or, in the *Tyro*,[41] the recognition by means of the cradle. However, some ways of using these tokens are better than others; for example, the recognition of Odysseus[42] through his scar is made in one way by his nurse and in another way by the swineherds. These recognitions, when made merely to gain credence, are less effective, as are all types of recognition used for such intentions; better are those that result from a reversal, as happens in the 'washing episode' in the *Odyssey*.

The second class of recognitions are those which are manufactured by the poet, and which are inartistic for that reason. An example occurs in *Iphigenia in Tauris*[43] when Orestes reveals who he is. While the identity of Iphigenia is revealed by means of the letter, Orestes himself is made to say what the poet here requires instead of what the plot demands; and this is not far removed from the fault I spoke about a moment ago, for he might have brought some tokens as well. Another example is 'the voice of the shuttle' in Sophocles' *Tereus*.[44]

A third kind is the recognition that is due to memory, when the sight of something leads to the required understanding. Thus [1455a] in *The Cyprians*, by Dicaeogenes, Teucer bursts into tears on seeing the picture, and in *The Tale of Alcinous* Odysseus also weeps when he hears the minstrel's lyre and remembers the past, and this is how these two are recognized.[45]

The fourth kind is the result of reasoning, such as is found in *The Choephori*: 'Someone who is like me has come; no one is like me except Orestes; therefore it is Orestes who has come.'[46] Another example is what the sophist Polyidus suggested in the case of Iphigenia: he said that it was likely enough that Orestes should reason that, as his sister had been sacrificed, so too it was his fate to be sacrificed. Then there is the episode in the *Tydeus* of Theodectes when the father has come to find his son, and realizes that he is himself to die; or that in the *Phineidae*[47] where, on seeing a particular place, the women infer that they are fated to die there, for it was there that they had been exposed at birth.

There is also a composite form of recognition arising from the fallacious reasoning of the audience, as in *Odysseus the False Messenger*.[48]

The fact that he alone can string the bow is manufactured by the poet and is a premise, as is his saying that he would know the bow which he had not seen; to make him reveal himself by the latter means when he is expected to do so by the former is false reasoning.

Of all the forms of recognition, the best is that which arises from the incidents themselves, when our amazement results from events that are probable, as happens in Sophocles' *Oedipus*, and again in the *Iphigenia* – for it was quite probable that she should wish to send off a letter. Recognitions of this kind are the only ones that dispense with such contrivances as tokens and necklaces. The next best are those that depend on reasoning.

CHAPTER 17

Some Rules for the Tragic Poet

In putting together his plots and working out the kind of speech to go with them, the poet should as far as possible keep the scene before his eyes. In this way, seeing everything very vividly, as though he were himself an eyewitness of the events, he will find what is appropriate, and will be least likely to overlook inconsistencies. Evidence of this is the censure laid on Carcinus,[49] who made Amphiaraus come out of a temple; this would have escaped notice if the episode had not been actually seen, but the audience took offence at it, and the play was not a success on the stage.

As far as possible, too, the dramatic poet should carry out the appropriate gestures as he composes his speeches, for of writers with equal abilities those who can actually make themselves feel the relevant emotions will be the most convincing – agitation or rage will be most vividly reproduced by one who is himself agitated or in a passion. Hence poetry is the product either of a man of great natural ability or of a madman; the one is highly responsive, the other beside himself.

As for the stories, whether he is taking over something ready-made or inventing for himself, the poet should first plan [**1455b**] the general outline, and then expand by working out appropriate episodes. What

I mean by planning the general outline may be illustrated from the *Iphigenia*, as follows: A young girl was offered as a sacrifice, and mysteriously disappeared from the view of her sacrificers; she was set down in another country, where it was the custom to sacrifice strangers to the goddess, and became the priestess of this rite. Some time later it happened that the priestess's brother arrived (the fact that the oracle had told him to go there and the purpose of his journey are matters that lie outside the plot). On his arrival he was seized, and was about to be sacrificed, when he revealed who he was, either in the way that Euripides makes it happen or, as Polyidus[50] suggests, by making the not-unnatural remark that not only his sister, it seemed, was fated to be sacrificed, but himself too; and thus he was saved.

When he has reached this stage the poet may supply the proper names and fill in the episodes, making sure that they are appropriate, like the fit of madness in Orestes which led to his capture, and his escape by the device of the purification.

In the plays the episodes are of course short; in epic poetry they are what supply the requisite length. The story of the *Odyssey*, for example, is not a long one. A man is kept away from his home for many years; Poseidon is watching him with a jealous eye, and he is alone. The state of affairs at home is that his wealth is being squandered by his wife's suitors, and plots are being laid against his son's life. After being buffeted by many storms he returns home and reveals his identity; he falls upon his enemies and destroys them, but preserves his own life. There you have the essential story of the *Odyssey*; the rest of the poem is made up of episodes.

CHAPTER 18

Further Rules for the Tragic Poet

Every tragedy has its complication and its denouement. The complication consists of the incidents lying outside the plot, and often some of those inside it, and the rest is the denouement. By complication I mean the part of the story from the beginning to the point immediately preceding the change to good or bad fortune; by denouement the part from the onset of this change to the end. In the *Lynceus* of Theodectes, for instance, the complication is what happened before the events of the play proper, together with the seizure of the boy and the revelation of the parents,[51] and the denouement extends from the accusation of murder to the end.

There are four kinds of tragedy, a number corresponding to that of the constituent parts that I spoke about.[52] There is complex tragedy, which depends entirely on reversal and recognition; tragedy of suffering, as in the various plays on Ajax [**1456a**] or Ixion; tragedy of character, as in *The Phthiotides* and the *Peleus*;[53] and fourthly, spectacular tragedy,[54] as in *The Phorcides*, in the *Prometheus*, and in plays with scenes in Hades. The poet should try to include all these elements, or, failing that, as many as possible of the most important, especially since it is the fashion nowadays to find fault with poets; just because there have been poets who excelled in the individual parts of tragedy, people expect that a single man should outdo each of them in his special kind of excellence. Properly speaking, tragedies should be classed as similar or dissimilar in complication and denouement. Many poets are skilful in complicating their plots but clumsy in unravelling them; a constant mastery of both techniques is what is required.

Bearing in mind what has often been said, the dramatic poet must be careful not to give his tragedy an epic structure, by which I mean one with a multiplicity of stories – as though one were to attempt a plot covering the whole story of the *Iliad*. By reason of its length, the *Iliad* can allow the proper development of its various parts, but in plays the results of such attempts are disappointing, as is proved by experience. For all the poets who have dramatized the destruction of Troy in its entirety, and not, like Euripides, only parts of it, or the whole of the story of Niobe, and not as Aeschylus did it, have either failed utterly or done badly in the dramatic competitions; and indeed even a play by Agathon[55] was a failure for this alone.

In the handling of reversals and of simple plots poets use amazement to achieve the effect they want;[56] this is tragic and appeals to our humanity. This happens when the clever man who is also wicked is outwitted, as Sisyphus was, or when the brave man who is also unscrupulous is worsted; and this is a likely enough result, as Agathon points out, for it is quite likely that many things should happen contrary to likelihood.

The Chorus should be regarded as one of the actors; it should be a part of the whole, and should assume a share in the action, as happens in Sophocles, but not in Euripides. With other playwrights the choral songs may have no more to do with the plot in hand than with any other tragedy; they are mere choral interludes, according to the practice first introduced by Agathon. But what difference is there between the singing of interpolated songs like these and the transference of a speech or a whole episode from one play to another?

CHAPTER 19

Thought and Diction

Now that the other elements of tragedy have been dealt with, it remains to say something about diction and thought. As far as thought is concerned, enough has been said about it in my treatise on rhetoric, for it more properly belongs to that study. Thought includes all the effects that have to be produced by means of language; among these are proof and refutation, the [1456b] awakening of emotions such as pity, fear, anger, and the like, and also exaggeration and depreciation. It is clear, too, that in the action of the play the same principles should be observed whenever it is necessary to produce effects of pity or terror, or of greatness or probability – with this difference, however, that here the effects must be made without verbal explanation, while the others are produced by means of language coming from the lips of a speaker, and are dependent on the use of language. For where would be the need of a speaker if the required effects could be conveyed without the use of language?

As for diction, one branch of study is the various forms of expression, an understanding of which belongs to the art of delivery and to the expert in that field: for example, what is a command, a prayer, a statement, a threat, a question, an answer? The poet's art is not seriously criticized according to his knowledge or ignorance of these things. For what would anyone think is wrong about the words which Protagoras censures on the grounds that the poet, intending a prayer, actually gives a command when he says, 'Sing of the wrath, Goddess'?[57] For, says Protagoras, to order a person to do or not to do something is a command. However, let us pass over this topic since it belongs to another art and not to the art of poetry.

CHAPTER 20

Some Linguistic Definitions

Diction in general is made up of the following parts: the letter, the syllable, the connecting word, the conjunction, the noun, the verb, the inflexion or case, and the statement.

A letter is an indivisible sound, not just any such sound, but one from which a composite sound may be produced; animals also, it is true, utter indivisible sounds, but none that I should describe as a letter. The different forms of this sound are the vowel, the semi-vowel, and the mute letter or consonant. A vowel is a letter which has an audible sound without any contact between the organs of speech. A semi-vowel (S or R, for instance) is given audible sound by such a contact. A mute is a letter which even with such contact has no sound of its own, but which becomes audible when combined with letters which possess sound; examples are G and D. The letters differ in sound according to the shape of the mouth and the places where they are produced; according as they are aspirated or not aspirated; according to their length or shortness; according as they have an acute, a grave, or a circumflex accent. However, the detailed study of these matters belongs to work on metre.

A syllable is a sound unit without meaning, made up of a mute and a sounded letter; for GR without an A is as much a syllable as it is with an A, as in GRA. But these distinctions are also the concern of metrical theory.

[1457a] A connecting word is a sound unit without significance

which neither hinders nor helps the production of a single significant utterance from the combination of several sounds, and which should not be put at the beginning of a phrase standing by itself; examples are *men*, *de*, *toi* and *de*. Alternatively it is a sound without significance capable of producing a single significant utterance from the combination of several sounds which are themselves significant; examples are 'around', 'about' and similar words.

A conjunction is a sound without significance which indicates the beginning or the end of a speech, or a dividing point in it, and its natural position is at either end or in the middle.

A noun is a composite of sounds with a meaning; it is independent of time, and none of its individual parts has a meaning in its own right. For in compounds we do not give separate meanings to the parts; in the name 'Theodorus', for instance, the '*-dorus*' part has in itself no meaning.

A verb is a composite of sounds with a meaning; it is concerned with time, and, as was the case with nouns, none of its individual parts has a meaning in its own right. The words 'man' and 'white' give no indication of time, but 'walks' and 'has walked' indicate respectively present and past time.

Case or inflexion in a noun or verb is that which gives the sense of 'of' or 'to' a thing, and the like, or indicates whether it relates to one or many, as with 'man' and 'men'. Alternatively it may signify types of intonation, as in question or command; 'walked?' and 'walk!' are verbal inflexions of this kind.

A statement is a composite of sounds with a meaning, and some parts of it have a meaning of their own. Not every statement is made up of verbs and nouns – the definition of a man, for example; it is possible to have a statement without verbs, but it will always have a part with a meaning of its own, as 'Cleon' has in the statement 'Cleon walks'. A statement may have unity in one of two ways, either in that it signifies one thing, or in that it achieves unity by a conjunction of several factors; the unity of the *Iliad*, for example, results from such a conjunction, that of the definition of a man from its signifying one thing.

CHAPTER 21

Poetic Diction

Nouns may be classified as simple, by which I mean those made up of elements which individually have no meaning, like the word 'earth' (*ge*), or as double or compound. These compounds may take the form either of a part which has a meaning combined with one which has no meaning – although within the compound no part has a separate meaning – or of parts which all have meanings. A noun may be triple or quadruple or multiple in form, like most of those from Massilia, for example, Hermocaicoxanthus.[58]

[**1457b**] Every noun is either a word in current use or a loan-word, a metaphor or an ornamental word, a poetic coinage or a word that has been expanded or abbreviated or otherwise altered.

By a word in current use I mean a word that everybody uses, and by a loan-word one that other peoples use. Obviously the same word can be both current and a loan-word, though not in relation to the same people; to the Cypriots, for example, *sigunon* is the current word for a spear, but to us it is a loan-word.

Metaphor is the application to one thing of a name belonging to another thing; the transference may be from the genus to the species, from the species to the genus, or from one species to another, or it may be a matter of analogy. As an example of transference from genus to species I give 'Here lies my ship',[59] for lying at anchor is a species of lying. Transference from species to genus is seen in 'Odysseus has indeed performed ten thousand noble deeds',[60] for 'ten thousand', which is a particular large number, is used here instead of the word 'many'. Transference from one species to another is seen in 'Draining off the life with the bronze' and 'Severing with the unyielding bronze';[61] here 'draining off' is used for 'severing', and 'severing' for 'draining off', and both are species of 'taking away'.

I explain metaphor by analogy as what may happen when of four things the second stands in the same relationship to the first as the fourth to the third; for then one may speak of the fourth instead of the second, and the second instead of the fourth. And sometimes people will add to the metaphor a qualification appropriate to the term which has been replaced. Thus, for example, a cup stands in the same relationship to Dionysus as a shield to Ares, and one may therefore call the cup Dionysus' shield and the shield Ares' cup. Or again, old age is to life as evening is to day, and so one may call the evening the old age of the day, or, like Empedocles, one may call old age the 'evening of life' or the 'sunset of life'.[62] In some cases there is no name for some of the terms of the analogy, but the metaphor can be used just the same. For example, to scatter seed is called sowing, but there is no word for the sun's scattering of its flame; however, this stands in the same relationship to sunlight as sowing does to seed, and hence the expression, 'sowing his god-created flame'.[63]

This kind of metaphor can also be used in another way; having called an object by the name of something else, one can deny it one of its attributes – for example, call the shield not Ares' cup, but a wineless cup.

A poetic coinage is a word which has not been in use among a people, but has been invented by the poet himself. There seem to be words of this kind, such as 'sprouters' for horns, and 'supplicator'[64] for priest.

[1458a] A word is expanded when it uses a longer vowel than is normal to it or takes on an extra syllable, and it is abbreviated when some part of it has been removed. Examples of expansion are *poleōs* for *poleōs* ('of a city'), and of abbreviation *kri* (for *krithē*, 'barley') and *dō* (for *dōma*, 'house'), and *ops* (for *opsis*, 'vision') in 'a single *ops* from both eyes'. An altered word is one in which part is left unchanged and part is coined, as when *dexiteron* ('righter') is used for *dexion* ('right') in 'on the righter breast'.[65]

Of the nouns themselves some are masculine, some feminine, and some neuter. Masculine are all that end in *n*, *r* and *s*, and in the compounds of *s*, that is, the two letters *ps* and *x*. Feminine are all those ending in the vowels that are always long, such as *ē* and *ō*, and in *a* among the vowels which may be lengthened. Thus there are equal numbers of masculine and feminine endings, for *ps* and *x* are compound forms of *s*. No noun ends in a mute consonant or in a short vowel. Only three end in *i*: *meli* ('honey'), *kommi* ('gum'), and *peperi* ('pepper'); and five end in *u*. The neuters may end in these vowels, and in *n* and *s*.

CHAPTER 22

Diction and Style

The greatest virtue of diction is to be clear without being commonplace. The clearest diction is that which consists of words in everyday use, but this is commonplace, and can be seen in the poetry of Cleophon and Sthenelus.[66] On the other hand, a diction abounding in unfamiliar usages has dignity, and is raised above the everyday level. By unfamiliar usages I mean loan-words, metaphors, expanded forms, and anything else that is out of the ordinary. However, the exclusive use of forms of this kind would result either in a riddle or in barbarism – a riddle if they were all metaphorical, barbarism if they were all loan words. The very essence of a riddle is to express facts in an impossible combination of language. This cannot be done by a mere succession of ordinary terms, but it can by the use of metaphors, as in the riddle, 'I saw a man welding bronze on another man with fire'[67] and similar examples. In the same way, the use of loan words leads to barbarism. What is needed, then, is some mixture of these various elements. For the one kind will prevent the language from being mean and commonplace, that is, the loan words, the metaphors, the ornamental terms, and the other figures I have described, while the everyday words will give clarity.

[1458b] Among the most effective means of achieving diction that is both clear and unusual is the use of expanded, abbreviated, and altered forms of words; the unfamiliarity due to this deviation from normal usages will raise the diction above the commonplace, while the retention of some part of the normal forms will make for clarity. It is not good criticism, therefore, to censure this type of language and to ridicule Homer for using it, as the elder Eucleides did when he said that it would be easy to write poetry if one were allowed to lengthen syllables whenever one liked, and when he lampooned this style in the lines, 'I

saw Epichares walking to Marathon' and 'not mixing his hellebore'.[68]

The too-obvious use of this style, then, is ridiculous; moderation is necessary in all kinds of diction. The same effect would be produced by anyone using metaphors, unfamiliar loan-words and other such devices ineptly and for the mere sake of raising a laugh. How great a difference is made by their being used properly may be seen in epic poetry if one replaces them with ordinary everyday words in the verse; anyone substituting common words for the unfamiliar words or for the metaphors and other devices mentioned would see the truth of what I am saying. For instance, Aeschylus and Euripides wrote the same line of iambics, with the change only of a single word; an unfamiliar word was substituted for an ordinary one, and one line is beautiful whereas the other is commonplace. This was the line as Aeschylus wrote it in his *Philoctetes*: 'The canker that eats the flesh of my foot.' For 'eats' Euripides put 'feasts upon'.[69]

Just suppose that in the line 'Now a paltry fellow, unseemly, and of no account', one were to use everyday words and say, 'Now a little, weak, ugly fellow.' Or suppose that for this line, 'setting down an unseemly stool and a paltry table', one were to substitute 'setting down a poor stool and a small table'. Or that for 'the headlands clamour' one were to substitute 'the headlands shout'.[70]

Then again, Ariphrades[71] ridiculed the tragedians for using expressions that no one would use in ordinary speech, such as 'from the house away' instead of 'away from the house', and 'thine', [**1459a**] and 'Achilles about' instead of 'about Achilles', and the like. By the very fact of not being normal idiom, all such usages as these raise the diction above the level of the commonplace; but Ariphrades failed to see this.

It is a fine thing to be able to make proper use of all the devices I have mentioned, including compound words and unfamiliar loan words, but far the most important thing to master is the use of metaphor. This is the one thing that cannot be learnt from anyone else, and it is the mark of great natural ability, for the ability to use metaphor well implies a perception of resemblances.

Of the different types of words, compound forms are best suited to dithyrambs, loan words to heroic verse, and metaphors to iambic verse. All these may, indeed, be fittingly used in heroic verse; but in iambic verse, which as far as possible models itself on speech, the only appropriate terms are those that anyone might use in prose speeches, and these are words in current use, metaphors, and ornamental words.

I need say no more now about tragedy and the art of representation by means of action.

CHAPTER 23

Epic Poetry

As for the art of representation in the form of narrative verse, clearly its plots should be dramatically constructed, like those of tragedies; they should centre upon a single action, whole and complete, and having a beginning, a middle, and an end, so that like a single complete organism the poem may produce its own special kind of pleasure. Nor should epics be constructed like histories, in which it is not the exposition of a single action that is required, but of a single period, and of everything that happened to one or more persons during this period, however unrelated the various events may have been. For just as the sea battle at Salamis and the engagement with the Carthaginians in Sicily[72] took place at the same time, but did not work towards the same end, so too in any sequence of time events may follow one another without producing any one single result. Yet most of our poets do this.

In this respect, too, as I have already said, Homer seems inspired in comparison with other poets, in that, although the Trojan War had a beginning and an end, he did not attempt to put the whole of it into his poem; the plot would have been too large to be taken in all at once, and, if he had limited its length, the diversity of its incident would have made it too complicated. As it is, he has selected one part of the story, and uses many other parts as episodes, such as the 'Catalogue of Ships' and other episodes with which he gives variety to the poem. Other epic poets write about one man, or a single period of time, or a single action made up of many parts; among such poets are the [1459b] authors of the *Cypria* and *The Little Iliad*.[73] Thus, while only one tragedy, or at most two, can be made out of the *Iliad* or the *Odyssey*, several can be made out of the *Cypria*, and more than eight out of *The Little Iliad*: a *Judgement of the Arms*, a *Philoctetes*, a *Neoptolemus*, a *Eurypylus*, an *Odysseus the Beggar*, a *Laconian Women*, a *Sack of Troy*, and a *Departure of the Fleet*, not to mention a *Sinon* and a *Trojan Women*.

CHAPTER 24

Epic Poetry (continued)

Furthermore, epic poetry must divide into the same types as tragedy, that is, the simple, the complex, that which turns on character, and that which turns on suffering. With the exception of song and spectacle, its constituent parts must also be the same, for it needs reversals and recognitions and sufferings, and moreover the thought and diction must be of good quality. All these things Homer was the first to use, and he did so with skill. Of his two poems the one, the *Iliad*, is simple in structure and a story of suffering, the other, the *Odyssey*, is complex (for it has recognitions throughout) and turns on character; moreover, they surpass all other poems in diction and in quality of thought.

Epic differs from tragedy in the length of its plot structure and in its metre. The limitations as to length that have already been indicated will suffice; that is to say, it must be possible for the beginning and the end to be embraced within a single view, and this will be the case if the plot structures are shorter than the ancient epics, but stretch to the length of a group of tragedies offered at a single hearing. It is the special advantage of epic that it may be of considerable length. In tragedy it is not possible to represent several parts of the story as taking place simultaneously, but only the part that is actually being performed on the stage by the actors; epic poetry, on the other hand, being narrative, is able to represent many incidents that are being simultaneously enacted, and, provided they are relevant, they increase the weight of the poem, and give it the merits of grandeur, variety of interest, and diversity in its episodes. Monotony soon bores an audience and can make tragedies fail.

Experience has shown that the heroic hexameter is the right metre for epic. If anyone were to write a narrative poem in some other metre, or in a variety of metres, it would seem inappropriate for, of all metres, the heroic hexameter has the greatest weight and stability, which enables it most readily to admit loan words and metaphors; and in this respect, too, the narrative form of representation is better than any other. The iambic and the trochaic tetrameter are metres expressing movement, the latter being suited to dancing, the former to action. However, it [1460a] would be even more out of place to mix several metres, as Chaeremon[74] did. And so no one has ever composed a poem on the grand scale in any other than the heroic measure; as I have said, nature herself teaches us to choose the right metre for our purposes.

Admirable as he is in so many other respects, Homer is especially so in this: he is the only poet who recognizes what part he himself ought to play in his poems. The poet should speak as little as possible in his own person, for it is not in that way that he represents actions. Other poets appear in their own person throughout their poems, and rarely impersonate others. But after a few prefatory words, Homer at once introduces a man, a woman, or some other person, no one of them lacking in character but each with distinctive characteristics.

The marvellous should of course be a feature of tragedy, but epic poetry, where the persons acting the story are not before our eyes, may include more of the inexplicable, which is the chief element in the marvellous. If it were brought on to the stage there would be something ridiculous about the pursuit of Hector,[75] with the Greeks merely standing there instead of pursuing him, and Achilles restraining them with a shake of the head; in the poem the absurdity is not apparent. The marvellous is a source of pleasure, as is shown by the fact that in passing on a piece of news everyone will add something extra so as to give pleasure.

Above all, Homer has taught other poets how to tell untruths as they ought to be told, that is, by false inference. If one thing exists or happens because another thing exists or happens, people think that, if the consequent exists or happens, the antecedent also exists; but this is not the case. Thus if a proposition were untrue, but there was something else which must be true or must happen if the proposition were true, the poet should supply the latter; for because we know that this is true, our soul falsely infers the truth of the original proposition. There is an example of this in the bath scene in the *Odyssey*.[76]

Probable impossibilities are to be preferred to improbable possibilities. Stories should not be constructed from irrational parts; anything irrational should as far as possible be excluded, or if not, at least kept out of the plot proper, like Oedipus not knowing how Laius died; it should not be admitted into the play, as in the *Electra* we have the messenger's report of the Pythian Games, or in the *Mysians* the business of the man's coming from Tegea to Mysia without speaking.[77] To say that otherwise the plot would have been spoilt is ridiculous; plots like these should not be devised in the first instance, but if a poet does employ such a plot and it appears that it could have been worked out more reasonably, then his endeavour is absurd as well.[78] Even in the *Odyssey* the irrational elements in the episode of Odysseus's being set ashore in Ithaca[79] would obviously not have been acceptable if they had been treated by an inferior poet; as [**1460b**] it is, Homer has managed to disguise their absurdity, charming it away by his other excellences.

The poet should take care to elaborate the diction in 'neutral' sections, that is, in passages where neither character nor thought is in question; on the other hand, diction that is too brilliant may obscure the presentation of character and thought.

CHAPTER 25

Critical Objections and Their Answers[80]

The way to get a clear idea of the various critical problems – their number, their nature, and the solutions to be offered – is to look at them as follows. Like the painter or any other image-maker, the poet represents things; necessarily, therefore, he must always represent things in one of three ways: either as they were or are, or as they are said to be or seem to be, or as they ought to be. His medium is language, which includes loan-words and metaphors and the various other modifications of language that we allow to poets. We must remember, too, that there are not the same standards of correctness in poetry as in politics or any other art. In poetry there are two kinds of fault, the one kind essential, the other incidental. If the poet has undertaken to represent [something, and has gone astray through][81] lack of skill, that is an essential fault. But if his error lies in what he sets out to do, if for instance he represents a horse with both its offside legs thrown forward, then that is an error in some special branch of knowledge (for example, medicine or some other technical subject), but no essential fault is involved. These, then, are the points to be considered in resolving problems of criticism.

Taking first problems relating to the essentials of the poetic art: if the poet has depicted something impossible, he is at fault indeed, but he is justified in doing it as long as the art attains its end, as I have described it, that is, as long as it makes this or some other part of the poem more striking. The pursuit of Hector[82] is a case in point. If, however, this end could have been achieved just as well, or better, by conforming to the requirements of the art, then there is no justification for the fault, for if possible a poem should be entirely free of faults. Then again, which of the two kinds of fault is actually in question, one that concerns the essentials of the poetic art or one that is merely incidental? It is a less serious fault not to know that a female deer has no horns than to make an unrecognizable picture of one.

Suppose next that a description is criticized as not being true. The answer might be, 'No, but it ought to be like that' – just as Sophocles said that he portrayed people as they ought to be, whereas Euripides portrayed them as they are. However, if neither of these claims fits the case, then an appeal might be made to tradition, as for example with the tales about the gods. Now it is possible that these tales are neither true nor improve on the truth, [**1461a**] but are what Xenophanes[83] said of them; nevertheless they are in accordance with tradition. In other cases the answer might be, not that it is better than the truth, but that it represents things as they used to be – for instance, in the matter of the spears: 'Their spears stood upright on their butt ends';[84] for that was then the custom, as it still is among the Illyrians.

In deciding whether something that has been said or done is morally good or bad, not only should we pay regard to the goodness or badness of the saying or deed itself, but we should also take into account the

93

persons by whom and to whom it was said or done, the occasion, the means, and the reason – whether, for example, to bring about a greater good, or to avert a greater evil.

Some criticisms may be answered by examining the diction;[85] an example is the loan-word in 'first the mules', where it is possible that Homer means 'sentinels', not 'mules'. Then there is Dolon, 'who indeed was evil of form'; here the reference is perhaps not to his deformed body but to his ugly face, for the Cretans use 'fair-formed' with the sense of 'fair-faced'. Then again, 'stronger mix the wine' may mean 'more quickly mix the wine', and not have the sense of 'unmixed', as though for drunkards.

Other expressions are metaphorical.[86] For example, 'then all gods and men slept through the night', but at the same time Homer says, 'and indeed when he gazed at the Trojan plain he wondered at the sound of reed-pipes and pan-pipes'. Here the word 'all' is metaphorically used instead of 'many', for 'all' is a species of plurality. So too 'alone without a share' is metaphorical, for the best-known representative is referred to as the only one.

Again, the solution may be a matter of pronunciation, as with the changes of Hippias of Thasos in 'we grant that he gain his prayer', and 'part of which rots in the rain';[87] or again of punctuation, as in Empedocles: 'at once mortal things were born that formerly learned immortal ways, and things unmixed formerly mixed';[88] or of ambiguity, as in 'more of the night has passed',[89] where 'more' is ambiguous; or of normal linguistic usage – wine mixed with water, for example, is normally called wine, and so one finds the phrase 'a greave of newly wrought tin';[90] and as iron-workers are called bronze-smiths, so too Ganymede[91] is said to pour wine for Zeus, although the gods do not drink wine. But this may also be explained as a metaphorical usage.

Whenever a word seems to involve some inconsistency of meaning, we ought to consider in how many ways it may be interpreted in the context – in, for example, 'there the brazen spear was stopped',[92] how many ways there are of taking 'there . . . was stopped'. We should think how best we shall avoid the fault [1461b] described by Glaucon[93] when he says that some people make unreasonable presuppositions, and go on to draw conclusions from their own adverse comments on the poet;

if his words conflict with the conclusions they have thus reached, they censure him as though he had actually said what they ascribe to him. This is what has happened in the case of Icarius. People believe that he was a Spartan, and therefore think it strange that Telemachus should not have met him when he went to Sparta.[94] But the truth of the matter may be, as the Cephallenians say, that Odysseus married one of their people, and that the name was Icadius, not Icarius. Thus it is probably through a mistake that this particular difficulty has arisen.

Generally speaking, then, the 'impossible' has to be justified on grounds either of poetic effect, or of an attempt to improve on reality, or of accepted tradition. As far as poetic effect is concerned, a convincing impossibility is preferable to an unconvincing possibility. Even though it is impossible that there should be such people as Zeuxis[95] used to paint, yet it is better so; for the artist should surpass the model.

Accepted tradition may justify the use of the irrational, as may the plea that there are times when it is not irrational, for it is probable enough that things should happen contrary to probability. Verbal inconsistencies should be examined in the same way as refutations in dialectical exercises in order to see whether the same thing is meant, in the same relation and with the same significance, before you blame the poet for contradicting either what he has himself said or what an intelligent person would assume to be true. However, irrationality and depravity are rightly censured when there is no need for them and they are not properly used, as no good use is made of the irrationality in Euripides' introduction of Aegeus in the *Medea*, or of the depravity of Menelaus in the *Orestes*.[96]

There are, then, five grounds on which a passage may be censured: that it is impossible, irrational, immoral, inconsistent, or technically at fault. And the answers are to be studied in the light of the twelve[97] criteria that I have already enumerated.

CHAPTER 26

Epic and Tragedy Compared

It may be asked which of the two forms of representation is the better, the epic or the tragic. If the better form is the less vulgar, and the less vulgar is always that which is designed to appeal to the better type of audience, then it is quite obvious that the form that represents everything is vulgar. And indeed, as though the audience will not grasp what is meant unless the performer himself adds something, they go in for a great deal of unnecessary movement; bad pipe-players, for instance, roll about if they have to represent a discus, and keep pulling at the leader of the chorus if they are performing *Scylla*.[98] This is what tragedy is like, we are told; it corresponds with what the older actors thought of their successors – for Mynniscus used to call Callipides 'the Ape' on the grounds that he overacted grossly, and the same was said of [**1462a**] Pindarus.[99] The tragic art as a whole, then, stands in the same relationship to the epic as these more recent actors do to the earlier. Thus epic is said to appeal to decent audiences who have no need of gestures, while tragedy appeals to inferior ones; so if it is vulgar it is obviously worse.

Now in the first place, this way of arguing is a criticism of acting, not of poetry, for it is also possible for a rhapsode to exaggerate his gestures while reciting an epic, as Sosistratus used to do, and for a singer too, like Mnasitheus[100] the Opuntian. Next, not all movement is to be rejected (any more than all dancing), but only that of inferior people; Callipides was subjected to the same criticism that is levelled against other actors now, that is, that they represent women who are not respectable. For another thing, tragedy achieves its effect even without movement, just as epic does, for its quality can be seen from reading it. So if tragedy is in other respects superior, this disadvantage is not necessarily inherent in it.

In the second place, tragedy has everything that epic has, and it can even use the epic metre; and as a not inconsiderable addition, it offers music and spectacle, the source of the most vivid pleasures. Again, it has vividness when read as well when performed. Moreover, this form of imitation [**1462b**] achieves its ends in shorter compass, and what is more compact gives more pleasure than what is extended over a long period. Just imagine the *Oedipus* of Sophocles spread out over as many lines as there are in the *Iliad*. Then there is less unity in the imitation of the epic poets, as is shown by the fact that any one work of this kind contains matter for several tragedies, so that, if these poets deal with a single plot, either it will appear truncated if it is briefly set out, or it will give the impression of being watered down if it observes the usual length of such poems; I mean one composed of several actions, such as the *Iliad* or the *Odyssey*, which have many parts, and each of a certain magnitude – and yet these poems are constructed as well as they could be, and each is, as far as this is possible, the representation of a single action.

If, therefore, tragedy is superior to epic in all these respects, and also in fulfilling its artistic function – for these forms of art ought to give, not just any kind of pleasure, but the kinds I have described – then obviously, in achieving its ends better than epic, it must be the better form of art.

This is all I have to say about tragedy and epic poetry, whether in general terms or in relation to their various forms and constituent parts; about the number and the characteristics of these parts; about the causes of their success or failure; and about the various critical problems and their solutions.

HORACE
The Art of Poetry

Supposing a painter chose to put a human head on a horse's neck, or to spread feathers of various colours over the limbs of several different creatures, or to make what in the upper part is a beautiful woman tail off into a hideous fish – could you help laughing when he showed you his efforts? You may take it from me, my dear Pisos,[1] that a book will have very much the same effect as these pictures if, like a sick man's dreams, the author's idle fancies assume such a shape that it is impossible to make a unity of head and tail. 'But,' you will say, 'the right [10] to take liberties of almost any kind has always been enjoyed by painters and poets alike.' I know that; we poets do claim this licence, and in our turn we concede it to others, but not to the point of associating what is wild with what is tame, of pairing snakes with birds or lambs with tigers.

Works that begin impressively and with the promise of carrying on in the heroic strain often have one or two purple passages tacked on to catch the eye, giving a description of Diana's grove and altar, the meanderings of a stream through a picturesque countryside, the River Rhine, or a rainbow. But this is not the right place for things of that kind. Perhaps, too, you know how to paint a cypress; [20] but what is the point of that if you are being paid to paint a shipwrecked man swimming for dear life? A potter sets out to make a two-handled wine-flagon: why, as his wheel spins, does it turn into an ordinary water-jug? In short, let it be anything you like, but at least let it be single and unified.

Most of us poets, father and sons worthy of their father, are led astray by the appearance of correctness. I try my hardest to be succinct, and merely succeed in being obscure; I aim at smoothness, only to find that I am losing fire and energy. One poet sets out to achieve the sublime, and falls into turgidity; another is over-cautious, and, nervous of spreading his wings, never leaves the ground. Yet another, wishing to vary the monotony of his single subject with something out of the ordinary, [30] introduces a dolphin into his woods, or puts a boar among his waves. If art is lacking, the avoidance of a petty fault may lead to a serious imperfection.

The poorest smith down by the Aemilian gladiatorial school will mould fingernails and reproduce wavy hair to the life, but the total effect of his work is unsatisfactory because he cannot put together the whole. Now if I set out to compose anything, I would no more want to be like him than to have a crooked nose, much though I might be admired for my dark eyes and black hair.

Choose a subject that is suited to your abilities, you who aspire to be writers; give long thought to what you are capable of undertaking, and what is beyond you. [40] A man who chooses a subject within his powers will never be at a loss for words, and his thoughts will be clear and orderly. The virtue and attraction of order, I think I am right in saying, is that the poet will at any moment be saying exactly what his poem at that moment requires; he will be keeping back points for the time being or leaving them out altogether, and showing what he thinks admirable and what beneath notice.

Furthermore, you will make an excellent impression if you use care and subtlety in placing your words and, by the skilful choice of setting, give fresh meaning to a familiar word. If it happens that you have to invent new terms for the discussion of abstruse topics, you will have a chance to coin words that were unknown [50] to the Cethegi in their loin-cloths,[2] and no one will object to your doing this, as long as you do it with discretion. New and recently coined words will win acceptance if they are borrowed from Greek sources and drawn upon sparingly. And, indeed, why should we Romans allow this privilege to Caecilius and Plautus, and refuse it to Virgil and Varius?[3] Why should I be grudged the right to add a few words to the stock if I can, when the language of Cato and Ennius[4] has enriched our native speech by the introduction of new terms? It has always been accepted, and always will be, that words stamped with the mint-mark of the day should be brought into currency. [60] As the woods change their foliage with the passing seasons, and the first leaves fall, so words die out with old age; and the newly born ones thrive and prosper just like human beings in the vigour of youth. We are all destined to die, we and all our works. Perhaps the land has been dug out and an arm of the sea let in, to give protection to our fleets from the northern gales (royal work!); or a marsh, long a barren waste on which oars were plied, has been put under the plough and produces food for the neighbouring towns; or a river has been made to change a course ruinous to the cornfields and turned into a straighter channel: whatever they are, the works of men will pass away. How much less likely are the glory and grace of language to have an enduring life! [70] Many terms that have now dropped out of use will be revived, if usage so requires, and others which are now in repute will die out; for it is usage which regulates the laws and conventions of speech.

Homer showed us in what metre the exploits of kings and commanders and the miseries of war were to be recorded. The elegiac couplet was first used as the vehicle for lament, but was later adopted for verses of thanksgiving; however, scholars argue about who devised this slighter elegiac form, and the case so far rests undecided. Rage armed Archilochus[5] with its own measure, the iambus; [80] the comic sock and the stately tragic buskin adopted this foot too, since it is appropriate for dialogue, is capable of drowning the noises of the audience, and is by its nature well suited to accompany action. To lyric poetry the Muse assigned the task of celebrating the gods and their offspring, the winner in a boxing match, and the horse that led the field; the task, too, of singing the woes of young lovers and the pleasures of wine.[6] If I have not the ability and skill to adhere to these well-defined functions and styles of poetic forms, why should I be hailed as a poet? Why out of false shame should I prefer to remain ignorant rather than to learn my craft? A comic subject is not susceptible of treatment in a tragic style, [90] and similarly the banquet of Thyestes[7] cannot be fitly described in the strains of everyday life or in those that approach the tone of comedy. Let each of these styles keep the appropriate place allotted to it. Yet even comedy at times uses elevated language, and an angry Chremes[8] rails in bombastic terms; while in tragedy Telephus and Peleus[9] often express their grief in prosaic language, and each of them in his poverty-stricken exile abandons his usual rant and his words a foot and a half long when he wants to move the spectator's pity with his lamentation.

It is not enough that poems should have beauty; if they are to carry the audience with them [100], they should have charm as well. Just as smiling faces are turned on those who smile, so is sympathy shown with those who weep. If you want to move me to tears, you must first feel grief yourself; then, Telephus and Peleus, your misfortunes will grieve me too, whereas, if your speeches are out of harmony with your feelings, I shall either fall asleep or burst out laughing. Sad words suit a mournful face, violent words the face of anger; sportive words become the playful face, and serious words the grave. For nature has so formed us that we first feel inwardly any change in our fortunes; it is she that cheers us or rouses us to anger, [110] she that torments us and bows us to the ground with a heavy burden of sorrow, and it is only afterwards that she expresses these feelings in us by means of the tongue. If the speaker's words are out of key with his fortunes, a Roman audience will cackle and jeer to a man. It will make a great difference whether a god or a hero is speaking, a man of ripe years or a hot-headed youngster in the pride of youth, a woman of standing or an officious nurse, a roving merchant or a prosperous farmer, a Colchian or an Assyrian, a man from Thebes or one from Argos.

Either follow tradition, or invent something that is consistent within itself, writer. [120] If you happen to be representing the illustrious Achilles, let him be energetic, passionate, ruthless, and implacable; let him say that laws are not meant for him, and think that everything must yield to the force of arms. Let Medea be fierce and indomitable, Ino tearful, Ixion faithless, Io a wanderer, and Orestes sorrowful. If you introduce an untried subject to the stage, or are so bold as to invent a new character, be sure that it remains the same all the way through as it was at the beginning, and is entirely consistent.

It is hard to express generalities in a particular way,[10] and it is better for you to be putting a Trojan poem into dramatic form [130] than that you should be first in the field with a theme hitherto unknown and unsung. A theme that is familiar can be made your own property as long as you do not waste your time on a hackneyed treatment; nor should you try to render your original word for word like a slavish translator, or in imitating another writer plunge yourself into difficulties from which shame, or the rules of the genre, prevent you from extricating yourself. And you must not, like the cyclic poet of old, begin: 'Of Priam's fate I'll sing and war's renown.'[11] What will emerge that can live up to such extravagant promises? The mountains will fall into labour, and there will be born – an absurd little mouse. [140] How much more to the purpose are the words of the man who makes no foolish undertakings: 'Tell me, Muse, of the man, who, after the fall of Troy, made himself acquainted with the ways of many men and their cities.'[12] This poet does not mean to let his flash of fire die away in smoke, but to make the smoke give way to light, so that he may then relate his tales of spectacular wonders, tales of Antiphates and Scylla and Charybdis and the Cyclops.[13] He does not trace Diomedes' return right back to the death of Meleager, or the Trojan War to the twin eggs of Leda.[14] All the time he is hurrying on to the crisis, and he plunges his hearer into the middle of the story as if it were already familiar to him; and [150] what he cannot hope to embellish by his treatment he leaves out. Moreover, so inventive is he, and so skilfully does he blend truth and falsehood, that the middle is not inconsistent with the beginning, nor the end with the middle.

I will tell you what I, and with me the public as a whole, look for in a play. If you want an appreciative hearer who will wait for the curtain and remain in his seat until the player calls out, 'Give us your applause', you must note the behaviour of people of different ages, and give the appropriate manners to characters of varying dispositions and years. The child who has just learnt to speak and to plant his feet firmly on the ground loves playing with his friends, [160] will fly into a temper and with as little reason recover from it, and will change every hour. The beardless youth who has at last got rid of his tutor finds his pleasures in horses and dogs and the grassy sports fields of the Campus Martius; pliant as wax, he is easily persuaded to vice, is stubborn with those who advise him, slow to provide for his needs, lavish with money, of high aspirations and passionate desires, and quick to abandon the objects of his fancy. When he is become a man in years and spirit, his inclinations change; he sets out to acquire wealth and influential connections, aims at securing public offices, and is careful to avoid doing anything which he would later find difficult to change. The old man is beset by many troubles; [170] he is acquisitive, and yet miserably holds back from what he has acquired and is afraid to use it; he is cautious and faint-hearted in all his dealings; he puts things off; clings to his hopes, is lazy, and fearful of the future; he is cantankerous, too, and querulous, and given to praising the days when he was a boy and criticizing and rebuking his juniors. The years as they approach bring with them many blessings, but many of these they take away as they recede. Thus, in order not to give a young man the characteristics of old age, or the child those of a grown man, you should always dwell upon the qualities that are appropriate to a particular time of life.

Actions are either performed on the stage, or reported as having taken place. [180] However, the mind is less actively stimulated by what it takes in through the ear than by what is presented to it through the trustworthy agency of the eyes – something that the spectator can see for himself. But you will not bring on to the stage anything that ought properly to be taking place inside, and you will keep out of sight many episodes that are to be described later by the eloquent tongue of a narrator. Medea must not butcher her children in the presence of the audience, nor the monstrous Atreus cook his dish of human flesh within public view, nor Procne be metamorphosed into a bird, nor Cadmus into a snake.[15] In disbelief and disgust I shall turn from anything of this kind that you show me. [190] If you want your play to be called for and given a second performance, it should not be either shorter or longer than five acts.[16] No god should intervene unless some entanglement develops which requires a deliverer to unravel it. And there should not be more than three speaking characters on the stage at the same time.

The Chorus should perform the role of an actor and the duty of a man, and should not sing anything between the acts that does not contribute to the plot and fit appropriately into it. It should side with the good characters and give them friendly advice, and should control those who are out of temper and show approval to those who are anxious not to transgress. It should commend moderation in the pleasures of the table, the blessings of law and justice, and times of peace when the gates lie open; [200] it should respect confidences, and should pray and beseech the gods to let prosperity return to the wretched and desert the proud.

At one time the pipe – not as now bound with brass and a rival to the trumpet, but simple and delicate in tone and with only a few stops – was sufficient to accompany and assist the Chorus; and its soft music filled rows of seats that were not yet overcrowded, where an audience small enough to be counted came together – simple, thrifty folk, modest and virtuous in their ways. But when a conquering race began to extend its territories, and cities grew in size, [210] and people could indulge themselves by drinking in the daytime on festal occasions without fear of censure, a greater freedom was allowed in the choice both of rhythms and melodies. For what taste could be expected in a crowd of uneducated men enjoying a holiday from work, when country bumpkins rubbed shoulders with townsfolk, and slum-dwellers with men of rank? Thus the pipe-player introduced wanton movements that were unknown in the style of earlier days, and trailed his robe as he made his way over the stage. The grave lyre, too, acquired new notes, and a headlong fluency brought with it a strange style of speech, in which wise thoughts and prophecies of the future became indistinguishable from the Delphic oracle.

[220] The poet originally competed in tragic verse for the paltry prize of a goat;[17] soon he introduced wild and naked satyrs on to the stage, and without loss of dignity tried his hand at a form of crude jesting; for an audience that was tipsy after observing the Bacchic rites and in a lawless mood could only be held by the attraction of some enticing novelty. But if jesting and mocking satyrs are to win approval, and a transition be made from the serious to the light-hearted, it must be done in such a way that no one who has been presented as a god or hero, and who a moment ago was resplendent in purple and gold, is transported into a dingy hovel and allowed to drop into the speech of the back streets, [230] or alternatively to spout cloudy inanities in an attempt to rise above vulgarity. Tragedy scorns to babble trivialities, and, like a married woman obliged to dance at a festival, will look rather shamefaced among the wanton satyrs. If ever I write satyric

dramas, my dear Pisos, I shall not be content to use merely the plain, unadorned language of everyday speech; I shall try not to depart so far from the tone of tragedy as to make no distinction between the speech of a Davus, or of a bold-faced Pythias who has managed to trick Simo out of a talent, and that of Silenus, who after all was the guardian and attendant of the young god Bacchus.[18] [240] I shall aim at a style that is newly fashioned from familiar elements, one that any writer might hope to achieve, yet would sweat and toil in vain when he attempted to do the same – such is the power of words that are used in the right places and in the right relationships, and such the grace that they can add to the commonplace when so used. If you are going to bring woodland Fauns[19] on to the stage, I do not think you should ever allow them to speak as though they had been brought up in the heart of the city; do not let them be too youthfully indiscreet in the lines you give them, or crack any filthy or obscene jokes. For such things give offence to those of knightly or freeborn rank and the more substantial citizens; these men do not take kindly to what meets with the approval of the masses, the buyers of roast beans and chestnuts, [250] nor do they give it a prize.

A long syllable following a short one is called an iambus, which is a fast-moving foot. Hence the name 'trimeters' became attached to the iambic line, although it produced six beats, and the metre was the same throughout the line. But not so very long ago, so that it might fall upon the ear with rather more weight and deliberation, the iambic line obligingly opened its ranks to the steady spondee, but did not extend its welcome to the point of giving way to it in the second or fourth foot. The true iambic measure is rarely found in the 'noble' trimeters of Accius;[20] and on the verse, too, [260] with which Ennius so ponderously burdened the stage lies the reproach of over-hasty and careless composition, or of ignorance of his art. Not everyone is critical enough to be aware of rhythmical faults in verse, and an indulgence has been shown to our Roman poets that true poets should not need. Is that a reason for loose and lawless writing on my part? Or should I assume that everyone will notice my transgressions, and therefore proceed cautiously, keeping within the bounds in which I may safely hope for indulgence? If I do so, I shall have escaped censure, indeed, but shall not have deserved any praise. For yourselves, my friends, you must give your days and nights to the study of Greek models. [270] But, you will say, your grandfathers were enthusiastic about the versification and wit of Plautus.[21] They were altogether too tolerant, not to say foolish, in their admiration of both these things in him, if you and I have any idea of how to discriminate between coarseness and graceful wit, and have the skill to recognize the right rhythm both by counting and by ear.

Thespis[22] is given the credit for having invented tragedy as a new genre; he is said to have taken his plays about to be sung and acted on wagons by players whose faces were smeared with the lees of wine. After him came Aeschylus, who devised the mask and the dignified robe of tragedy; it was he who laid down a stage with modest planks, [280] and who introduced the grand style into tragedy and increased the actor's height with buskins. These playwrights were succeeded by those of the Old Comedy, which enjoyed considerable favour; but its freedom degenerated into vice and violence which had to be curbed by law. This law was observed, and the Chorus, deprived of its right to be abusive, fell into a shamed silence.

Our own poets have tried their hand in every style; and they have enjoyed some of their greatest successes when they have had the courage to turn aside from the paths laid down by the Greeks and sing of deeds at home, and this in both tragedies and comedies with Roman themes. Indeed Latium would be no less renowned in literature than she is in valour and the arts of war, [290] were it not that her poets, one and all, shrink from the tedious task of polishing their work. But you, descend-ants of Numa Pompilius,[23] you must have nothing to do with any poem that has not been trimmed into shape by many a day's toil and much rubbing out, and corrected down to the smallest detail.

Because Democritus[24] believes that native genius is a happier thing than wretched art, and will not allow sane poets a place on Mount Helicon, a good many will not take the trouble to trim their nails and their beards; they haunt solitary places, and keep away from the public baths. For a man will gain the repute and title of poet, they think, [300] if he never submits to the ministrations of the barber Licinus a head that all the hellebore[25] of all the Anticyras in the world could never reduce to sanity. What an ass I am to purge the bile out of my system as the season of spring comes along! Otherwise no man would write better poetry. But the game's not worth the candle. So I will play the part of a whetstone, which can put an edge on a blade, though it is not itself capable of cutting. Even if I write nothing myself, I will teach the poet his duties and obligations; I will tell him where to find his resources, what will nourish and mould him as a poet, what he may, and may not, do with propriety, where the right course will take him, and where the wrong.

The foundation and fountain-head of good composition is wisdom. [310] The Socratic writings will provide you with material, and if you look after the subject matter the words will come readily enough. The man who has learnt his duty towards his country and his friends, the kind of love he should feel for a parent, a brother, and a guest, the obligations of a senator and of a judge, and the qualities required in a general sent out to lead his armies in the field – such a man will certainly know the qualities that are appropriate to any of his characters. I would lay down that the skilled imitator should look to human life and character for his models, and from there derive a language that is true to life. Sometimes a play that has attractive maxims and well-drawn characters, [320] even if it lacks grace and has little depth or artistry, will catch the fancy of an audience, and keep its attention more firmly than verse which lacks substance but is filled with well-sounding trifles.

To the Greeks the Muses gave native wit and the ability to turn phrases, and there was nothing they craved more than renown. We Romans in our schooldays learn long calculations for dividing the *as* into a hundred parts. 'Here, young Albinus, you tell me: if you take an *uncia* from a *quincunx*, what's left? Come on now, you could have answered by now.' 'A *triens*.' 'Good! You'll be able to look after yourself all right. If you add an *uncia*, what does that come to?' [330] 'A *semis*.' When once this corroding lust for profit has infected our minds, can we hope for poems to be written that are worth rubbing over with cedar oil and storing away in cases of polished cypress?

Poets aim either to benefit or to please, or to combine the giving of pleasure with some useful precepts for life. When you are giving precepts of any kind, be succinct, so that receptive minds may easily grasp what you are saying and retain it firmly; when the mind has plenty to cope with, anything superfluous merely goes in one ear and out of the other. Works invented to give pleasure should be as true to life as possible, and your play should not demand belief for just anything that catches your fancy; you should not let the ogress Lamia gobble up a child, and later bring it out of her belly alive. [340] The ranks of elder citizens will disapprove of works lacking in edification, while the haughty Ramnes[26] will have nothing to do with plays that are too serious. The man who has managed to blend usefulness with pleasure wins everyone's approbation, for he delights his reader at the same time as he instructs him. This is the book that not only makes money for the booksellers, but is carried to distant lands and ensures a lasting fame for its author.

However, there are faults that we should be ready to forgive; for the lyre string does not always give the note intended by the mind and hand, [350] and the bow will not always hit the mark at which it aims. When there are plenty of fine passages in a poem, I shall not take exception to occasional blemishes which the poet has carelessly let slip, or which his fallible human nature has not guarded against. What, then, is our conclusion about this? Just as the literary scribe gets no indulgence if he keeps on making the same mistake however often he is warned, and the lyre player is laughed at if he always goes wrong on the same string, so the poet who is often remiss seems to me another Choerilus,[27] whose two or three good lines I greet with an amused surprise; at the same time I am put out when the good Homer nods, [360] although it is natural that slumber should occasionally creep over a long poem.

A poem is like a painting:[28] the closer you stand to this one the more it will impress you, whereas you have to stand a good distance from that one; this one demands a rather dark corner, but that one needs to be seen in full light, and will stand up to the keen-eyed scrutiny of the critic; this one only pleased you the first time you saw it, but that one will go on giving pleasure however often it is looked at.

A word to you, the elder of the Piso boys. Though you have been trained by your father to form sound judgements and have natural good sense, take this truth to heart and do not forget it: that only in certain walks of life does the second-rate pass muster. An advocate or barrister [370] of mediocre capacity falls short of the eloquent Messala in ability, and knows less than Aulus Cascellius,[29] yet he is not without his value;

on the other hand, neither gods nor men – nor, for that matter, booksellers – can put up with mediocrity in poets. Just as music that is out of tune, a coarse perfume, or poppy-seeds served with bitter Sardinian honey give offence at a pleasant dinner party, for the meal could just as well have been given without them, so is it with a poem, which is begotten and created for the soul's delight; if it falls short of the top by ever so little, it sinks right down to the bottom. A man who does not understand the game keeps away from the equipment of the field, [380] and if he has no skill with the ball or discus or hoop, he stands quietly aside so that the crowds round the side-lines will not roar with laughter at his expense; yet the man who knows nothing about poetry has the audacity to write it. And why not? he says. He's free, and a free man by birth, and above all he is rated as a knight in wealth and has an excellent record.

You, I am sure, will not say or do anything counter to the will of Minerva;[30] you have judgement and sense enough for that. But if at any time you do write anything, submit it to the hearing of the critic Maecius, and your father's and mine as well; then put your parchment away and keep it for nine years. You can always destroy [390] what you have not published, but once you have let your words go, they cannot be taken back.

While men still roamed the forests, they were restrained from bloodshed and a bestial way of life by Orpheus, the sacred prophet and interpreter of the gods – that is why he is said to have tamed tigers and savage lions. Amphion, too, the founder of Thebes, is credited with having moved stones by the strains of his lyre, and led them where he would with this sweet blandishment. This, once, was wisdom: to distinguish between public and private things, between sacred and profane, to discourage indiscriminate sexual union and make rules for married life, to build towns, and to inscribe laws on tablets of wood. [400] For this reason honour and fame were heaped upon the bards, as divinely inspired beings, and upon their songs. After them the illustrious Homer and Tyrtaeus[31] fired the hearts of men to martial deeds with their verses. In song, too, oracles were delivered, and the way to right living taught; the favour of kings was sought in Pierian strains; and festivals were devised as a close to the long toils over the year. So there is no need for you to blush for the Muse, with her skill in song, and for Apollo the god of singers.

The question has been asked whether a fine poem is the product of nature or of art. I myself cannot see what study can do without a rich vein of natural talent, or, [410] on the other hand, what can be achieved by native genius unless it is cultivated – so true is it that each requires the help of the other, and that they enter into a friendly compact with each other. The athlete who strains to reach the winning-post has trained hard as a boy and put up with a great deal, sweating, shivering in the cold, and keeping away from women and wine; the piper who plays at the Pythian games has first had to learn his art under a stern master. Yet nowadays it is enough for a man to say: 'I write marvellous poems – the devil take the hindmost! It would be dreadful if I fell behind and had to admit that I know absolutely nothing about what, after all, I've never learnt.'

Like the auctioneer who gathers a crowd round him anxious to buy his wares, [420] the poet who has plenty of property and plenty of money accumulating interest is a standing invitation to flatterers to swarm round for what they can make out of him. But if he is a man who can put on a first-class dinner in proper style, or stand security for a poor man of little credit, or rescue him when he is tied up in a dismal lawsuit, I shall be surprised if the lucky fellow can tell a true friend from a false. And you, if you have given or intend to give anyone a present, do not ask him in the first flush of his delight to listen to your own poems. 'Lovely!' he will exclaim. 'That's excellent – it's absolutely first rate!' He will turn quite pale with emotion, and will even be so amiable as to [430] squeeze out a tear or two; he will dance with excitement, or beat the ground with his foot. Just as at a funeral the paid mourners are almost more active and vocal than those who are really suffering deeply, so the mock admirer shows more appreciation than the man who is sincere in his praise. It is said that when kings are anxious to test thoroughly whether a man is worthy of their friendship, they put him to the trial with wine, and ply him with many cups. If you are going to write poetry, see to it that you are never put upon by people with the hidden cunning of the fox.

When anything was read to Quintilius Varus,[32] he would say: 'You must put this right – and this too, please.' If after two or three ineffectual attempts you said you could not do any better, [440] he would tell you to get rid of the passage; the lines were badly turned and would have to be hammered out again. If you chose to defend a weakness rather than correct it, he would not say another word, nor waste any effort in trying to prevent you from regarding yourself and your work as unique and unrivalled. An honest, sensible man will condemn any lines that are lifeless, will find fault with them if they are rough, and will run his pen through any that are inelegant; he will cut out any superfluous adornment, will force you to clarify anything that is obscure, will draw attention to ambiguities, and point out everything that needs changing; [450] in fact, he will prove another Aristarchus.[33] He will not say, 'Why should I quarrel with a friend over trifles?' Those trifles will bring his friend into serious trouble once he has been mocked and become an object of ridicule.

Just as happens when a man is plagued by a nasty rash, or by jaundice, or a fit of lunacy, so men of sense are afraid to have any dealings with a mad poet, and keep clear of him; but children boldly follow him about and tease him. While he is wandering about, spouting his lines with his head in the air like a fowler intent on his game, he can fall into a well or pit, [460] and no one will bother to pull him out however long he goes on shouting to the passers-by for help. And if anyone should take the trouble to lend a hand and let down a rope, 'How do you know he didn't jump down there on purpose,' I shall say, 'and doesn't want to be rescued?' and I shall tell the story of the Sicilian poet Empedocles' death. Eager to be regarded as one of the immortal gods, Empedocles[34] in cold blood leapt into the flames of Etna. And poets should have the right to take their own lives. To save a man who does not want to be saved is as good as murdering him. This is not the first time he has tried, and if he is pulled out he will not immediately become a normal human being and abandon his desire to win notoriety by his death. [470] Nor is it very clear why he goes on trying to write poetry – whether because he has defiled his father's ashes, or sacrilegiously violated a place struck by lightning. It is certain, at any rate, that he is raving mad, and like a bear that has been strong enough to burst the bars of its cage, he makes everyone, learned and ignorant alike, take to their heels when he embarks on his pitiless recitations. He will fasten on to anyone he manages to catch, and read him to death – just like a leech that will not drop off your skin until it is gorged with blood.

LONGINUS

On the Sublime

INTRODUCTION

Caecilius' Treatise and Its Shortcomings

As you will remember, my dear Postumius Terentianus,[1] when we were working together on Caecilius'[2] little treatise on the sublime, it seemed to us too trivial a handling of the subject as a whole; it showed no grasp of the main points, and offered its readers little of the practical help that it should be the writer's main object to supply. In any systematic treatise two things are essential: first, there must be some definition of the subject; second, in order of treatment but of greater importance, there must be some indication of the methods by which we may ourselves reach the desired goal. Now Caecilius, assuming us to be ignorant, sets out to establish the nature of the sublime by means of innumerable examples; but he leaves out of account, apparently considering it unnecessary, the means by which we may be enabled to raise our faculties to the proper pitch of grandeur. However, we ought perhaps rather to praise him for the conception itself and the industry he has shown in carrying it out than to find fault with him for his deficiencies.

CHAPTER I

First Thoughts on Sublimity

Since you have urged me in my turn to write down my thoughts on the sublime for your gratification, we should consider whether my views contain anything of value to men in public life. And as your nature and your sense of fitness prompt you, my dear friend, you will help me to form the truest possible judgements on the various details; for it was a sound answer that was given by the man who, when asked what we have in common with the gods, replied, 'Benevolence and truth.'

As I am writing for a man of such erudition as yourself, Terentianus, I almost feel that I can dispense with a long preamble showing that sublimity consists in a certain distinction or excellence of discourse, and that it is from this source alone that the greatest poets and prose writers have acquired their pre-eminence and won for themselves an eternity of fame. For the effect of elevated language is not to persuade the hearers, but to amaze them; and at all times, and in every way, what transports us with wonder is more telling than what merely persuades or gratifies us. The extent to which we can be persuaded is usually under our own control, but these sublime passages exert an irresistible force and mastery, and get the upper hand with every hearer. Inventive skill and the proper order and disposition of material are not manifested in a good touch here and there, but reveal themselves by slow degrees as they run through the whole texture of the composition; on the other hand, a well-timed stroke of sublimity scatters everything before it like a thunderbolt, and in a flash reveals the full power of the speaker. But I should think, my dear Terentianus, that you could develop these points and others of the same kind from your own experience.

CHAPTER 2

Is There an Art of the Sublime?

Before going any farther, I must take up the question whether there is such a thing as an art of sublimity or emotion, for some people think that those who relate matters of this kind to a set of artistic precepts are on a completely wrong track. Genius, they say, is innate; it is not something that can be learnt, and nature is the only art that begets it. Works of nature are spoilt, they believe, are indeed utterly debased when they are reduced to the bare bones of rules and systems. However, I suggest that there is a case for the opposite point of view when it is considered that, although nature is for the most part subject only to her own laws where matters of emotion and elevation are concerned, she is not given to acting at random and wholly without system. Nature is the first cause and the fundamental creative principle in all activities, but the function of a system is to prescribe the degree and the right moment for each, and to lay down the clearest rules for use and practice. Furthermore, grandeur is exposed to greater dangers when it is left to itself without the ballast and stability of knowledge; it needs the curb as often as the spur.

Speaking of the life of mankind as a whole, Demosthenes[3] declares that the greatest of all blessings is good fortune, and that next to it comes good counsel, which, however, is no less important, since its absence leads to the complete destruction of what good fortune brings. Applying this to literature, we might say that nature fills the place of good fortune, and art that of good counsel. Most important, we must remember that the very fact that certain effects of literature derive from nature alone cannot be learnt from any other source than art. If then the critic who censures those who want to learn this art would take these points into consideration, he would no longer, I imagine, regard the study of the topic I am treating as superfluous and unprofitable.

(Here two pages of the manuscript are missing)

CHAPTER 3

Defects That Militate Against Sublimity

. . . Quell they the oven's far-flung splendour-glow!
Ha, let me but one hearth-abider mark –
One flame-wreath torrent-like I'll whirl on high;
I'll burn the roof, to cinders shrivel it! –
Nay, now my chant is not of noble strain.[4]

Such things as this are not tragic, but pseudo-tragic – the 'flame-wreaths', the 'vomiting forth to heaven', making Boreas a pipe-player, and all the rest. They are turbid in expression, and the imagery is confused rather than suggestive of terror; each phrase, when examined in the light of day, sinks gradually from the terrifying to the contemptible.

Now even in tragedy, which by its very nature is majestic and admits of some bombast, misplaced tumidity is unpardonable; still less, I think, would it be appropriate to factual discourse. This is why people laugh at Gorgias[5] of Leontini when he writes of 'Xerxes, the Zeus of the Persians', or of 'vultures, animated sepulchres'. Similarly certain expressions of Callisthenes[6] are ridiculed as being high-flown and not sublime; still more are some of Cleitarchus[7] – a frivolous fellow who, in the words of Sophocles, blows 'on tiny little pipes without control of breath'. Such effects will be found also in Amphicrates and Hegesias and Matris,[8] for often when they believe themselves to be inspired they are not really carried away, but are merely being puerile.

Tumidity seems, on the whole, to be one of the most difficult faults to guard against. For somehow or other, all those who aim at grandeur in the hope of escaping the charge of feebleness and aridity fall naturally into this very fault, putting their trust in the maxim that 'to fall short of a great aim is at any rate a noble failure'. As in the human body, so also in discourse swellings are bad things, mere flabby insincerities that will probably produce an effect opposite to that intended; for as they say, there is nothing drier than a man with dropsy.

Tumidity, then, arises from the desire to outdo the sublime. Puerility, on the other hand, is the complete antithesis of grandeur, for it is entirely low and mean-spirited, and is indeed the most ignoble of faults. What then is puerility? Is it not, surely, a thought which is pedantically elaborated until it tails off into frigidity? Writers slip into this kind of fault when they strive for unusual and well-wrought effects, and above all for attractiveness, and instead flounder into tawdriness and affectation.

Related to this there is a third type of fault in impassioned writing which Theodorus[9] called the 'pseudo-bacchanalian'. This is misplaced or hollow emotion where none is called for, or immoderate passion where restraint is what is needed. For writers are often carried away, as though by drunkenness, into outbursts of emotion which are not relevant to the matter in hand, but are wholly personal, and hence tedious. To hearers unaffected by this emotionalism their work therefore seems atrocious, and naturally enough, for while they are themselves in an ecstasy, their hearers are not. However, I am leaving this matter of the emotions for treatment in another place.

CHAPTER 4

Frigidity

Of the second fault I mentioned, that is, frigidity, there are plenty of examples in Timaeus,[10] in other respects a writer of some ability, and not incapable of occasional grandeur – a man, indeed, of much learning and inventiveness. However, while he was very fond of criticizing the failings of others, he remained blind to his own, and his passion for continually embarking upon odd conceits often led him into the most trifling puerilities. I shall give you only one or two examples from this author, since Caecilius has anticipated me with most of them. In his eulogy of Alexander the Great he says of him that 'he gained possession of the whole of Asia in fewer years than Isocrates[11] took to write his *Panegyric* advocating war against the Persians'. How remarkable is this comparison of the great Macedonian with the sophist! For it is obvious, Timaeus, that, seen in this light, the Spartans were far inferior in prowess to Isocrates, since they took thirty years over the conquest of Messene, whereas he took no more than ten over the composition of his *Panegyric*. Then look at the way in which he speaks of the Athenians captured in Sicily:[12] 'They had behaved sacrilegiously towards Hermes and mutilated statues of him, and it was for this reason that they were punished, very largely through the efforts of a single man, Hermocrates the son of Hermon, who on his father's side was descended from the outraged god.' I am surprised, my dear Terentianus, that he does not write of the tyrant Dionysius that, 'having been guilty of impious conduct towards Zeus and Heracles, he was therefore deprived of his sovereignty by Dion and Heracleides'.[13] But why speak of Timaeus when even such demigods as Xenophon and Plato, though they were trained in the school of Socrates, forget themselves at times for the sake of such trivial effects? In his *Constitution of Sparta* Xenophon writes: 'In fact you would hear their voices less than those of marble statues, and would turn aside their gaze less easily than those of bronze figures; and you would think them more modest even than the maidens in their eyes.'[14] It would have been more characteristic of Amphicrates than Xenophon to speak of the pupils of our eyes as modest maidens. And how absurd to ask us to believe that every single one of them had modest eyes, when it is said that the shamelessness of people is revealed in nothing so much as in their eyes! 'You drunken sot with the eyes of a dog,'[15] as the saying goes. However, Timaeus could not let Xenophon keep even this frigid conceit to himself, but laid his thieving hands on it. At all events, speaking of Agathocles, and how he abducted his cousin from the unveiling ceremony when she had been given in marriage to another man, he asks, 'Who would have done this if he had not had harlots in his eyes instead of maidens?'

As for the otherwise divine Plato, he says, when he means merely wooden tablets, 'They will inscribe memorials of cypress-wood and place them in the temples';[16] and again, 'With regard to walls, Megillus, I would agree with Sparta that the walls be allowed to remain lying asleep in the ground, and not rise again.' And Herodotus' phrase for beautiful women, when he calls them 'tortures for the eyes',[17] is not much better. However, Herodotus can in some measure be defended, for it is barbarians who use this phrase in his book, and they are drunk.

All the same, it is not right to display triviality of mind, even through the mouths of people such as these, and thereby lay oneself open to the censure of later ages.

CHAPTER 5

The Origins of Literary Impropriety

All these ignoble qualities in literature arise from one cause – from that passion for novel ideas which is the dominant craze among the writers of today; for our faults spring, for the most part, from very much the same sources as our virtues. Thus while a fine style, sublime conceptions, yes, and happy turns of phrase, too, all contribute towards effective composition, yet these very factors are the foundation and origin, not only of success, but also of its opposite. Something of the kind applies also to variations in manner, to hyperbole, and to the use of the plural for the singular, and I shall show later the dangers which these devices seem to involve. At the moment I must cast about and make some suggestions as to how we may avoid the defects that are so closely bound up with sublimity.

CHAPTER 6

Criticism and the Sublime

The way to do this, my friend, is first of all to get a clear understanding and appreciation of what constitutes the true sublime. This, however, is no easy undertaking, for the ability to judge literature is the crowning achievement of long experience. Nevertheless, if I am to speak by way of precept, we can perhaps learn discrimination in these matters from some such considerations as those which follow.

CHAPTER 7

The True Sublime

It must be understood, my dear friend, that, as in everyday life nothing is great which it is a mark of greatness to despise, so is it with the sublime. Thus riches, honours, reputation, sovereignty, and all the other things which possess in marked degree the external trappings of a showy splendour, would not seem to a sensible man to be great blessings, since contempt for them is itself regarded as a considerable virtue; and indeed people admire those who possess them less than those who could have them but are high-minded enough to despise them. In the same way we must consider, with regard to the grand style in poetry and literature generally, whether certain passages do not simply give an impression of grandeur by means of much adornment indiscriminately applied, being shown up as mere bombast when these are stripped away – passages which it would be more noble to despise than to admire. For by some innate power the true sublime uplifts our souls; we are filled with a proud exaltation and a sense of vaunting joy, just as though we had ourselves produced what we had heard.

If an intelligent and well-read man can hear a passage several times, and it does not either touch his spirit with a sense of grandeur or leave more food for reflection in his mind than the mere words convey, but with long and careful examination loses more and more of its effectiveness, then it cannot be an example of true sublimity – certainly not unless it can outlive a single hearing. For a piece is truly great only if it can stand up to repeated examination, and if it is difficult, or, rather, impossible to resist its appeal, and it remains firmly and ineffaceably in the memory. As a generalization, you may take it that sublimity in all its truth and beauty exists in such works as please all men at all times. For when men who differ in their pursuits, their ways of life, their ambitions, their ages, and their manners all think in one and the same way about the same works, then the unanimous judgement, as it were, of discordant voices induces a strong and unshakeable faith in the object of admiration.

CHAPTER 8

Five Sources of Sublimity

It may be said that there are five particularly fruitful sources of the grand style, and beneath these five there lies as a common foundation the command of language, without which nothing worth while can be done. The first and most important is the ability to form grand conceptions, as I have explained in my work on Xenophon. Second comes the stimulus of powerful and inspired emotion. These two elements of the sublime are very largely innate, while the remainder are the product of art – that is, the proper formation of the two types of figure, figures of thought and figures of speech, together with noble diction, which in its turn may be resolved into the choice of words and the use of imagery and elaborated language. The fifth source of grandeur, which embraces all those I have already mentioned, is dignified and elevated word-arrangement.

We must consider, then, what is involved under each of these heads, with a preliminary reminder that Caecilius has left out of account some of the five divisions, one of them obviously being that which relates to emotion. Now if he thought that these two things, sublimity and emotion, were the same thing, and that they were essentially bound up with each other, he is mistaken. For some emotions can be found that are mean and not in the least sublime, such as pity, grief, and fear; and on the other hand many sublime passages convey no emotion, such as, among countless examples, Homer's daring lines about the Aloadae:

Keenly they strove to set Ossa upon Olympus, and upon Ossa the forest-clad Pelion, that they might mount up to heaven;

and the still greater conception that follows:

And this would they have accomplished . . .[18]

With the orators, again, their eulogies, ceremonial addresses, and display speeches contain touches of majesty and grandeur at every point, but as a rule lack emotion; thus emotional speakers are the least effective eulogists, while, on the other hand, those who excel as panegyrists avoid emotionalism. But if Caecilius believed that emotion contributes nothing at all to the sublime, and for this reason considered it not worth mentioning, once again he was making a very serious mistake; for I would confidently maintain that nothing contributes so decisively to grandeur as noble emotion in the right setting, when, filled as it were with frenzy and enthusiasm, it breathes a kind of divine inspiration into the speaker's words.

CHAPTER 9

Natural Greatness

Now since the first of these factors, that is to say, natural greatness, plays the most important part of them all, here too, even though it is a gift rather than an acquired characteristic, we should do all we can to train our minds towards greatness, perpetually impregnating them, so to speak, with noble thoughts. By what means, you will ask, is this to be done? Well, I have written elsewhere to this effect: 'Sublimity is the echo of a noble mind.' Thus, even without being spoken, a simple idea will sometimes of its own accord excite admiration by reason of its nobility; for example, the silence of Ajax in 'The Calling Up of the Dead'[19] is grand, more sublime than any words.

First, then, it is absolutely necessary to indicate the source of this power, and to show that the truly eloquent man must have a mind that is not mean or ignoble. For it is not possible for those whose thoughts and habits are mean and servile throughout their lives to produce anything that is remarkable or worthy of immortal fame; no, greatness of speech is the province of those whose thoughts are deep, and this is why lofty expressions come naturally to the most high-minded men. Alexander's reply[20] to Parmenio when he said, 'I would have been content . . .'

(Here six pages of the manuscript are missing)

. . . the distance from earth to heaven; and it might be said that this is the stature of Homer as much as of Strife.[21]

Quite different from this is Hesiod's description of Trouble – if indeed *The Shield* is to be ascribed to Hesiod: 'Rheum was running from her nostrils.'[22] The image he has presented is not powerful, but offensive. But see how Homer exalts the heavenly powers:

And as far as a man can see with his eyes into the hazy distance as he sits upon a mountain-peak and gazes over the wine-dark sea, even so far is the leap of the loudly neighing steeds of the gods.[23]

He measures their mighty leap in terms of cosmic distances. Might one not exclaim, from the supreme grandeur of this, that if the steeds of the gods make two leaps in succession they will no longer find room on the face of the earth? And magnificent also are the images he conjures up for the Battle of the Gods:

And round them rolled the trumpet-tones of the wide heavens and of Olympus. And down in the underworld Hades, monarch of the realm of the shades, leapt from his throne and cried aloud in dread, lest the earth-shaker Poseidon thereafter should cleave the earth apart, and reveal to the gaze of mortals and immortals alike those grim and festering abodes which the very gods look upon with abhorrence.[24]

You see, my friend, how the earth is split from its foundations upwards, how Tartarus itself is laid bare, how the whole universe is turned upside down and torn apart, and everything alike, heaven and hell, things mortal and immortal, shares in the conflict and peril of the combat.

And yet, awe-inspiring as these things are, if they are not taken as allegory, they are altogether ungodly, and do not preserve the canons of propriety. In his accounts of the wounds suffered by the gods, their quarrels, their vengeful actions, their tears, their imprisonment, and all their manifold passions, Homer seems to me to have done everything in his power to make the men of the Trojan war gods, and the gods men. But while for us mortals, if we are miserable, death is appointed as a refuge from our ills, Homer has given the gods immortality, not only in their nature, but also in their misfortunes.

But far superior to the passages on the Battle of the Gods are those which represent the divine nature as it really is, pure, majestic, and undefiled; for example, the lines on Poseidon, in a passage on which many others before me have commented:

And the far-stretched mountains and woodlands, and the peaks, and the Trojan city and the ships of the Achaeans trembled beneath the immortal feet of Poseidon as he strode forth. And he went on to drive over the swelling waters, and from all round the monsters of the deep came from their hiding-places and gambolled about him, for they knew their lord. And the sea parted her waves in joy, and onwards they flew.[25]

So, too, the lawgiver of the Jews, no ordinary person, having formed a worthy conception of the power of the Divine Being, gave expression to it when at the very beginning of his *Laws* he wrote: 'God said' – what? – 'let there be light, and there was light; let there be land, and there was land.'[26]

I should not, I think, seem a bore, my friend, if I were to put before you still one more passage from Homer – one dealing with human affairs – in order to show how he habitually associates himself with the sublimity of his heroic themes. All of a sudden the battle of the Greeks is plunged into the impenetrable darkness of night, and then Ajax, utterly at a loss what to do, cries out:

Father Zeus, do but rescue the sons of Achaea from out of the gloom, make the sky clear, and grant that we may see with our eyes. So long as it be in the light of day, even destroy us.[27]

These are truly the feelings of an Ajax. He does not beg for life, for this plea would be too base for the hero: but since in the crippling darkness he can turn his courage to no noble purpose, he is angered that this prevents him from getting on with the fight, and prays for the immediate return of daylight, resolved at least to find a death worthy of his valour, even though Zeus should oppose him. Here Homer shares in the inspiration of the fray, and is affected by it just as if he himself

is raging madly, like Ares the spear-hurler, or as when ruinous flames rage among the hills, in the thickets of a deep forest, and foam gathers about his lips.[28]

However, throughout the Odyssey, which for a number of reasons must be taken into consideration, Homer shows that when great genius falls into decline, a love of story-telling characterizes its old age. For it is clear on many grounds that he produced this work as his second composition, particularly from the fact that throughout the Odyssey he introduces remnants of the experiences at Troy as episodes. Indeed, he there pays tribute of mourning and lamentation to his heroes as persons already long known. In fact, the Odyssey is nothing other than an epilogue to the Iliad:

There lies Ajax the great warrior, there Achilles, there too Patroclus, peer of the gods in counsel; and there too my own dear son.[29]

It was, I suppose, for the same reason that, writing the Iliad in the prime of life, he made the whole body of the work dramatic and vivid, whereas the greater part of the Odyssey is narrative, as is characteristic of old age. Thus, in the Odyssey, Homer may be likened to the setting sun: the grandeur remains but without the intensity; for no longer there does he maintain the same pitch as in those lays of Troy. There is not the consistent level of sublimity which nowhere lapses into mediocrity, nor is there the same closely packed profusion of passions, nor the versatility and realism studded with images drawn from real life. As though the ocean were withdrawing into itself and remaining quietly within its own bounds, from now on we see the ebbing of Homer's greatness as he wanders in the realms of the fabulous and the incredible. In saying this I have not forgotten the storms in the Odyssey and the episode of the Cyclops and other things of the kind. I am speaking of old age, but it is, after all, the old age of Homer. Nevertheless, in every one of these passages the fabulous predominates over the real.

As I said, I have digressed in this way in order to show how very easily a great spirit in his decline may at times be misled into writing nonsense; examples are the episodes of the wine-skin,[30] of the men whom Circe turned into swine, and whom Zoilus[31] described as 'wailing piglets', of Zeus nurtured by the doves like a nestling, and of Odysseus remaining without food on the wreck for ten days, and the incredible story of the killing of the suitors. For how else are we to describe these things than as veritable dreams of Zeus?

There is another reason why these comments should be made on the *Odyssey*, and that is that you should understand how the decline of emotional powers in great writers and poets gives way to the portrayal of character. For the realistic depiction of the way of life in Odysseus' household is like this, and constitutes what is in effect a comedy of manners.

CHAPTER 10

The Selection and Organization of Material

Next we must consider whether there is anything else that makes for sublimity of style. Now as we naturally associate with all things certain elements that are inherent in their substance, so it necessarily follows that we shall find one source of the sublime in the unerring choice of the most felicitous of these elements, and in the ability to relate them to one another in such a way as to make of them a single organism, so to speak. For the first procedure attracts the hearer by the choice of matter, the second by the cumulative effect of the ideas chosen. For example, Sappho in her poetry always chooses the emotions attendant on the lover's frenzy from among those which accompany this passion in real life. And wherein does she demonstrate her excellence? In the skill with which she selects and fuses the most extreme and intense manifestations of these emotions:

A peer of the gods he seems to me, the man who sits over against you face to face, listening to the sweet tones of your voice and the loveliness of your laughing; it is this that sets my heart fluttering in my breast. For if I gaze on you but for a little while, I am no longer master of my voice, and my tongue lies useless, and a delicate flame runs over my skin. No more do I see with my eyes, and my ears hum. The sweat pours down me, I am all seized with trembling, and I grow paler than the grass. My strength fails me, and I seem little short of dying.[32]

Are you not astonished at the way in which, as though they were gone from her and belonged to another, she at one and the same time calls up soul and body, ears, tongue, eyes, and skin; how, uniting opposites, she freezes while she burns, is both out of her senses and in her right mind? And all this is done so that not one emotion alone may be seen in her, but a concourse of emotions. All such emotions are experienced by lovers, but it is, as I said, the selection of the most striking of them and their fusion into a single whole that have given the poem its distinction.

In the same way Homer in describing storms singles out their most terrifying properties. The author of the *Arimaspeia*[33] thinks the following passage to be awe-inspiring:

This also to our minds is a great marvel. There are men dwelling in the waters of the ocean, far away from land. Wretched creatures they are, for grievous is the trouble they undergo, fixing their gaze upon the stars and their spirit upon the waters. Often, methinks, they lift up their hands to the gods, and with their hearts raised heavenwards they pray in their misery.

It is obvious to anyone, I imagine, that this passage is more elegant than terrifying. But how does Homer set about it? Let us choose one out of many possible examples:

And he fell upon them like a wave which, swollen by the storm-winds beneath the lowering clouds, burst furiously over a hurrying ship. And the ship is all lost in foam, and the terrifying blast roars in the sail, and the souls of the crew are seized with a fearful shuddering, for barely can they slip out from under the clutch of death.[34]

Aratus made an attempt to adapt this same idea to his own purposes: 'And a slender plank wards off destruction.'[35] However, he has made it trivial and elegant instead of terrifying. Furthermore, by saying that a plank keeps away destruction, he has kept the danger within bounds – after all, the plank does keep it away. On the other hand, Homer does not for a moment limit the terror, but draws a picture of his sailors again and again, all the time, on the brink of destruction with the coming of each wave. Moreover, in 'out from under the clutch of death' he has exerted an abnormal force in thrusting together prepositions not usually compounded, and has thus twisted his language to bring it into conformity with the impending disaster; and by this compressed language he has supremely well pictured the disaster and all but stamped on the diction the very image of the danger – 'slip out from under the clutch of death.' Not dissimilar is the passage of Archilochus,[36] relating to the shipwreck, and that in which Demosthenes, describing the bringing of the news, begins, 'For it was evening . . .' It might be said that these writers have polished up and fitted together the very best points, finding no place among them for anything frivolous, undignified or pedantic. For such faults as these ruin the whole, by introducing gaps and crevices, as it were, into the grand expressions that have been built together into a coherent structure.

CHAPTER II

Amplification

A merit associated with those already presented is that which is called amplification, that is, when the matters under discussion or the points of an argument allow of many pauses and many fresh starts from section to section, and the grand phrases come rolling out one after another with increasing effect.

This may be managed either by the rhetorical development of a commonplace, or by exaggeration, whether facts or arguments are to be stressed, or by the building up of actions or emotions. There are, indeed, countless forms of amplification. Yet the speaker must be aware that, without the help of sublimity, none of these methods can of itself achieve its effect, except no doubt in the expression of pity or disparagement. In other forms of amplification, when you take away the element of the sublime, it will be like taking the soul out of the body; for their vigour will be completely drained away without the sustaining power of the sublime.

However, in the interests of clarity I must briefly indicate how my present precepts differ from those about which I have just spoken, that is, the marking-out of the most striking points and their organization into a single whole, and in what general respects sublimity is to be distinguished from the effects of amplification.

CHAPTER 12

Amplification Defined

Now the definition of the writers on rhetoric is not, in my view, acceptable. Amplification, they say, is language which invests the subject with grandeur. But obviously this definition could apply equally well to sublimity and to the emotional and the figurative styles, since these too invest language with some degree of grandeur. As I see it, they are to be distinguished from one another by the fact that sublimity consists in elevation, amplification in quantity; thus sublimity is often contained in a single idea, whereas amplification is always associated with quantity and a certain amount of redundancy. To sum it up in general terms, amplification is the accumulation of all the small points and topics bearing on the subject-matter; it adds substance and strength to the argument by dwelling on it, differing from proof in that, while the latter demonstrates the point at issue . . .

(*Here two pages of the manuscript are lost*)

. . . extremely rich; like some ocean, he often swells into a mighty expanse of grandeur. From this I should say that, where language is concerned, Demosthenes, being more concerned with the emotions, shows much fire and vehemence of spirit, whilst Plato, standing firmly based upon his supreme dignity and majesty, though indeed he is not cold, has not the same vehemence.

It seems to me that it is on these same grounds, my dear Terentianus – if we Greeks may be allowed an opinion in this matter – that Cicero is to be differentiated from Demosthenes in his use of the grand style. Demosthenes is characterized by a sublimity which is for the most part rugged, Cicero by profusion. Demosthenes, by reason of his force, yes, and his speed and power and intensity, may be likened to a thunderbolt or flash of lightning, as it were burning up or ravaging all that is before him. But Cicero is, in my opinion, like a wide-spreading conflagration that rolls on to consume everything far and wide; he has within him an abundance of steady and enduring flame which can be let loose at whatever point he desires, and which is fed from one source after another.

However, you Romans should be able to form a better judgement in this matter. But the right place for the Demosthenean sublimity and intensity is in passages where vehemence and powerful emotions are involved, and where the audience are to be swept off their feet in amazement. On the other hand, profusion is in order when it is necessary to flood them with words. It is for the most part appropriate to the treatment of rhetorical commonplaces, and of perorations and digressions; well suited, too, to all descriptive and epideictic writings, to works of history and natural philosophy, and to a number of other types of literature.

CHAPTER 13

Plato and the Sublime: Imitation

Now, although Plato – for I must return to him – flows with such a noiseless stream, he none the less achieves grandeur. You are familiar with his *Republic* and know his manner. 'Those, therefore,' he says, 'who have no experience of wisdom and goodness, and are always engaged in feasting and similar pleasures, are brought down, it would seem, to a lower level, and there wander about all their lives. They have never looked up towards the truth, nor risen higher, nor tasted of any pure and lasting pleasure. In the manner of cattle, they bend down with their gaze fixed always on the ground and on their feeding-places, grazing and fattening and copulating, and in their insatiable greed for these pleasures they kick and butt one another with horns and hoofs of iron, and kill one another if their desires are not satisfied.'[37]

Provided that we are ready to give him due attention, this author shows us that, in addition to those already mentioned, there is another way that leads to sublimity. And what kind of a way is this? It is the imitation and emulation of the great writers and poets of the past. Let us steadfastly keep this aim in mind, my dear fellow. For many authors are inspired by the spirit of others – just as we are told that the Pythian priestess, when she approaches the tripod where there is a cleft in the ground which, they say, breathes out a divine vapour, is impregnated thence with the heavenly power, and by virtue of this afflatus is at once inspired to speak oracles. So too, as though also issuing from sacred orifices, certain emanations are conveyed from the genius of the men of old into the souls of those who emulate them, and, breathing in these influences, even those who show very few signs of inspiration derive some degree of divine enthusiasm from the grandeur of their predecessors.

Was Herodotus alone a most Homeric writer? No, for even earlier there was Stesichorus,[38] and Archilochus, and above all others Plato, who for his own use drew upon countless tributary streams from the great Homeric river. I should perhaps have had to prove this had not people like Ammonius[39] selected and recorded detailed examples.

Now this procedure is not plagiarism; rather it is like the reproduction of good character in statues or other works of art. I do not think there would have been so fine a bloom on Plato's philosophical doctrines, or that he would so often have embarked on poetic subject-matter and phraseology, had he not been striving heart and soul with Homer for first place, like a young contestant entering the ring with a long-admired champion, perhaps showing too keen a spirit of emulation in his desire to break a lance with him, so to speak, yet getting some profit from the endeavour. For as Hesiod says, 'This strife is good for mortals.'[40]

And indeed the fight for fame and the crown of victory are noble and very well worth the winning, where even to be worsted by one's predecessors carries no discredit.

CHAPTER 14

Some Practical Advice

It is well, then, that we too, when we are working at something that demands grandeur both of conception and of expression, should carefully consider how perhaps Homer might have said this very thing, or how Plato, or Demosthenes, or (in history) Thucydides, might have given it sublimity. For conjured up before our eyes, as it were, by our spirit of emulation, these great men will raise our minds to the standards of which we have formed a mental image.

Still more will this be so if we put to ourselves the further query, 'How would Homer or Demosthenes, if he had been present, have listened to this passage of mine, and how would it have affected him?' For indeed it would be a great feat to bring our own utterances before such a jury or audience, and to make a pretence of submitting our writings to the scrutiny of such heroic judges and witnesses.

It would be even more stimulating if you added the question, 'What kind of hearing should I get from all future ages if I wrote this?' But if anyone shrinks from saying anything that will outlast his own time and age, the conceptions of his mind are obviously obscure and incomplete, and are bound to miscarry, never to be brought forth whole and perfect for a life of posthumous fame.

CHAPTER 15

Visualization

Furthermore, my dear boy, dignity, grandeur, and urgency are to a very large degree derived from visualization (*phantasia*). That, at any rate, is the term I use for what some people call the production of images. In a general way the term *phantasia* is used of any mental conception, from whatever sources it presents itself, which gives rise to speech; but in current usage the word is applied to passages in which, carried away by enthusiasm and emotion, you imagine you are actually seeing the subject of your description, and bring it before the eyes of your audience. You will have noticed that *phantasia* means one thing with orators and another with poets – that in poetry its aim is to astonish, in oratory to produce vividness of description, though indeed both seek to stir the emotions.

Mother, I beseech you, do not set upon me those blood-reddened and snake-like hags. See there, see there, they approach, they leap upon me![41]

and again, 'Ah! She will slay me! Whither shall I fly?'[42] In these passages the poet himself saw the Furies, and he almost compelled his audience, too, to see what he had visualized.

Now Euripides expends his highest powers in giving tragic expression to these two passions, madness and love, and he is more brilliantly successful with these, I think, than with any others, although he is not afraid to make incursions into other forms of visualization. While he is very far from possessing a natural grandeur, yet on many occasions he forces himself to tragic heights, and where sublimity is concerned, each time, in the words of Homer, 'he lashes his ribs and flanks on both sides with his tail, and goads himself on to the fight.'[43]

For example, when the Sun hands the reins to Phaethon, he says: 'And do not as you drive venture into the Libyan sky, for being tempered with no moisture it will burn up your wheel.'[44] And he goes on, 'But speed your course towards the seven Pleiades.' And hearing this, the boy took hold of the reins, and lashed the flanks of his winged team, and they winged their path up to the cloudy ridges of the sky. And hard behind rode his father, astride the Dog-Star's back, schooling his son: 'Drive that way! Now this way guide the chariot, this way!'

Now, would you not say that the soul of the poet goes into the chariot with the boy, sharing his danger and joining the horses in their flight? For he could never have visualized such things had he not been swept along, keeping pace with those celestial bodies. You will find the same in the words he gives to Cassandra: 'Yet, you Trojans, lovers of horses . . .'[45]

Aeschylus, too, ventures on images of a most heroic cast, as when he says in his *Seven against Thebes*:

Seven resistless warrior-captains have slit a bullock's throat over an iron-rimmed shield, and have brushed their hands over the bullock's blood and sworn an oath by War and Havoc and Terror, the lover of blood . . .[46]

Here they pledge themselves by a joint oath to a pitiless death. Sometimes, however, Aeschylus introduces ideas that are unfinished and crude and harsh; yet Euripides in a desire to emulate him comes dangerously near to committing the same faults. For example, in Aeschylus the palace of Lycurgus at the appearance of Dionysus is described in unusual terms as being divinely possessed: 'Then the house is in an ecstasy, and the roof is inspired with Bacchic frenzy.'[47] Euripides has expressed the same idea differently, softening it down: 'And the whole mountain joined with them in their Bacchic frenzy.'

Sophocles,[48] too, has made excellent use of visualization in describing the death of Oedipus as he entombs himself amid portents from the sky, and in his account of how, at the departure of the Greeks, Achilles shows himself above his tomb to those who are sailing away, a scene which I think no one has depicted more vividly than Simonides. But it would be out of the question to quote all the examples.

However, as I have said, those from the poets display a good deal of exaggeration of a somewhat fabulous kind, and everywhere exceed the bounds of credibility, whereas the finest feature of visualization in oratory is always its adherence to reality and truth. Whenever the texture of the speech becomes poetical and fabulous, and falls into all sorts of impossibilities, such deviations seem strange and unnatural. Our brilliant modern orators, for example, see Furies, heaven help us, just as though they were tragedians, and, noble fellows that they are, they cannot even understand that when Orestes says, 'Be off, for you are one of my avenging Furies clasping my waist to hurl me down to hell,'[49] he is imagining this because he is mad.

What, then, is the effect of visualization in oratory? Among other things, it can infuse much passion and energy into speeches, but when it is combined with factual arguments it not only persuades the hearer, but actually masters him.

'Suppose,' says Demosthenes,[50] to give an example, 'suppose that at this very moment an uproar were to be heard in front of the courts, and someone were to tell us that the prison had been broken open and the prisoners were escaping, there is no one, old or young, so irresponsible that he would not give all the help in his power; moreover, if someone were to come and tell us that so-and-so was the person who let them out, he would at once be put to death without a hearing.' Then of course there is Hyperides,[51] who was put on trial when he had proposed the enfranchisement of the slaves after the great defeat; his answer was that it was not himself, the advocate, who had framed the measure, but the battle of Chaeronea. Here the orator has at one and the same time developed an argument and visualized the event, and his conception has therefore transcended the bounds of mere persuasion. In all such cases our ears always, by some natural law, seize upon the stronger element, so that we are attracted away from the demonstration of fact to the astonishing effect of the visualization, and the argument lies below the surface of the accompanying brilliance. And it is not unreasonable that we should be affected in this way, for when two forces are combined to produce a single effect, the greater always attracts to itself the virtues of the lesser.

I have gone far enough in my discussion of sublimity of thought, as it is produced by greatness of mind, imitation, or visualization.

CHAPTER 16

Rhetorical Figures: Adjuration

We next come to the topic of rhetorical figures, for they too, when properly handled, will contribute in no small measure, as I have said, to the effect of grandeur. However, since it would be a long and indeed endless business to consider them all closely at this stage, I shall now explain a few of those which make for grandeur of utterance, simply in order to confirm my proposition.

In the following passage Demosthenes is putting forward an argument in support of his policy. What was the natural way of doing this?

You were not wrong, you who undertook the struggle for the freedom of the Greeks, and you have a precedent for this here at home. For those who fought at Marathon were not wrong, nor those at Salamis, nor those at Plataea.[52]

But when, as though suddenly carried away by divine inspiration and possession, he uttered his oath by the champions of Greece, 'By those who risked their lives at Marathon, it cannot be that you were wrong', it would seem that, by his use of this single figure of adjuration, which I here give the name of apostrophe, he has deified his ancestors by suggesting that we ought to swear by men who have died such deaths as we swear by gods; he has instilled into his judges the spirit of the men who stood there in the forefront of the danger, and has transformed the natural flow of his argument into a passage of transcending sublimity, endowing it with the passion and the power of conviction that arise from such an unheard of and extraordinary oath. At the same time he has infused into the minds of his audience words which act in some sort as an antidote and a remedy, so that, uplifted by these eulogies, they come to feel just as proud of the war against Philip as of the triumphs at Marathon and Salamis. By all these means he has been able to carry his hearers away with the figure he has employed.

It is said, indeed, that Demosthenes found the germ of this oath in Eupolis:[53] 'For by the fight I fought at Marathon, no one of them shall vex my heart and not pay for it.' But there is nothing grand about the mere swearing of an oath; we must take into account the place, the manner, the circumstances, and the motive. In the Eupolis there is nothing but an oath, and that addressed to the Athenians while they were still enjoying prosperity and in no need of consolation. Moreover, the poet has not in his oath deified the warriors in order to engender in his audience a high opinion of their valour, but has wandered away from those who risked their lives to something inanimate, that is, the fight. In Demosthenes the oath is designed for men who have suffered defeat, so that the Athenians may no longer regard Chaeronea as a disaster; and at the same time it is, as I said, a proof that no wrong has been done, an example, a confirmation, a eulogy, and an exhortation. And since the orator was likely to be faced with an objection, 'You are speaking of a defeat that resulted from your policy, yet your oath relates to victories,' in what follows he keeps on the safe side and measures every word, showing that even when inspired it is necessary to remain sober. 'Those who risked their lives at Marathon,' he says, 'and those who fought aboard ship at Salamis and Artemisium, and those who stood shoulder to shoulder at Plataea.' Nowhere does he speak of the 'victors'; everywhere he cunningly avoids mention of the result, since it was a happy one and the reverse of what happened at Chaeronea. Thus he anticipates objections and carries his audience with him. 'To all of whom, Aeschines,' he adds, 'the state gave a public funeral, not only to those who were successful.'

CHAPTER 17

Rhetorical Figures and Sublimity

While on this topic, my dear friend, I must not omit an observation of my own, which, however, shall be quite concisely stated. This is that rhetorical figures by their nature reinforce the sublime, and in their turn derive a marvellous degree of support from it. I will tell you where and how this happens. The cunning use of figures is peculiarly subject to suspicion, and engenders impressions of hidden traps and plots and fallacies. This is true when the speech is addressed to a judge with absolute authority, and still more to despots, kings, or rulers in high places, for such a one immediately becomes angry if, like a simple child, he is caught on the wrong foot by the rhetorical devices of a highly skilled orator. Accepting the fallacy as a personal insult, he sometimes turns quite savage, and even if he masters his rage, he becomes utterly impervious to the persuasive quality of the speech. Thus a rhetorical figure would appear to be most effective when the fact that it is a figure is concealed.

Sublimity and the expression of strong emotion are, therefore, a wonderfully helpful antidote against the suspicion that attends the use of figures. The cunning artifice remains out of sight, surrounded by the brilliance of beauty and sublimity, and all suspicion is put to flight. Sufficient evidence of this is the passage already mentioned, 'I swear by the men of Marathon!' But by what means has the orator here concealed his figure? Obviously by its very brilliance. For in much the same way as dim lights vanish in the radiance of the sun, so does the all-pervading effluence of grandeur utterly obscure the artifices of rhetoric.

Something of the same kind occurs also in painting. For although light and shade as represented by colours may lie side by side on the same surface, it is the light that first catches the eye and seems not only to stand out, but also to be much nearer. So also is it with literature: by some natural affinity and by their brilliance, expressions of emotion and sublimity lie nearer to our hearts, and always catch our attention before the figures, overshadowing their artistry, and keeping it out of sight, so to speak.

CHAPTER 18

Rhetorical Questions

But what are we to say on the matter of questions and answers? Does not Demosthenes[54] aim at enhancing the vigour and effectiveness of his speeches very considerably by the very way in which he exploits the specific character of these figures?

Now tell me, do you want to go about asking one another, 'Is there any news?' For what stranger news could there be than that of a Macedonian conquering Greece? 'Is Philip dead?' 'No, but he is ill.' What difference does it make to you? For even if anything should happen to him, you will soon invent another Philip. And again, 'Let us sail against Macedonia,' he says. 'But where shall we land?' someone asks. The mere fact of our fighting will find out the weak spots in Philip's strategy.

If this had been given as a bald statement, it would have been completely ineffective; but as it is, the inspired rapidity in the play of question and answer, together with the device of meeting his own objections as though they were someone else's, has not only added to the sublimity of his words, but also given them greater conviction, and all this by the use of this particular figure. For a display of emotion is more effective when it seems not to be premeditated on the part of the speaker, but to have arisen from the occasion; and this method of asking questions and providing your own answers gives the appearance of being a natural outburst of emotion. People who are being questioned by others are stirred into answering the questions spontaneously, and with energy and complete candour; in the same way the rhetorical figure of question and answer beguiles the audience into thinking that each deliberately considered point has been struck out and put into words on the spur of the moment. Furthermore – for the following passage has been accepted as one of the most sublime in Herodotus . . .

(Here two pages of the manuscript are missing)

CHAPTER 19

Asyndeton, or the Omission of Conjunctions

. . . the words come gushing out, as it were, set down without connecting links, and almost outstripping the speaker himself. 'And, locking their shields,' says Xenophon,[55] 'they pressed forward, fought, slew, were slain.'

Then there are the words of Homer's Eurylochus: 'We came through the oak-coppice, as you bade, renowned Odysseus. We saw amid the forest-glens a beautiful palace.'[56] The phrases, disconnected, but none the less rapid, give the impression of an agitation which at the same time checks the utterance and urges it on. And the poet has produced such an effect by his use of asyndeton.

CHAPTER 20

The Accumulation of Figures

A combination of figures in one phrase usually has a very moving effect, when two or three unite in a kind of partnership to add force, persuasiveness, and beauty. Thus, in Demosthenes' speech against Midias you will find examples of asyndeton interwoven with the figures of anaphora and vivid description: 'For the aggressor might do many things, some of which the victim would be unable to describe to anyone else, by his manner, his looks, his voice.'[57] Then, in order that the speech may not, as it proceeds, remain at a standstill as far as these particular effects are concerned (for standing still connotes calm, whereas emotion, being an upheaval or agitation of the soul, connotes disorder), he at once hurries on to fresh examples of asyndeton and anaphora: 'By his manner, his looks, his voice, when he acts with insolence, when he acts with hostility, when he strikes you with his fists, when he strikes you like a slave.' In this way the orator does just the same as the aggressor; he belabours the judges' minds with blow after blow. He goes on from here to make yet another hurricane onslaught: 'When he strikes you with his fists,' he says, 'when he beats you about the face – this rouses you, this drives a man mad when he is not used to being trampled underfoot. No one could bring out the terrible nature of such an occurrence by merely describing it.' Thus all the way through, although with continual variations, he preserves the essential character of the repetitions and the asyndeta, and thus too his order is disordered, and similarly his disorder embraces a certain element of order.

CHAPTER 21

Conjunctions: Some Disadvantages

Now, if you will, try putting in the conjunctions, in the manner of Isocrates[58] and his disciples: 'Furthermore, this too must not be overlooked, that the aggressor might do many things, first by his manner, then by his looks, and then again by his mere voice.' If you amplify it like this, phrase by phrase, you will see that, if the drive and ruggedness of the emotion is toned down into smoothness by the use of the conjunctions, it loses its sting and its fire is immediately quenched. If you bind up the arms of a runner you will deprive him of his speed; in exactly the same way emotion resents being hampered by conjunctions and other appendages of the kind, for it then loses its freedom of motion and the impression it gives of being shot from a catapult.

CHAPTER 22

The Figure of Hyperbaton, or Inversion

Hyperbata, or inversions, must be put into the same class. These consist in the arrangement of words or ideas out of their normal sequence, and they carry, so to speak, the genuine stamp of powerful emotion. People who really are angry or frightened or indignant or carried away by jealousy or any other feeling – for there are innumerable forms of emotion, and indeed no one would be able to say just how many – often, after they have brought forward one point, will rush off on a different tack, dropping in other points without rhyme or reason, and then, under the stress of their agitation, they will come right round to their original position. Dragged rapidly in every direction as if by a veering wind, they will keep altering the arrangement of their words and ideas, losing their natural sequence and introducing all sorts of variations. In the same way the best authors will use hyperbaton in such a way that imitation approaches the effects of nature. For art is perfect only when it looks like nature, and again, nature hits the mark only when she conceals the art that is within her.

This may be exemplified by the words of Dionysius the Phocaean in Herodotus:[59] 'For our affairs stand on a razor's edge, men of Ionia, whether we are to be free men or slaves, and runaway slaves at that. Now, therefore, if you are prepared to accept hardships, straightway there is toil for you, but you will be able to overcome your enemies.' Here the normal order would have been, 'O men of Ionia, now is the time for you to take toil upon you; for our affairs stand on a razor's edge.' However, the speaker has transposed 'men of Ionia', starting at once with the thought of the fear, as though in this pressing danger he would not even address his hearers first. Furthermore, he has inverted the order of his ideas; for instead of saying that they must endure toil, which is the point of his exhortation, he first gives them the reason why they must toil when he says, 'Our affairs stand on a razor's edge.' Thus what he says does not seem premeditated, but forced out of him.

Thucydides is even more skilful in his use of inversions to dissociate things which are by their nature one and indivisible. Demosthenes, though indeed he is not as wilful as Thucydides, is the most extravagant of all in his use of this kind of figure, and through inversions he gives the impression of great vehemence and, what is more, of speaking impromptu; moreover, he carries his audience with him to share in the dangers of his long inversions. For he will often hold up the sense of what he has begun to express, and meanwhile he will in a strange and unlikely order pile one idea on top of another, drawn from any kind of source and just dropped into the middle of what he is saying, inducing in his hearer the fear that the whole structure of the sentence will fall to pieces, and compelling him in his agitation to share in the risk the speaker is taking; and then unexpectedly, after a long interval, he will bring out the long-awaited phrase just where it is most effective, at the very end, and thus, by the very audacity and recklessness of his inversions, he astonishes the listener all the more. I forbear to give examples, since there are so many of them.

CHAPTER 23

Polyptoton: Interchange of Singular and Plural

The figures called polyptota[60] (accumulations, variations, and climaxes) are, as you know, very powerful auxiliaries in the production of elegance and of every kind of sublime and emotional effect. Observe, too, how greatly an exposition is diversified and enlivened by changes in case, tense, person, number, and gender. In the matter of number, I can say that the decorative quality of a passage is not only enhanced by words which are singular in form, but which on close examination are found to have a plural meaning, as in 'Straightway a countless host ranged along the beaches send out a cry, "Tunny!" '[61]

But it is more noteworthy that at times the use of the plural in place of the singular has a more resounding effect, and impresses us by the very idea of multitude implied in the plural number. This is exemplified by Sophocles in some lines spoken by Oedipus:

O marriages, marriages, it is you that begot me and gave me birth, and then brought to light again the same seed, and showed fathers, brothers, and sons as being all kindred blood, and brides, wives, and mothers, too, and all the foulest deeds that are done among men.[62]

All these relate to a single name, that of Oedipus, with that of Jocasta on the other side; however, the expansion of the number serves to pluralize the misfortunes as well.

There is the same kind of multiplication in the line, 'Forth came Hectors, and Sarpedons too';[63] and again in Plato's passage[64] on the Athenians, which I have also quoted in another work: 'For no Pelopes nor Cadmuses nor Aegyptuses and Danauses, nor any other hordes of barbarians by birth share our home with us, but we who are pure Greeks and not semi-barbarians live here', and the rest of it. For naturally the facts sound more impressive from this accumulation of names in groups. However, this should not be done except on occasions when the subject admits of amplification or redundancy or exaggeration or emotionalism – any one or more of these; for to be hung all over with bells is altogether the mark of a sophist.

CHAPTER 24

Polyptoton: Conversion of Plural to Singular

Furthermore, the opposite process, the contraction of plurals to singulars, sometimes achieves an outstanding effect of sublimity. 'Afterwards,' says Demosthenes,[65] 'the whole Peloponnese was at variance.' Again, 'And when Phrynicus produced his play *The Capture of Miletus* the theatre burst into tears.'[66] To compress the number from multiplicity into unity gives a stronger impression of a single entity. In both examples the reason for the striking effect is, I think, the same. Where the words are singular, to turn them into the plural suggests an unexpected burst of emotion; where they are plural, and are fused into a fine-sounding singular, the change in the opposite direction produces an effect of surprise.

CHAPTER 25

Polyptoton: Interchange of Tenses

Again, if you introduce circumstances that are past in time as happening at the present moment, you will turn the passage from mere narrative into vivid actuality. 'Someone,' says Xenophon,[67] 'has fallen under Cyrus' horse and, being trampled on, strikes the horse in the belly with his sword. It rears and throws Cyrus, and he falls to the ground.' Thucydides is particularly fond of this device.

CHAPTER 26

Polyptoton: Variations of Person, or Personal Address

In the same way the change of person is striking, and often makes the hearer feel that he is moving in the thick of the danger: 'You would say that they met in the shock of war, all unwearied and undaunted, so impetuously did they rush into the fray.'[68] Then there is Aratus' 'Do not in that month entrust yourself to the surges of the ocean.'[69]

Herodotus does much the same kind of thing: 'From the city of Elephantine you will sail upwards, until you come to a level plain; and after you have crossed this tract, you will board again another ship and sail for two days, and then you will come to a great city whose name is Meroe.'[70] Do you see, my friend, how he takes your mind through the places in question, and transforms hearing into sight. All such passages, by their direct personal form of address, bring the hearer right into the middle of the action being described. And when you seem to be addressing, not the whole audience, but a single member of it – 'But you would not have known for which of the armies the son of Tydeus fought'[71] – you will affect him more profoundly, and make him more attentive and full of active interest, if you rouse him by these appeals to him personally.

CHAPTER 27

Polyptoton: Conversion to the First Person

Again, there are times when a writer, while speaking of a character, suddenly breaks off and converts himself into that character. A figure of this kind is in a way an outburst of emotion:

And with a far-echoing shout Hector cried out to the Trojans to rush against the ships and leave the blood-spattered spoils. And if I spy anyone who of his own will holds back from the ships, I will surely bring about his death.[72]

Here the poet has taken upon himself the presentation of the narrative, as is appropriate, and then suddenly, without any warning, has attributed the abrupt threat to the angry chieftain. Had he inserted, 'Hector said so and so', it would have given a frigid effect; as it is, the change in form of the passage has anticipated the sudden change of speakers. Accordingly this figure is useful when a sudden crisis will not give the author time to linger, but compels him to change at once from one character to another. There is another example in Hecataeus:[73] 'Ceyx took this badly and at once ordered the descendants to depart. For it is not in my power to help you. Therefore, in order that you may not perish yourselves and injure me, take yourselves off to some other country.'

In his *Aristogeiton*,[74] Demosthenes has by a rather different method used change of person to indicate a rapid play of emotion. 'And will none of you,' he says, 'be found to feel disgust and indignation at the violence of this vile and shameless creature, who – O, you most abominable of men – whose unbridled speech is not shut in by gates and doors which might well be opened . . .' With his sense incomplete, he has made a sudden change, and in his indignation has all but split a single phrase between two persons – 'who – O, you most abominable . . .' Thus, while he has turned his speech round to address Aristogeiton, and seems to have abandoned his argument, yet with this display of emotion he has intensified it all the more. The same thing occurs in Penelope's speech:[75]

Herald, why have those highborn suitors sent you here? Is it to tell the handmaids of the godlike Odysseus to cease from their labours and prepare a banquet for them? Would that they had never wooed me, nor elsewhere gathered together, that this now were the latest and last of their feasting, you that assemble together and waste so much of our substance, the store of the prudent Telemachus. Nor did you ever in the bygone days of your childhood hear from your fathers what manner of man Odysseus was.'

CHAPTER 28

Periphrasis

No one, I think, would dispute that periphrasis contributes to the sublime. For, as in music, the sweetness of the dominant melody is enhanced by what are known as the decorative additions, so periphrasis often harmonizes with the direct expression of a thought and greatly embellishes it, especially if it is not bombastic or inelegant, but pleasantly tempered.

This is pretty well illustrated by Plato at the beginning of his *Funeral Oration*:[76] 'We have given these men the tribute that is their due, and having gained this, they proceed along their appointed path, escorted publicly by their country, and each man privately by his kinsfolk.' Death, you see, he calls 'their appointed path', and their having been granted the accustomed rites he describes as a kind of 'public escort on the part of their native land'. Surely he has considerably increased the dignity of his conception here. Has he not made music of the unadorned diction that was his starting point, surrounding it, as it were, in the melodious harmonies of his periphrasis?

Then there is Xenophon: 'You regard toil as the guide to a life of pleasure; you have garnered in your hearts the best of all possessions and the fittest for warriors. For nothing rejoices you so much as praise.'[77] By rejecting 'you are willing to work hard' in favour of 'you make toil the guide to a life of pleasure', and by expanding the rest of the sentence in the same way, he has added to his eulogy a certain grandeur of thought. And this is true also of that inimitable sentence in Herodotus:[78] 'Upon those Scythians who despoiled her temple the goddess inflicted a female malady.'

CHAPTER 29

The Dangers of Periphrasis

However, periphrasis is a hazardous business, more so than any other figure, unless it is used with a certain sense of proportion. For it quickly falls flat, smacking of empty chatter and dullness of wit. This is why even Plato,[79] who always uses figures with skill, but sometimes with a certain lack of timeliness, is mocked when he says in his *Laws* that 'neither golden nor silvern treasure should be allowed to establish itself and dwell in a city'; so that if he had been forbidding people to possess herds, says the critic, he would obviously have said 'ovine and bovine treasure'.

However, my digression on the use of figures and their bearing on the sublime has gone on long enough, my dear Terentianus. They are all means of increasing the animation and the emotional impact of style, and emotion plays as large a part in the production of the sublime as the study of character does in the production of pleasure.

CHAPTER 30

The Proper Choice of Diction

Since, in discourse, thought and diction are for the most part mutually interdependent, we must further consider whether any other elements that come under the heading of diction remain to be studied. It is probably superfluous to explain to those who already know it how wonderfully the choice of appropriate and high-sounding words moves and enchants an audience, and to remind them that such a choice is the highest aim of all orators and authors; for of itself it imparts to style at once grandeur, beauty, charm, weight, force, power, and a certain lustre such as blooms on beautiful statues; it endows the facts as it were with a living voice. For beautiful words are in truth the very light of thought. Yet it would not do to use such grand diction all the time, for to apply great and stately terms to trifling matters would be like putting a big tragic mask on a tiny child. However, in poetry and . . .

(Here four pages of the manuscript are missing)

CHAPTER 31

Familiar Language

. . . and productive; so too is Anacreon's 'No longer do I care for the Thracian filly'.[80] In this way also that unusual term employed by Theopompus[81] deserves praise, for by reason of the analogy implied it seems to me to be highly expressive, although Caecilius for some reason finds fault with it: 'Philip,' says Theopompus, 'had a genius for stomaching things.' A common phrase is sometimes much more expressive than elegant diction, for, being taken from everyday life, it is at once recognized, and carries the more conviction from its familiarity. Thus, in connection with a man whose greedy nature makes him put up patiently and cheerfully with things that are shameful and sordid, the words 'stomaching things' are extremely vivid. Much the same may be said of Herodotus' expressions:[82] 'Cleomenes in his madness cut his own flesh into strips with a dagger until, having made mincemeat of himself, he perished;' and 'Pythes continued fighting on the ship until he was all cut into shreds.' These phrases are on the very edge of vulgarity, but their expressiveness saves them from actually being vulgar.

CHAPTER 32

Metaphor

With regard to the appropriate number of metaphors, Caecilius appears to side with those who lay down that two, or at most three, should be brought together in the same passage. Demosthenes is again the standard in this context. The appropriate occasion for their use is when the emotions come pouring out like a torrent, and irresistibly carry along with them a host of metaphors. 'Men,' he says, 'who are steeped in blood, who are flatterers, who have each of them mutilated the limbs of their own fatherlands, who have pledged their liberty by drinking first to Philip, and now to Alexander, measuring their happiness by their bellies and their basest appetites, and who have uprooted that liberty and that freedom from despotism which were to the Greeks of earlier days the rules and standards of integrity.'[83] Here the orator's indignation against the traitors casts a veil over the number of figurative expressions he has used.

Now Aristotle and Theophrastus declare that the following phrases have a softening effect on bold metaphors: 'as if', and 'as it were', and 'if one may put it like this', and 'if one may venture the expression'; for the qualifications, they say, mitigate the boldness. I accept this, but at the same time, as I said when I was talking about rhetorical figures, the timely expression of violent emotions, together with true sublimity, is the appropriate antidote for the number and boldness of metaphors. For the onward rush of passion has the property of sweeping everything before it, or rather of requiring bold imagery as something altogether indispensable; it does not allow the hearer leisure to consider the number of metaphors, since he is carried away by the enthusiasm of the speaker.

Furthermore, in the handling of commonplaces and of description nothing so much confers distinction as a continuous series of metaphors. It is by this means that the anatomy of the human body is superbly depicted in Xenophon,[84] and still more divinely in Plato.[85] The head, says Plato, is a citadel, and the neck is constructed as an isthmus between the head and the breast; and the vertebrae, he says, are set below like pivots. Pleasure tempts men to evil, and the tongue is the touchstone of taste. The heart is the fuel store of the veins, the fountain from which the blood begins its vigorous course, and it keeps its station in the guardhouse of the body. The various passages he calls the lanes. 'And for the thumping of the heart which takes place when danger is imminent or when anger is rising, when it becomes fiery hot, the gods,' he says, 'have devised some relief by implanting the lungs, which, being soft and bloodless, and pierced inwardly with pores, serve as a kind of buffer, so that when anger boils up in the heart, it may throb against a yielding substance and not be damaged.' The seat of the desires he compares with the women's apartments, and that of anger with the men's. Then the spleen is the napkin of the entrails, from which it is filled with waste matter, and swells and festers. 'And after this,' he says, 'they covered everything over with flesh, which they put there, like felt matting, as a protection against attacks from outside.' And he called the blood the fodder of the flesh, adding that, 'in order to provide nourishment, they irrigated the body, cutting channels as is done in gardens, so that, the body being perforated with conduits, the rivulets of the veins might flow on as though from some never-failing source.' And when the end comes, he says, the cables of the soul, like those of a ship, are loosed, and she is set free. These and innumerable similar metaphors form a continuous succession. But those I have mentioned are enough to show that figurative language is a natural source of grandeur, and that metaphors contribute to sublimity; and also that it is emotional and descriptive passages that most gladly find room for them.

However, it is obvious, even without my stating it, that the use of metaphors, like all the other beauties of style, is liable to lead to excess. In this respect Plato himself is much criticized, on the ground that he is often carried away by a kind of linguistic frenzy into harsh and intemperate metaphors and bombastic allegory. 'For it is not easy to see,' he says, 'that a city needs to be mixed like a bowl of wine, in which the strong, raging wine seethes as it is poured in, but when it is chastened by another god who is sober, its association with such good company turns it into an excellent and temperate drink.'[86] To call water 'a sober god', say the critics, and to describe mixing as 'chastening', is to use the language of a poet, who is not in fact sober.

Caecilius, too, has picked on such defects as these, and in the works he has written in praise of Lysias[87] he has actually dared to represent Lysias as being in all respects superior to Plato. But here he has given way to two uncritical emotions; for although he is even fonder of Lysias than of himself, his hatred for Plato altogether surpasses his love for Lysias. However, he is merely being contentious, and his assumptions are not, as he thought, generally accepted. For he prefers the orator, on the grounds that he is faultless and unblemished, to Plato, who often made mistakes. But this is not the truth of the matter, nor anything like the truth.

CHAPTER 33

Superiority of Flawed Sublimity to Flawless Mediocrity

Suppose we take some writer who really may be considered flawless and beyond reproach. In this context we must surely ask ourselves in general terms, with reference to both poetry and prose, which is superior, grandeur accompanied by a few flaws, or mediocre correctness, entirely sound and free from error though it may be. Yes, and further, whether in literature the first place should rightly be given to the greater number of virtues, or to virtues which are greater in themselves. For these questions are proper to a study of sublimity, and for every reason they should be resolved.

Now I am well aware that the highest genius is very far from being flawless, for entire accuracy runs the risk of descending to triviality, whereas in the grand manner, as in the possession of great wealth, something is bound to be neglected. Again, it may be inevitable that men of humble or mediocre endowments, who never run any risks and never aim at the heights, should in the normal course of events enjoy a greater freedom from error, while great abilities remain subject to danger by reason of their very greatness. And in the second place, I know that it is always the less admirable aspects of all human endeavours that are most widely noticed; the remembrance of mistakes remains ineradicable, while that of virtues quickly melts away.

I have myself observed a good many faults in Homer and our other authors of the highest distinction, and I cannot say that I enjoy finding these slips; however, I would not call them wilful errors, but rather careless oversights let in casually and at random by the heedlessness of genius. I am none the less certain that the greater virtues, even if they are not consistently shown throughout the composition, should always be voted into the first place – for the greatness of mind that they represent, if for no other reason. Now Apollonius reveals himself in his *Argonautica* as an impeccable poet, and Theocritus is extremely successful in his pastorals, apart from a few surface blemishes. Yet would you not rather choose to be Homer than Apollonius?

And again, is Eratosthenes[88] in his *Erigone*, which is an entirely flawless little poem, a greater poet than Archilochus, with all his disorganized flood and those surges of divine inspiration which are so difficult to bring under the control of rules? Again, in lyric poetry would you choose to be Bacchylides rather than Pindar? And in tragedy Ion of Chios[89] rather than Sophocles? Bacchylides and Ion are, it is true, faultless and elegant writers in the polished manner. But Pindar and Sophocles seem at times to burn up everything before them as they go, although their fire is often unaccountably quenched, and they lapse into a most miserable flatness. Yet would anyone in his senses put the whole series of Ion's works on the same footing as the single play of *Oedipus*?

CHAPTER 34

Hyperides and Demosthenes

If good points in composition were judged by their number rather than their greatness, then Hyperides would be ranked altogether higher than Demosthenes. For he has more variety of tone than Demosthenes, and more numerous merits. In every branch of his art he is very nearly in the first rank, like the pentathlete; in each contest he is inferior to the champions among his rivals, but comes first among the amateurs.

Now Hyperides not only imitates all the virtues of Demosthenes except his skill in composition; he has also with uncommon success taken to his province the merits and graces of Lysias. For he talks plainly, when this is required, and does not make all his points in the same tone, like Demosthenes. He has, too, a gift for characterization, seasoned with charm and simplicity. Moreover, he has considerable wit, a most urbane raillery, good breeding, a ready skill in handling irony, a fund of jokes which, in the Attic manner, are neither tasteless nor ill bred, but always to the point, a clever touch in satire, and plenty of comic force and pointed ridicule combined with a well-directed sense of fun – and all this invested with an inimitable elegance. He is very well endowed by nature with the power to awaken pity. He has a superb facility for narrating myths copiously and for pursuing a theme with fluency. For example, his story of Leto is somewhat poetic in manner, whereas his *Funeral Oration*[90] is an example of the epideictic style which could not, I think, be bettered.

Demosthenes, on the other hand, is not good at describing character. He lacks fluency and smoothness, and has no capacity for the epideictic style. In general he partakes of none of the merits that have just been listed. When he is forced into attempting a joke or a witticism, he does not so much raise laughter at what he says as make himself the object of laughter, and when he wants to exert a little charm, he comes nowhere near doing so. If he had tried to write the little speeches on Phryne or Athenogenes,[91] he would have made us think even more highly of Hyperides.

All the same, in my opinion the virtues of Hyperides, many as they may be, are wanting in grandeur; the productions of a sober-hearted fellow, they are staid and do not disturb the peace of mind of the audience – certainly no one who reads Hyperides is frightened by him. But when Demosthenes takes up the tale, he displays the virtues of great genius in their highest form: a sublime intensity, living emotions, copiousness, readiness, speed, where it is appropriate, and his own unapproachable power and vehemence. Having, I say, made himself master of all the riches of these mighty, heaven-sent gifts – for it would not be right to call them human – he invariably, by reason of the virtues he possesses, puts down all his rivals, and this even where the qualities he does not possess are concerned; it might be said, indeed, that he overpowers with his thunder and lightning the orators of every age. One could more easily outface a descending thunderbolt than meet unflinchingly his continual outbursts of emotion.

CHAPTER 35

Plato and Lysias

In the case of Plato and Lysias there is, as I have said, a further point of difference. Lysias is much inferior to Plato in both the greatness and the number of his merits, and at the same time he surpasses him in his faults even more than he falls short of him in his virtues.

What, then, was in the mind of those godlike authors who, aiming at the highest flights of composition, showed no respect for detailed accuracy? Among many other things this – that nature has adjudged us men to be creatures of no mean or ignoble quality. Rather, she has brought us into life, into the whole universe, as though inviting us to some great festival, there to be spectators at her games and the keenest competitors; and thus from the first she has implanted in our souls an unconquerable passion for all that is great and for all that is more divine than ourselves. For this reason the entire universe does not satisfy the contemplation and thought that lie within the scope of human endeavour; our ideas often go beyond the boundaries by which we are circumscribed, and if we look at life from all sides, observing how in everything that concerns us the extraordinary, the great, and the beautiful play the leading part, we shall soon realize the purpose of our creation.

This is why, by some sort of natural instinct, we admire, not, surely, the small streams, beautifully clear though they may be, and useful too, but the Nile, the Danube, the Rhine, and even more than these the Ocean. The little fire that we have kindled ourselves, clear and steady as its flame may be, does not strike us with as much awe as the heavenly fires, in spite of their often being shrouded in darkness; nor do we think our flame a greater marvel than the craters of Etna, whose eruptions throw up from their depths rocks and even whole mountains, and at times pour out rivers of that earth-born, spontaneous fire. In all such circumstances, I would say only this, that the useful and the necessary are readily available to man, whereas what is out of the ordinary always excites our wonder.

CHAPTER 36

Sublimity and Literary Fame

Now with regard to authors of genius, whose grandeur always has some bearing on questions of utility and service, it must be observed at the outset that, while writers of this quality are far from being faultless, yet they all rise above the human level. Other attributes prove their possessors to be men, but sublimity carries one up to where one is close to the majestic mind of God. Freedom from error escapes censure, but greatness excites admiration as well. It need scarcely be added that each of these outstanding authors time and again redeems all his failures by a single happy stroke of sublimity; and, most decisive of all, that if we were to pick out all the blunders of Homer, Demosthenes, Plato, and all our other really great authors, and were to put them all together, it would be found that they amounted to a very small part, say rather an infinitesimal fraction, of the triumphs achieved by these heroes in their works. That is why the judgement of all ages, which envy itself cannot convict of perversity, has awarded them the palm of victory, guarding it as their inalienable right, and likely so to preserve it 'as long as rivers run and tall trees flourish'.[92]

As for the writer who maintains that the faulty Colossus is not superior to Polyclitus' spearman,[93] one obvious retort, among many others, is to point out that meticulous accuracy is admired in art, grandeur in the works of nature, and that it is by nature that man is endowed with the power of speech. Moreover, in statues we look for the likeness of a man, whereas in literature, as I have said, we look for something transcending the human. However, to revert to the doctrine with which I began my treatise, since freedom from faults is usually the result of art, and excellence, however unevenly sustained, is due to genius, it is right that art should always provide assistance to nature, for in co-operation the two may bring about perfection.

So much it has been necessary to say in order to resolve the problems before us. But everyone is welcome to his own taste.

CHAPTER 37

Comparisons and Similes

Closely related to metaphors – for we must go back to them – are comparisons and similes, which differ only in this. . . .

(*Here two pages of the manuscript are missing*)

CHAPTER 38

Hyperbole

. . . and such expressions as, 'Unless you carry your brains trodden down in your heels'.[94] One must therefore know in each case where to draw the line, for sometimes if one overshoots the mark one spoils the effect of the hyperbole, and if such expressions are strained too far they fall flat, and sometimes produce the opposite effect to that which was intended. Isocrates,[95] for example, unaccountably lapsed into childishness through the ambition which led to his fondness for exaggeration. The theme of his *Panegyric* is that Athens is superior to Sparta in the benefits that she has conferred on the Greeks, but at the very beginning he declares: 'Moreover, words have such power that they can make what is grand humble, and endow petty things with greatness; they can express old ideas in a new way, and discuss what has just happened in the style of long ago.' 'Do you then by these means, Isocrates,' says someone, 'intend to interchange the roles of the Athenians and the Spartans?' For in his eulogy of the power of language he has all but made a prefatory announcement to his auditors that he himself is not to be trusted. Perhaps then, as I said earlier about rhetorical figures, the best hyperboles are those which conceal the fact that they are hyperboles. And this happens when, under the influence of powerful emotion, they are used in connection with some great circumstance, as is the case with Thucydides when he speaks of those who perished in Sicily. 'For the Syracusans,' he says, 'went down and began their slaughter, especially of those who were in the river. And the water was immediately polluted; but none the less it was drunk, thick though it was with mud and blood, and most of them still thought it was worth fighting for.'[96] That a drink of mud and blood should still be worth fighting for is made credible by the height of the emotions excited by the circumstances.

The same is true of Herodotus' account of those who fought at Thermopylae. 'In this place,' he says, 'as they were defending themselves with their daggers, such of them as still had daggers, and with their very hands and mouths, the barbarians buried them with missiles.'[97] Here you may ask what is meant by fighting against armed men 'with their very mouths', and being 'buried with missiles'. At the same time the expressions carry conviction, for the incident does not seem to be introduced for the sake of the hyperbole, but the hyperbole seems to take its rise quite plausibly from the incident. For as I keep on saying, actions and feelings which come close to sweeping us off our feet serve as a justification and a remedy for any kind of daring phraseology. This is why comic expressions, even when they reach the point of being incredible, yet seem plausible because they are so laughable, as in 'The field he had was smaller than a Spartan letter.'[98] For laughter, too, is an emotion, related as it is to pleasure.

Hyperboles may apply just as much to petty things as to great, an overstraining of the facts being the common element. In a sense, ridicule is the exaggeration of pettiness.

CHAPTER 39

Composition, or Disposition of Material

The fifth of the factors contributing to the sublime which I specified at the beginning remains to be dealt with, my friend, and that is the arrangement of the words in due order. On this matter I have already in two treatises given an adequate account of such conclusions as I could reach; for my present purpose I need only add the essential fact that men find in a harmonious arrangement of sounds not only a natural medium of persuasion and pleasure, but also a marvellous instrument of grandeur and emotion. For does not the pipe instil certain emotions into those that hear it, seeming to carry them away and fill them with a divine frenzy? Does it not give rhythmic movement, and compel the hearer to conform to the rhythm and adapt himself to the tune, even if he is not in the least musical? Then the tones of the lyre, though meaningless in themselves, often cast a wonderful spell, as you know, by the variety of their sounds and the interplay and harmonious blending of the notes.

Yet these are mere semblances, spurious counterfeits of persuasion, and not, as I have mentioned, a genuine expression of human nature. Now composition is a kind of harmony of words which are natural to man, and which affect not his hearing alone but his very soul; and it stirs up manifold patterns of words, thoughts, deeds, beauty, and melody, all of which are born and bred in us; moreover, by the blending of its myriad tones it brings into the hearts of the bystanders the actual emotion of the speaker, and always induces them to share it; and finally it builds up an accumulation of phrases into a grand and harmonious structure. Are we not to believe that by these means it casts a spell on us, and draws our thoughts towards what is majestic and dignified and sublime, and all else that it embraces, gaining a complete mastery over our minds? But it is madness to dispute on matters which are the subject of such general agreement, since experience is sufficient proof.

An idea which seems sublime, and which is certainly to be admired, is that which Demosthenes applies to his decree: 'This decree caused the peril which at that time encompassed the city to pass away just like a cloud.'[99] But its ring owes no less to the harmony than to the thought, for its delivery rests entirely on the dactylic rhythms, which are the noblest of rhythms and make for grandeur – which is why the heroic measure, the most beautiful of known measures, is composed of dactyls . . . (*A phrase is missing here*) And indeed, if you moved it wherever you liked away from its proper place, and said, 'This decree, just like a cloud, caused the peril at that time to pass away', or if you cut out a single syllable and said, 'Caused to pass away like a cloud', you would realize how far the harmony of sound chimes in with the sublimity. For 'just like a cloud' ('*hōsper nephos*') starts off with a long rhythm, consisting of four metrical beats, and if you remove a single syllable and write 'like a cloud' ('*hōs nephos*'), by this abbreviation you at once mutilate the effect of grandeur. And again, if you stretch the phrase out with 'caused to pass away just as if a cloud', the meaning is the same, but it no longer falls on the ear with the same effect because, by the drawing out of the final beats, the sheer sublimity of the passage is robbed of its solidity and of its tension.

CHAPTER 40

The Structure of the Sentence

Among the chief agents in the formation of the grand style is the proper combination of the constituent members – as is true of the human body and its members. Of itself no single member, when dissociated from any other, has anything worthy of note about it, but when they are all mutually interconnected they make up a perfect whole. Similarly, when the elements of grandeur are separated from one another, they carry the sublimity along with them, dispersing it in every direction; but when they are combined into a single organism, and, moreover, enclosed within the bonds of harmony, they form a rounded whole, and their voice is loud and clear, and in the periods thus formed the grandeur receives contributions, as it were, from a variety of factors. I have, however, sufficiently demonstrated that many writers both of prose and poetry who have no natural gift of sublimity, and may indeed lack the capacity for grandeur, and who for the most part employ common and popular words which carry no extraordinary associations, have nevertheless, by merely combining and fitting these words together in the right order, achieved dignity and distinction and an appearance of grandeur – among many others Philistus,[100] for example, Aristophanes at times, and Euripides as a rule.

After the slaughter of his children Heracles says, 'I am loaded with woes, and there is no room for more.'[101] The expression is very ordinary, but it becomes sublime by reason of its aptness to its setting. If you fit the passage together in any other way, you will realize that Euripides is a poet rather by virtue of his power of composition than of his ideas. Writing of Dirce being pulled apart by the bull, he says: 'And wheresoever he chanced to wheel around, he seized and dragged them all along, woman, rock, oak, now this, now that.'[102] This idea is excellent in itself, but gains further strength from the fact that the rhythm is not hurried or, as it were, carried along on rollers, but the words are propped up by one another and derive support from the pauses, and take their stand in a firmly based grandeur.

CHAPTER 41

Some Impediments to Sublimity

Where the sublime is concerned nothing has so debasing an effect as effeminate or agitated rhythms, such as pyrrhics ($\smile\smile$), trochees ($-\smile$) and dichorees ($-\smile-\smile$), which drop right down to the level of dance music. For all over-rhythmical passages are at once felt to be cheap and affected; the monotonous jingle seems superficial, and does not penetrate our feelings – and the worst of it is that, just as songs distract the audience's attention from the action of the play and forcibly claim it for themselves, so also an over-rhythmical style does not communicate the feeling of the words, but only of the rhythm. And so there are times when the hearers foresee the likely endings and themselves beat time for the speaker, and anticipate him in setting the step, as in a dance.

Equally wanting in grandeur are passages which are too close-packed, or cut up into tiny phrases and words with short syllables, giving the impression of being roughly and unevenly held together with pins.

CHAPTER 42

Conciseness

Furthermore, excessive conciseness in expression reduces sublimity, for grandeur is marred when it is too closely compressed. You must take this to mean, not compression that is properly used, but what is entirely broken up into fragments and thus frittered away. For excessive conciseness curtails the sense where brevity goes straight to the point. It is obvious that the converse holds for fully extended expressions: what is developed at unseasonable length is lifeless.

CHAPTER 43

Triviality of Expression, and Amplification

The use of trivial words terribly disfigures passages in the grand style. For example, as far as the conception goes, the storm in Herodotus[103] is marvellously described, but the description contains certain details which are, heaven knows, too far below the dignity of the subject. One might perhaps instance 'when the sea boiled', where the word 'boiled' is so cacophonous as to detract greatly from the sublimity. Then 'the wind', he says, 'flagged'; and 'an unpleasant end' awaited those who were clinging to the wreck. The phrase 'flagged' is uncouth, and lacks dignity, and 'unpleasant' is inappropriate to so great a disaster.

Similarly, when Theopompus[104] had given a marvellous account of the Persian King's descent into Egypt, he spoiled the whole description by the use of some trivial words. 'For which city and which tribe of all those in Asia,' he says, 'did not send envoys to the King? And what thing of beauty or value, whether product of the earth or work of art, was not brought to him as an offering? Were there not many costly coverlets and mantles, purple and white and multi-coloured, many pavilions of gold furnished with all things needful, many robes of state and costly couches? Further, there was silver and gold plate richly wrought, goblets and mixing-bowls, some of which you might have seen studded with jewels, others embellished in a cunning and costly fashion. In addition to these there were countless myriads of weapons, both Greek and barbarian, and beasts of burden beyond number, and sacrificial victims fattened for the slaughter; and many bushels of spices, and bags and sacks and pots of onions and all other useful things; and such a store of preserved flesh from every kind of victim as to form piles so large that anyone approaching them from a distance took them for mounds and hills confronting them.'

Here Theopompus runs from the sublime to the trivial where he ought, on the contrary, to have been heightening his effects. By mixing bags and spices and sacks with the wonderful report of the equipment as a whole, he has almost given the impression of a cook-shop. Suppose that among all those decorative objects, among the golden and jewelled mixing bowls, the silver plate, the pavilions of pure gold, and the goblets – suppose that someone had actually brought paltry bags and sacks and placed them in the midst of all these, it would have been an unseemly sight. Well, in the same way the untimely introduction of such words as these as it were disfigures and debases the description. He could have given a general account of the 'hills' which he says were piled up, and, with regard to the rest of the provisions, he could have spoken of wagons and camels and a host of baggage-animals laden with everything that ministers to the luxury and the pleasures of the table; or he could have called them piles of all kinds of grain and of all that conduces to fine cooking and good living; or if he had to put it so explicitly, he could have spoken of all the delicacies of caterers and fine cooks.

In sublime passages we ought not to resort to sordid and contemptible terms unless constrained by some extreme necessity. We should use words that suit the dignity of the subject, and imitate nature, the artist who has fashioned man, for she has not placed in full view our private parts or the means by which our whole frame is purged, but as far as possible has concealed them, and, as Xenophon says,[105] has put their passages into the farthest background so as not to sully the beauty of the whole figure.

However, there is no urgent need to enumerate in detail the things that lead to triviality. For as I have previously indicated the qualities that furnish style with nobility and sublimity, it is obvious that their opposites will for the most part make it mean and ugly.

CHAPTER 44

The Decay of Eloquence

However, one problem remains to be cleared up which, in view of your love of learning, my dear Terentianus, I shall not hesitate to add – a problem which a certain philosopher recently put to me. 'I wonder,' he said, 'as no doubt do many other people, why it is that in our age there are men well fitted for public life who are extremely persuasive, who are keen and shrewd, and especially well endowed with literary charm, and yet really sublime and transcendent natures are, with few exceptions, no longer produced. Such a great and world-wide dearth of literature attends our age! Are we to accept the well-worn view,' he went on, 'that democracy is the kindly nurse of great men, and that great men of letters have flourished only under democracy and perished with it? For freedom, they say, has the power to foster noble minds and to inspire them with hope, and with it there spreads the keenness of mutual rivalry and an eager competition for the first place. Furthermore, by reason of the prizes which are open to all in republics, the intellectual gifts of orators are continually sharpened by practice and as it were kept bright by rubbing, and, as might be expected, these gifts shine forth free in a free world. Nowadays,' he continued, 'we seem to be schooled from childhood onwards in justified slavery, all but swaddled in the infancy of our minds in slavish customs and observances, and never tasting of the finest and most productive source of eloquence, by which I mean freedom; and thus we emerge as nothing but sublime flatterers.'

This, he maintained, was the reason why, although all other faculties may fall to the lot even of slaves, no slave ever becomes an orator; for the fact that he has no freedom of speech, and that he lives as it were in prison immediately breaks out, bludgeoned into him by habit. As

Homer puts it, 'The day of our enslavement takes away half our manhood.'[106] 'And so,' went on the philosopher, 'just as the cages in which they keep the Pygmies, or dwarfs, as they call them, not only stunt the growth of those who are imprisoned in them, if what I hear is true, but also shrink them by reason of the fetters fixed round their bodies, so all slavery, however just it may be, could well be described as a cage of the soul, a common prison-house.'

However, I took him up and said: 'It is easy, my good sir, and a characteristic of human nature, always to be finding fault with the present state of affairs. But consider whether it may be that it is not the peace of this world of ours that corrupts great natures, but much rather this endless war which holds our desires in its grasp, yes, and further still the passions that garrison our lives nowadays and utterly devastate them. For the love of money, that insatiable sickness from which we all now suffer, and the love of pleasure make us their slaves, or rather, one might say, sink our lives (body and soul) into the depths; for love of money is a disease that makes us petty-minded, and the love of pleasure is utterly ignoble.

'On further reflection, indeed, I do not see how, if we value the possession of unlimited wealth, or, to give the truth of the matter, make a god of it, we can prevent the evils that naturally attend it from entering our souls. For vast and unlimited wealth is closely followed – step by step, as they say – by extravagance, and no sooner has the one opened the gates of cities and houses than the other comes in and joins it in setting up house there. With the passing of time, according to the philosophers, they build nests in our lives, and soon set about begetting offspring, giving birth to pretentiousness, vanity, and luxury – no bastards these, but very much their true-born issue. And if these children of wealth are allowed to reach maturity they soon breed in our hearts implacable masters, insolence and lawlessness and shamefulness. This will inevitably happen, and then men will no longer lift up their eyes nor take any thought for their future good name; the ruin of their lives will gradually be completed as their grandeur of soul withers and fades until it sinks into contempt, when they become lost in admiration of their mortal capabilities and neglect to develop the immortal.

'A man who has accepted a bribe for a verdict would never be a sound and unbiased judge of what is just and honourable, for a corrupt judge must necessarily regard his own private interests as honourable and just. And where bribery now governs all our lives, and we hunt others to death, and lay traps for legacies, and bargain our souls for gain from any and every source, having become slaves to luxury, can we expect, in this pestilential ruin of our lives, that there should still remain an unbiased and incorruptible judge of works which possess grandeur or enduring life, and that he would not be overcome by his passion for gain? For such men as we are, indeed, it is perhaps better that we should be ruled than live in freedom. If we were given complete liberty, like released prisoners, our consuming greed for our neighbours' possessions might flood the world in a deluge of evil.'

In short, I maintained that what wears down the spirit of the present generation is the apathy in which, with few exceptions, we all pass our lives; for we do no work nor show any enterprise from any other motives than those of being praised or being able to enjoy our pleasures – never from an eager and honourable desire to serve our fellows.

'It is best to leave these things be',[107] and to pass on to the next problem, that is, the emotions, about which I previously undertook to write in a separate treatise, for they seem to me to share a place in literature generally, and especially in the sublime . . .

(The rest is lost)

NOTES

PLATO: *Ion*

Plato (*c.* 429–347 BC) stands with Socrates and Aristotle as one of the shapers of the whole intellectual tradition of the West. He came from a family that had long played a prominent part in Athenian politics, and it would have been natural for him to follow the same course. He declined to do so, however, disgusted by the violence and corruption of Athenian political life, and sickened especially by the execution in 399 of his friend and teacher, Socrates. Inspired by Socrates' inquiries into the nature of ethical standards, Plato sought a cure for the ills of society not in politics but in philosophy, and arrived at his fundamental and lasting conviction that those ills would never cease until philosophers became rulers or rulers philosophers. At an uncertain date in the early fourth century BC he founded the Academy in Athens, the first permanent institution devoted to philosophical research and teaching, and the prototype of all Western universities.

His literary works are almost all in the form of philosophical dialogues, which probably reflect Socrates' methods of teaching and practising philosophy through conversation. These dialogues, in which Plato himself never appears, are presented as dramatized conversations, usually between Socrates and one or more interlocutors, and they typically proceed by means of question and answer.

The *Ion*, one of Plato's earlier dialogues, dates probably from the 390s BC. It consists of a conversation between Socrates and Ion, a rhapsode or professional reciter of epic poetry, who travelled round Greece competing at contests and festivals. Its chief interest lies in the questions it raises about the nature of poetic inspiration and the sources of the poet's art.

1. *Asclepius at Epidaurus*: Epidaurus in the Peloponnese was a centre for the worship of Asclepius, god of healing, in whose honour a festival was held, which included athletic and musical contests.

2. *Panathenaea*: A festival celebrated annually by the Athenians in honour of their patron goddess, Athena. Once every four years the ceremony was held on a grander scale and included contests in music and athletics. A distinctive feature of this enlarged festival, the Great Panathenaea, was the contest between Homeric rhapsodes, to which Socrates refers here.

3. *Metrodorus . . . Glaucon*: Metrodorus (and possibly Stesimbrotus also) interpreted Homer allegorically. The identity of Glaucon is uncertain, although he may be the commentator on Homer mentioned by Aristotle, *Poetics* 1461b.

4. *Homeridae*: A guild of reciters, known in Chios by the sixth century, who claimed descent from Homer.

5. *Polygnotus*: One of the most famous painters working in Athens in the mid fifth century BC. He was born in Thasos and later given Athenian citizenship.

6. *Daedalus . . . Theodorus of Samos*: Daedalus was a legendary craftsman, known for his exceptionally lifelike statues. Epeius, with the help of Athena, made the wooden horse of Troy. Theodorus was a well-known craftsman of the sixth century BC.

7. *Olympus . . . Phemius*: Legendary exponents of the four types of musical activity just mentioned. Olympus was said to have invented pipe playing; Thamyras was the Thracian lyre player who challenged the Muses to a contest; Orpheus charmed nature itself with his singing; Phemius is the bard forced to sing for the entertainment of the suitors in the *Odyssey*.

8. *Corybantic worshippers*: The Corybantes were mythical attendants of the Phrygian mother-goddess, Cybele, whose cult involved wild orgiastic dancing. Like their mythical counterparts, participants in Corybantic ritual engaged in frenzied dancing which was believed to have therapeutic powers.

9. *dithyrambs . . . iambics*: Dithyrambs were choral songs in honour of Dionysus; encomia were songs of praise in honour of men, as opposed to hymns in honour of gods; the iambic metre was used in poems of invective such as Aristotle describes in chapter four of the *Poetics*.

10. *paean*: a song in praise of Apollo. Nothing is known about Tynnichus.

11. *Odysseus . . . Priam*: Odysseus reveals himself to the suitors in *Odyssey* 22; Achilles pursues Hector round the walls of Troy in *Iliad* 22; the pitiful passages referred to include the lamentations for Hector in *Iliad* 22 and 24.

12. *Lean over . . . the stone*: *Iliad* 23.335–40.

13. *with Pramnian . . . as relish*: *Iliad* 11.639–40.

14. *She went . . . ravenous fish*: *Iliad* 24.80–82.

15. *Wretched men . . . spread about*: *Odyssey* 20.351–7.

16. *A bird . . . the wind*: *Iliad* 12.200–207.

17. *My city*: Ephesus was a member of the Delian league, the alliance which was formed after the Persian wars, and which became increasingly controlled by Athens during the course of the fifth century BC. Little is known of the characters mentioned by Socrates as examples of foreigners who were appointed to offices at Athens.

PLATO: *Republic* 2.376 – 3.398

The *Republic*, Plato's most ambitious work, belongs to his so-called middle period, and was probably composed between 380 and 370 BC, though it cannot be dated with certainty. The dialogue takes place between Socrates and a group of friends, and its subject is the nature of justice. After a preliminary discussion in which various definitions of justice are considered and rejected, Socrates is challenged to prove that living a just life is not merely an expedient way of gaining external rewards but intrinsically beneficial to the individual. Is the just life really better than the unjust life? This is the question which the *Republic* as a whole is designed to answer. But Socrates points out that, in order to answer this question, it will first of all be necessary to discover what justice actually is. He suggests, therefore, that they should look for justice on a large scale, that is, justice in the *polis*, the city or state, before considering the nature of justice in the individual. The city which Socrates envisages is based on the principles of specialization and division of labour: each person will do only one job, and that job will be the one to which he is particularly suited by nature. Justice is the harmony which exists when each class in society performs its proper function for the benefit of the community as a whole.

In the sections of books two and three presented here, Socrates is concerned with the guardian class who will defend the city in warfare. Later on we learn that the guardians will be divided into two classes: rulers and auxiliaries. The top class will be trained in philosophy and are destined to become philosopher kings, whose special task will be to rule the state. But at this stage Socrates is concerned with the guardian class as a whole, and the question of what sort of education they should receive in order to equip them for their task. This is the context in which the first of two important and highly influential discussions of poetry in the *Republic* takes place. The conversation is put into the mouths of Socrates and Plato's brother, Adeimantus.

1. *music*: Greek education was based on *mousike*, that is, all the arts over which the Muses presided: poetry, music, song and dance.
2. *Ouranos . . . on him*: According to the myth in Hesiod's *Theogony* (lines 154–82

and 453–506), Kronos castrated his father Ouranos, and then swallowed his own children through fear of being usurped. However, Zeus escaped this fate and eventually deposed his father.

3. *a pig*: The usual sacrifice for initiates at the Eleusinian mysteries because it was cheap and easily obtainable.

4. *embroidered on robes*: The battle of the giants against the gods was traditionally depicted on the robe woven for the statue of Athena at the Panathenaea (see n. 2 of the *Ion*).

5. *Two urns . . . the earth*: Iliad 24.527–32.

6. *Pandarus . . . Zeus*: the story is told at Iliad 4.69–104.

7. *The gods . . . cities*: Odyssey 17.485–6.

8. *For the life-giving . . . Argos*: A fragment from a lost play of Aeschylus, the *Xantriae*.

9. *the dream sent by Zeus*: Iliad 2.1–34.

10. *he sang . . . my child*: A fragment from an unknown play of Aeschylus.

11. *I would rather . . . dead*: Odyssey 11.489–91. The following six quotations are: Iliad 20.64–5; Iliad 23.103–4; Odyssey 10.495; Iliad 16.856–7; Iliad 23.100–101; Odyssey 24.6–9.

12. *Cocytus and Styx*: Rivers in Hades whose names mean 'Wailing' and 'Hateful' respectively.

13. *Lying . . . down*: Iliad 24.10–13. The following four quotations are: *Iliad* 22.414–15; Iliad 18.54; Iliad 22.168–9; Iliad 16.433–4.

14. *Unquenchable . . . hall*: Iliad 1.599–600.

15. *Anyone . . . timbers*: Odyssey 17.383–4.

16. *Friend . . . word*: Iliad 4.412. Contrary to what Plato says, the next quotation does not follow on in the standard text of Homer. In fact the lines are a conflation of Iliad 3.8 and 4.431.

17. *Drunkard . . . deer*: Iliad 1.225.

18. *The tables . . . cups*: Odysseus' words at Odyssey 9.8–10. The following quotation is from Odyssey 12.342.

19. *Zeus*: The story is told at Iliad 14.294–351.

20. *Hephaestus . . . Aphrodite*: Odyssey 8.266–332.

21. *He struck . . . before*: Odyssey 20.17–18.

22. *Gifts . . . kings*: A traditional saying, attributed by some to Hesiod.

23. *Phoenix*: Iliad 9.515–605.

24. *Achilles . . . ransom*: The episodes referred to occur in Iliad 19, where Achilles accepts Agamemnon's gifts, and Iliad 24, where Priam offers him ransom in return for Hector's body.

25. *You have wronged . . . power*: Iliad 22.15 and 22.20.

26. *River-god*: Scamander. The story is told in Iliad 21.130–32 and 21.212–382.

27. *The lock of his hair . . . dead*: Iliad 23.138–51. The subsequent references are to *Iliad* 24.14–18 and 23.175–7.

28. *Theseus . . . Zeus*: These two heroes carried off Helen, and attempted to abduct Persephone from Hades.

29. *Close kin . . . flows fresh*: From a lost play by Aeschylus, the *Niobe*, to which Plato also refers at *Republic* 380.

30. *The point*: That is, that only the just person can be truly happy.

31. *He entreated . . . people*: Iliad 1.15–16.

32. *Dithyrambs*: See n. 9 on the *Ion*.

33. *Imitate a woman . . . in labour*: The particular examples of unsuitable female behaviour in this passage suggest that Plato is thinking of tragic heroines such as Niobe, Phaedra or Medea. In his lost play *Auge*, Euripides is said to have portrayed the heroine giving birth in a temple. All these roles would have been played by men, hence dramatic mimesis often involved males impersonating females. The issue of gender inversion in Greek theatre had already been exploited for its comic possibilities by Aristophanes, particularly in the *Thesmophoriazusae*, discussed above in the Introduction, section 2.

34. *Horses neighing . . . and so on*: Plato is probably thinking here of the onomatopoeic use of language rather than of the direct mimicry of actual sounds.

35. *The appropriate musical mode . . . rhythm*: The assumption is that different forms of musical expression are needed for the representation of different characters. But since the good man will confine his imitations for the most part to good men performing good actions, his style will be correspondingly uniform.

PLATO: *Republic* 10.595–608

Plato returns to the subject of poetry in the final book of the *Republic*. In the intervening section of the dialogue we have been introduced to the central doctrines of Plato's metaphysics and psychology: the theory of Forms (n. 2), and the tripartite theory of the soul (n. 1). Both of these theories are now invoked in order to explain further Plato's hostility to poetry, an issue which is here treated in a far more trenchant manner than in the earlier books. There Plato was concerned to reform existing poetry through censorship, and was primarily interested in the effects of poetry on the young, whereas now his aim is to remove the poetry of Homer, the tragedians and all the great masterpieces of classical literature from Greek culture altogether. There may be a place for certain types of poetry in Plato's ideal state, for example, hymns to the gods and songs in praise of good men, but such work will be strictly controlled, and poets will be subject to the dictates of the rulers. The speakers are Socrates and Plato's brother, Glaucon.

1. *Parts of the soul*: In book four Plato distinguished between three parts or elements in the soul: the reasoning part, the spirited part, and the desiring part. Here it is signalled that the division of the soul into parts has a direct bearing on the banishment of mimetic poetry, though the connection between the two is by no means clear, as the puzzlement of the interlocutor makes clear.

2. *Form*: A reference to Plato's theory of Forms, which here, as elsewhere, is introduced as being familiar to, and accepted by, Socrates' interlocutors. No systematic account of the theory is given, but it assumes a distinction between the true objects of knowledge, existing in a timeless and unchanging reality, which can only be apprehended by reason, and the less real particulars of everyday life, which are perceived by the senses.

3. *Asclepius . . . his sons*: In Homer, Asclepius, god of healing, has two sons to whom he has passed on the skills of healing. But the term 'sons of Asclepius' came to be used of physicians in general.

4. *Homeridae*: See *Ion*, n. 4.

5. *Thales . . . Anacharsis*: Thales, one of the Seven Wise Men, was well known for his practical wisdom. Anacharsis was said to have invented the anchor and the potter's wheel.

6. *Creophylus*: The name, meaning 'meat-stock', suggests boorishness rather than culture, a tradition to which Sir Andrew Aguecheek alludes in *Twelfth Night* (Act 1, scene 3): 'I am a great eater of beef and I believe that does harm to my wit.'

7. *Protagoras . . . Prodicus*: Two of the best-known fifth-century BC sophists. The tremendous enthusiasm of Protagoras' followers is vividly depicted in the opening scene of the Platonic dialogue named after him.

8. *Iambic or epic*: Iambic is the metre of tragedy; the reference to epic is clearly to Homer, whom Plato regards as the originator of tragedy.

9. *Encomia*: See *Ion*, n. 9.

10. *"Yapping bitch . . . starve"*: We do not know the source of any of these quotations.

ARISTOTLE: *Poetics*

Aristotle was born at Stagira, in the dominion of the kings of Macedonia, in 384 BC. For twenty years he studied at Athens in the Academy of Plato, on whose death in 347 he left, and some time later became tutor to the young

Alexander the Great. When Alexander succeeded to the throne of Macedonia in 336, Aristotle returned to Athens and established his school and research institute, the Lyceum, to which his great erudition attracted a large number of scholars. After Alexander's death in 323, anti-Macedonian feeling drove Aristotle out of Athens, and he fled to Chalcis in Euboea, where he died in 322. His writings, which were of extraordinary range, profoundly affected the whole course of ancient and medieval philosophy, and they are still eagerly studied and debated by philosophers today.

The *Poetics* as it stands is a difficult and elusive text, not least because it is almost certainly a series of lecture notes for use in a private educational context rather than a polished work intended for publication. Like almost all the texts of Aristotle we possess, it belongs to his so-called 'esoteric' works, that is, works which were written not for the general public, but for teaching purposes. Aristotle published several works on poetry, including a dialogue in three books *On Poetry* and six books of *Homeric Problems*. These no longer survive, but Aristotle seems to draw on them in the *Poetics* (see nn. 38 and 80), which no doubt contains material from more than one period of his career. The *Poetics* cannot be dated, but it appears to be a late work, since it presupposes in the reader a knowledge of other mature works by Aristotle, especially the *Ethics*, the *Politics* and the *Rhetoric*. The text as we have it probably represents lecture notes which Aristotle used for the instruction of his students at the Lyceum.

1. *Dithyrambic poetry*: See *Ion*, n. 9. The pipe (*aulos*) and the lyre (*kithara*) were the two main instruments used in Greek music.

2. *Use of the voice*: the reference is to vocal mimicry, such as that of animal sounds, rather than to articulate speech.

3. *Sophron and Xenarchus*: Sicilian writers, father and son, who were writing in the latter part of the fifth century BC. Sophron is said to have influenced Plato's dialogues.

4. *Empedocles*: The fifth-century BC pre-Socratic philosopher who wrote his treatises *On nature* and *Purifications* in hexameter verse. He is also referred to in chapter 21 (see nn. 61 and 62) and in chapter 25 (n. 88).

5. *Chaeremon*: a fourth-century BC tragedian, mentioned also at 1460a. Little is known of the work referred to here.

6. *Nomic poetry*: The nome, like the dithyramb, was a choral lyric song.

7. *Polygnotus*: See *Ion*, n. 5. Little is known about the other two painters mentioned, but at *Politics* 1340a36 Aristotle makes a similar contrast between Polygnotus and Pauson.

8. *Cleophon . . . Deiliad*: Cleophon is a fourth-century BC tragic poet mentioned also at 1458a20; Hegemon composed epic burlesques in the late fifth century BC; Nicochares was an Athenian comic poet of the early fourth century BC. The *Deiliad* ('the tale of a coward') is a mock-epic title, analogous to the *Iliad*, the tale of Ilium (Troy).

9. *Timotheus and Philoxenus*: Both were dithyrambic poets of the late fifth and the early fourth century BC, known as musical and stylistic innovators. Philoxenus is known to have depicted the Cyclops, Polyphemus, as a caricature of the Sicilian tyrant Dionysius I. Timotheus' treatment was presumably more serious, but we cannot be sure of Aristotle's point because the text is defective here. Timotheus is also mentioned at 1454b30 and 1461b32.

10. *People doing things . . . Magnes*: The word 'drama', literally 'a thing done', derives from the verb *dran*, 'to do', an etymology which is used in support of the Dorians' claim to have invented drama, as Aristotle points out at the end of this chapter. Megara was a Dorian city in mainland Greece, where democracy was established by the mid sixth century BC. Megara Hyblaea, a Dorian colony in Sicily, was said to have been the birthplace of Epicharmus, a comic poet active in the late sixth and early fifth century BC. Aristotle exaggerates in saying that he was 'much earlier' than Chionides and Magnes, the earliest recorded Athenian comic poets, who were working in the 480s and 470s BC.

11. *Margites*: A lost burlesque narrative, not now attributed to Homer, in a mixture of hexameters and iambic trimeters, on the exploits of an incompetent hero, who 'knew many things, but knew them all badly'. The earliest known invective poems are those of the seventh century BC poet Archilochus.

12. *Dithyramb*: See *Ion*, n. 9. The implication is that tragedy originated when the leader of the dithyramb began to perform solos in response to the chorus, the first step towards the emergence of an independent actor. The same process is envisaged for comedy in relation to the songs sung to accompany ritual processions carrying the phallus in honour of Dionysus.

13. *Satyric style*: Satyrs were lewd and drunken followers of Dionysus. Satyr plays, with their choruses of satyrs, were a regular feature of the dramatic contests at Athens in the classical period, and were composed by tragedians for performance after each set of three tragedies. The only complete surviving satyr play is the *Cyclops* of Euripides. Aristotle here implies that tragedy developed out of satyric drama, or something like it, a view which might seem to conflict with what he has just said about tragedy's relation to the dithyramb. All that can be said with certainty is that satyr play, dithyramb and tragedy were all connected with the worship of Dionysus.

14. *Granted a chorus*: The archon, the chief annual magistrate at Athens, was responsible for selecting the dramatists who were to compete at the festival of the City Dionysia, and for assigning to each of them a wealthy citizen, a *choregos*, who would finance the cost of the production. Comedy was first officially performed in this way at Athens in 486 BC.

15. *Crates*: An Athenian comic poet active between about 450 and 430 BC.

16. *Hexameters . . . comedy*: Epic is discussed in chapters 23–4. No discussion of comedy survives, but it is likely to have been part of a second book of the *Poetics*, now lost.

17. *Catharsis*: On the meaning of this term, see Introduction, section 5.

18. *These, it may be said . . . thought*: Text and interpretation here are uncertain.

19. *Zeuxis and Polygnotus*: Zeuxis, a famous painter of the late fifth and early fourth century BC, is also mentioned at 1461b. On Polygnotus, see 1448a and *Ion*, n. 5.

20. *It is said . . . occasion*: Text and meaning are uncertain here.

21. *By now . . . actual people*: Whereas Aristophanes and the poets of Old Comedy had satirized individuals such as Cleon and Socrates in the manner of the 'iambic poets' referred to in chapter 4, by the mid fourth century BC this practice had been abandoned.

22. *Agathon's Antheus*: Agathon, an Athenian tragic poet active in the late fifth century BC, is also mentioned at 1456a. The dramatic setting of Plato's *Symposium* is a party to celebrate his first victory in 416 BC. He is parodied in Aristophanes' *Thesmophoriazusae*, discussed in the Introduction, section 2. Nothing is known of his *Antheus*.

23. *Oedipus . . . who he was*: Sophocles, *Oedipus Tyrannus* 925–1085.

24. *Lynceus*: A lost play by Aristotle's contemporary Theodectes, also referred to at 1455b.

25. *Iphigenia*: Euripides' *Iphigenia in Tauris* 727–826. The recognition scene is also referred to in chapters 14, 15 and 16, and the plot of the play is summarized in chapter 17.

26. *Anapaests or trochees*: Rhythms suitable for marching and dancing, which were generally used in choral entrance songs.

27. *Alcmaeon . . . Telephus*: Alcmaeon, like Orestes, killed his mother to avenge his father; Oedipus killed his father and married his mother; Meleager and Telephus killed their uncles; Thyestes ate his children's flesh, served up to him by his brother, Atreus, in revenge for Thyestes' adultery with his wife.

28. *Alcmaeon . . . Odysseus*: Astydamas was a leading tragic poet of the mid fourth century BC. In this lost play Alcmaeon killed his mother without knowing who she was. In *The Wounded Odysseus*, a lost play by Sophocles, Telegonus, son of Odysseus by Circe, fought and fatally wounded his father in ignorance of his identity.

29. *Haemon . . . Antigone*: The messenger in Sophocles' *Antigone* 1231–7 describes how Haemon fails to kill his father and then kills himself.

30. *Cresphontes . . . Helle*: The *Cresphontes* is a lost play by Euripides; on the *Iphigenia* see n. 25 – the scene referred to here occurs at 727ff.; the author and theme of the *Helle* are unknown.

31. *Female . . . manliness*: The word *andreia*, translated here as 'manliness', also means 'courage'. Aristotle's point is that women may be courageous, but not in the same way as men. Compare *Politics* 1260a20–24 and 1277b20–25 for the view that courage and the other virtues differ between men and women.

32. *Menelaus . . . Orestes*: Menelaus' cowardice in refusing to help his nephew in Euripides' *Orestes* (see especially lines 682ff.) is 'unnecessary' in that the plot does not require it. The same example is used at 1461b12.

33. *Scylla*: A lost dithyramb by Timotheus (see n. 9), also mentioned at 1461b32, in which Odysseus laments his comrades who had been eaten by the monster Scylla.

34. *Melanippe's speech*: In Euripides' lost play, *Melanippe*, the heroine's speech, which survives in fragments, shows a knowledge of scientific cosmogony and a cleverness in argument that was thought inappropriate for a woman.

35. *Iphigenia at Aulis*: In Euripides' play, when Iphigenia hears that she is to be sacrificed by her father so that the Greek fleet may set sail for Troy, she first begs for her life (1211ff.), but later offers to die for Greece (1368ff.).

36. *Ex machina*: The *machina* was a crane-like device from which gods were suspended over the stage at the end of a play to pronounce on the fate of the characters. Aristotle objects that divine intervention of this sort was often misused in order to bring about an arbitrary resolution of the plot, citing as examples Medea's escape in the chariot of the sun in Euripides' play (1317ff.), and Athene's intervention at *Iliad* 2.155ff., which prevented the Greeks from leaving Troy.

37. *Homer . . . harshness*: The text here is uncertain.

38. *Arising . . . mistakes*: The sense of this passage has never been adequately explained. The 'published work' referred to in the next sentence is probably the dialogue *On Poets*.

39. *Spearhead . . . bear*: A birthmark in the shape of a spearhead indicated descent from the 'earthborn', the men who sprang from the dragon's teeth sown by Cadmus. The source of the quotation is unknown.

40. *Carcinus . . . Thyestes*: Carcinus was a fourth-century BC tragic poet. Nothing is known of his *Thyestes*, but a star was the birthmark of the descendants of Pelops, including Thyestes.

41. *Tyro*: A lost play by Sophocles in which Tyro recognized her sons from the boat in which they had been set adrift as children.

42. *The recognition of Odysseus*: At *Odyssey* 19.386ff. the nurse Eurycleia recognizes Odysseus unexpectedly when she washes his feet and sees his scar, whereas at

Odyssey 21.193ff. Odysseus proves his identity to the herdsmen by deliberately showing them his scar.

43. *Iphigenia in Tauris*: See n. 25. Orestes confirms his identity to his sister by describing various things in their old home, including a tapestry that she herself had woven. Aristotle's point is that he might as well have produced a token, as in the least artistic kind of recognition.

44. *Tereus*: Tereus was married to Procne, but raped her sister Philomela and then cut out her tongue. Philomela revealed what had happened by weaving her story into a tapestry, hence the 'voice of the shuttle'.

45. *These two are recognized*: Dicaeogenes was a tragedian and dithyrambic poet of the late fifth century BC. Nothing is known of his *Cyprians*. In *Odyssey* 8.521ff., Odysseus weeps when the bard sings of the fall of Troy, and Alcinous then asks him who he is.

46. *Someone . . . has come*: Electra reasons thus in Aeschylus' *Choephori* 168–211.

47. *Polyidus . . . Phineidae*: Also mentioned at 1445b10, but otherwise unknown. Nothing is known of the *Tydeus* by Theodectes, the rhetorician and tragic poet referred to at 1452a27–9 (n. 24) and 1455b29–32, or of the *Phineidae*.

48. *Odysseus the False Messenger*: An unknown play. The text and meaning of the following sentence are obscure.

49. *Carcinus*: See n. 40. Nothing is known of the play referred to here.

50. *Polyidus*: See 1455a and n. 47.

51. *And the revelation of the parents*: The text is uncertain here. On Theodectes' *Lynceus*, see 1452a and n. 24.

52. *A number . . . spoke about*: A problematic statement, since at 1450a7–14 Aristotle spoke of six constituent parts, not four.

53. *The Phthiotides and the Peleus*: Both were probably by Sophocles, though Euripides also wrote a *Peleus*.

54. *Spectacular tragedy*: The text is damaged here and the translation is based on a conjecture which makes sense of the examples cited, though we cannot be certain which particular plays Aristotle has in mind: Aeschylus wrote a play on the Phorcides, three hideous old women who guarded the Gorgons, and his *Prometheus* trilogy contained some spectacular effects. An alternative suggestion for the fourth kind of tragedy is that it should be 'simple', to link up with the types of epic and tragedy discussed at the beginning of chapter 24.

55. *Agathon*: See n. 22.

56. *In the handling . . . want*: Text and interpretation are uncertain here.

57. *Sing . . . Goddess*: The opening of the *Iliad*. On Protagoras see above, n. 7 to Plato, *Republic* 10.

58. *Hermocaicoxanthus*: A compound formed from the name of three separate rivers in Phocaea, the area from which the founders of the Greek colony Massilia (Marseilles) originally came. The text is uncertain here.

59. *Here lies my ship*: Odyssey 1.185.

60. *Odysseus . . . deeds*: Iliad 2.272.

61. *Draining . . . bronze*: Empedocles (see n. 4) fragments 138 and 143. The first refers to the killing of a man, the second to drawing off water in a bronze vessel.

62. *Empedocles . . . life*: The text is uncertain here and it is not clear which phrase is being attributed to Empedocles.

63. *Sowing . . . flame*: From an unknown source.

64. *Sprouters . . . supplicator*: The first word (*ernuges*) is unknown; the second (*areter*) occurs three times in Homer.

65. *On the righter breast*: Iliad 5.393.

66. *Cleophon and Sthenelus*: On Cleophon see 1448a and n. 8. Sthenelus was probably the late fifth-century BC tragic poet whose style was mocked by Aristophanes, fragment 158.

67. *I saw . . . fire*: The riddle describes the medical use of a cupping glass to draw blood.

68. *I saw . . . hellebore*: The lines parody the metrical licence found in Homer. Eucleides is otherwise unknown.

69. *The canker . . . upon*: Aeschylus, fragment 253; Euripides, fragment 792.

70. *Now a paltry fellow . . . headlands shout*: The three quotations are from Odyssey 9.515, 20.259 and Iliad 17.265.

71. *Ariphrades*: Otherwise unknown.

72. *Salamis . . . Sicily*: According to Herodotus 7.166, the battles at Salamis and at Himera in Sicily took place on the same day in 480 BC.

73. *Cypria . . . Iliad*: Two poems, both lost, from the so-called Epic Cycle. The former told of the events leading up to the Trojan War, the latter continued the story from the end of the *Iliad*.

74. *Chaeremon*: See 1447b and n. 5.

75. *The pursuit of Hector*: Iliad 22.131ff.

76. *Odyssey*: At 19.220ff. the disguised Odysseus tells Penelope that he has seen Odysseus, and she believes him because he describes his appearance accurately. The fallacy is that she infers the truth of the antecedent from the truth of the consequent.

77. *Electra . . . speaking*: In Sophocles' *Electra*, 680–763, a fictitious account is given of Orestes' death in a chariot race at the Pythian games, which is an anachronism because the games were founded centuries after the time of Orestes. Both Aeschylus and Sophocles wrote plays entitled the *Mysians*. The story concerned Telephus, who, having killed his uncle in Tegea, travelled to

Mysia in Asia Minor without speaking to anyone because of the blood guilt he had incurred.

78. *If a poet . . . absurd as well*: Text and interpretation are uncertain here.

79. *Irrational elements . . . Ithaca*: *Odyssey* 13.116ff.

80. *Critical Objections*: This difficult chapter summarizes points which must have been discussed at far greater length in the six books of Aristotle's lost *Homeric Problems*.

81. *Something . . . through*: The text is damaged here.

82. *Hector*: See 1460a and n. 75.

83. *Xenophanes*: Philosopher and poet (*c.* 570–*c.* 475) who criticized the anthropomorphic conception of the gods, and denounced the traditional stories of their immorality.

84. *Their spears . . . ends*: *Iliad* 10.152–3.

85. *Diction*: The examples in this paragraph are from *Iliad* 1.50 (why should Apollo have inflicted the plague on animals?), *Iliad* 10.316 (how can Dolon be both 'evil of form' and 'swift of foot'?) and *Iliad* 9.203 (the Greeks normally drank wine mixed with water).

86. *Metaphorical*: The first example is from *Iliad* 10.1–2, slightly misquoted, with 10.11–13. The second is found at *Iliad* 18.489 and *Odyssey* 5.275: the Bear is not the only constellation which never sets, but the most famous one.

87. *Hippias . . . rain*: Hippias is unknown. The first example was in Aristotle's text of the *Iliad* at 2.15 (though in ours it occurs at 21.297). By a change of accent Hippias turns 'we grant' into the imperative 'grant', so that Zeus is not guilty of deception in relation to the false dream that was sent to Agamemnon. The second example is at *Iliad* 23.328 where a change of accent and breathing produces the required sense.

88. *Empedocles . . . mixed*: Empedocles (see n. 4) fragment 35.14–15. The required sense is produced by inserting a comma: '. . . things unmixed formerly, mixed.'

89. *More . . . passed*: *Iliad* 10.252–3.

90. *A greave . . . tin*: *Iliad* 21.592.

91. *Ganymede*: *Iliad* 20.234. The gods drank nectar, not wine.

92. *There . . . stopped*: *Iliad* 20.272 where there is inconsistency because Aeneas' spear pierces two layers of bronze on Achilles' shield, but is stopped by a layer of gold, which must have been on the outside.

93. *Glaucon*: Unknown, but see Plato's *Ion* 530d with n. 3 above.

94. *Icarius . . . Sparta*: Father of Penelope in the *Odyssey*. But Homer does not say that he was a Spartan.

95. *Zeuxis*: See 1450a and n. 19. The text is uncertain here.

96. *Aegeus . . . Orestes*: *Medea* 663ff. On Menelaus, see 1454a and n. 32.

97. *Twelve*: There is no scholarly agreement on how to make sense of this number.

98. *Scylla*: See n. 33 above.

99. *Mynniscus . . . Pindarus*: An actor who performed in Aeschylus' later plays (in the 460s BC), and won a prize for acting in 422. Callippides won a prize in 418, and, according to Xenophon, *Symposium* 3.11, was known for his ability to make an audience weep. Pindarus is unknown.

100. *Sosistratus . . . Mnasitheus*: Both unknown.

HORACE: *The Art of Poetry*

Horace was born in 65 BC at Venusia in Apulia. His father, though once a slave, had made enough money as a revenue official to send his son to well-known teachers in Rome and subsequently to the university at Athens. While he was there Julius Caesar was assassinated, and Brutus, on his way to Macedonia, offered Horace a command in the Republican army, which he accepted, and fought on the losing side at Philippi. Although his family's property was confiscated, he was allowed to return to Rome, where he served as a clerk to the treasury. Later he was introduced by his friends Virgil and Varius to Maecenas, the great patron of letters, who in the course of time became his close friend and conferred many benefits on him, including the famous Sabine farm. From now on Horace was free from financial worries, and he moved among the leading poets and statesmen of Rome. His work, which included the *Epodes*, *Satires*, *Odes* and *Epistles*, was admired by Augustus, and, indeed, after Virgil's death in 19 BC he was virtually Poet Laureate. Horace died in 8 BC, soon after Maecenas.

As a major poet himself Horace was not merely a detached observer, but had deeply held views about the kind of poetry that was needed in Augustan Rome. In his *Epistle to Augustus* (*Epistles* 2.1), a verse epistle like the *Art of Poetry*, but addressed to the emperor himself, Horace attacked the literary conservatism of his contemporaries, who worshipped the Roman writers of the past simply because they were old, and praised Augustus for his judgement and taste in recognizing the achievements of Horace's contemporaries, Virgil and Varius. In the *Epistle to Florus* (*Epistles* 2.2) he satirized the popular but shallow poets of the day, and gave his own view of poetic technique, especially the need for the most careful revision in order to ensure that the best words have been found and set down in the best order.

These themes are taken up and expanded in the *Epistle*, known since Quintilian so named it in the first century AD as the *Ars Poetica* or *Art of Poetry*.

One of the puzzles about this poem is that it has virtually nothing to say about the genres of poetry which Horace himself wrote: lyric poetry in particular is passed over in silence. But the poem's focus on tragedy and the long section on satyric drama (lines 220–50) are probably to be explained in terms of the source or sources on which Horace draws, as mentioned in the Introduction, section 7. Its date is uncertain, but many scholars regard it as a late work, composed *c.* 10 BC.

1. *My dear Pisos*: The identity of the father and two sons, the Pisos, to whom the poem is addressed, is uncertain.

2. *The Cethegi in their loin-cloths*: i.e. early Romans.

3. *Caecilius . . . Varius*: Caecilius (d. 168 BC) and Plautus (d. *c.* 184) – both wrote comedies adapted from Greek. Varius was an Augustan poet and friend of Virgil, who prepared the *Aeneid* for publication after Virgil's death in 19 BC.

4. *Cato and Ennius*: Cato the Censor (234–149 BC), orator and historian, brought Ennius (239–169 BC) to Rome in 204. The latter was a prolific writer in several genres, including tragedy and comedy, but his most famous work was the *Annales*, an epic account of Roman history in eighteen books.

5. *Archilochus*: The Greek poet of the seventh century BC, the earliest known writer of invective poetry in the iambic metre. Compare Aristotle, *Poetics*, chapter 4 with n. 11.

6. *To lyric poetry . . . wine*: Greek lyric poetry included hymns to the gods and heroes, odes (such as those of Pindar) celebrating victories in the games, and amatory and sympotic poems (such as those of Sappho, Alcaeus, and Anacreon).

7. *The banquet of Thyestes*: A favourite subject for tragedy. See Aristotle, *Poetics*, chapter 13 with n. 27.

8. *Chremes*: A typical father's name in New Comedy, where the irate father is a stock figure.

9. *Telephus and Peleus*: On these tragic characters see Aristotle, *Poetics*, chapter 13 with n. 27, chapter 24 with n. 77, and chapter 18 with n. 53.

10. *It is hard . . . way*: The interpretation of this line (*difficile est proprie communia dicere*) is much disputed. The translation adopted here assumes that Horace is referring to the difficulty of treating new subjects or types of character (the 'generalities') which have not yet been particularized by tradition. Compare Aristotle's remarks on the differences between poetry and history in *Poetics*, chapter 9. It is better, therefore, to stick to finding new ways of dealing with familiar subjects.

11. *Of Priam's . . . renown*: The particular source of this quotation is unknown, but the point is that as a poem it promises too large a topic. For the contrast between the poets of the epic cycle and Homer, see Aristotle, *Poetics*, chapter 23 with n. 73.

12. *Tell me . . . cities*: The opening of the *Odyssey*.

13. *Tales . . . Cyclops*: The tales told in *Odyssey*, books 9–12.

14. *Twin eggs of Leda*: A reference to the birth of Helen.

15. *Atreus . . . snake*: On Atreus, see Aristotle, *Poetics*, n. 27. Procne, having served up her murdered son, Itys, to his father, Tereus, in revenge for the latter's treatment of her sister, Philomela (see Aristotle, *Poetics*, n. 44), was changed into a swallow or, alternatively, a nightingale. According to the myth, Cadmus, founder of Thebes, was turned into a snake. See, for example, Euripides, *Bacchae*, 1330–39.

16. *Five acts*: It is not clear how this so-called 'five-act law' can be applied to Greek tragedy, but the comedies of Menander seem to have been divided into five acts with choral interludes in between.

17. *The prize of a goat*: An allusion to the derivation of the word 'tragedy' from *tragos* (goat), allegedly because the prize in the competition for tragedy was originally a goat. On satyric drama, see Aristotle, *Poetics*, chapter 4 with n. 13.

18. *Davus . . . Bacchus*: Davus, Pythias and Simo are typical names in comedy. Silenus was the leader of the satyrs and teacher of Dionysus (Bacchus).

19. *Fauns*: The Roman equivalent of satyrs.

20. *Accius . . . Ennius*: Accius (170 – c. 86 BC) was a Roman tragic poet, known, and sometimes mocked, for the grandeur of his style. On Ennius, see n. 4.

21. *Plautus*: The comedies of Plautus (early second century BC) are the earliest works of Latin literature to have survived complete. Horace criticizes him in the *Epistle to Augustus* (lines 170–76) for his portrayal of character.

22. *Thespis*: Nothing certain is known of him, and the tradition that he invented tragedy is open to suspicion. Compare Aristotle's account of the origins of tragedy in *Poetics*, chapter 4.

23. *Numa Pompilius*: An early king of Rome from whom the Piso clan claimed descent.

24. *Democritus*: A fifth-century Greek philosopher who seems to have attached importance to the idea of poetic inspiration, and is thought to have influenced Plato's views on the subject, as in, for example, *Ion* 533–5 and *Phaedrus* 245, quoted in the Introduction, section 4.

25. *Hellebore*: Used in the treatment of madness, it grew in Anticyra in central Greece. According to the ancient theory of humours, madness was thought to arise from an excess of black bile, which could be purged by hellebore.

26. *Ramnes*: One of the three centuries, or ranks, of knights, who here represent the aristocratic young bloods of the day.

27. *Choerilus*: An inferior epic poet of the time of Alexander the Great. There were said to have been only seven good lines in his poem on the exploits of Alexander.

28. *A poem is like a painting*: The parallel between poetry and painting goes back at least as far as Simonides, the Greek poet of the late sixth and early fifth centuries BC, who is credited with saying, 'Painting is silent poetry, and painting poetry that speaks'. The analogy between the two is exploited by both Plato and Aristotle, and it evidently became a commonplace of literary theory. But Horace's '*ut pictura, poesis*' is the classic formulation, which gave rise to a wide-ranging discourse on the relationship of the two arts in the Italian Renaissance and beyond.

29. *Messalla . . . Cascellius*: The former (64 BC–AD 8) was a prominent general, patron (the poet, Tibullus, was one of his clients) and orator, the latter a distinguished lawyer, born *c.* 104 BC.

30. *Minerva*: i.e. Athene, patron goddess of wisdom and learning.

31. *Tyrtaeus*: An elegist of the seventh century BC, who inspired the Spartans in their struggles against the Messenians.

32. *Quintilius Varus*: A friend of both Horace and Virgil. His death was lamented by Horace in *Odes* 1.24.

33. *Aristarchus*: The great Alexandrian scholar and critic (*c.* 216–145 BC), famous for his work on Homer.

34. *Empedocles*: See Aristotle, *Poetics*, n. 4. Various tales were told about the mysterious circumstances surrounding his death.

LONGINUS: *On the Sublime*

Both the author and the date of this treatise are uncertain. The manuscript tradition refers to its author as 'Dionysius Longinus' or 'Dionysius or Longinus', and until the nineteenth century it was confidently ascribed to Cassius Longinus, an eminent rhetorician of the third century AD. But internal evidence suggests an earlier date. In particular the final chapter on the decay of eloquence is reminiscent of arguments put forward in Tacitus' *Dialogue on Orators* (late first century AD), and this theme is something of a commonplace amongst writers of the period. Most experts now believe that *On the Sublime* was written sometime during the first century AD by an otherwise unknown author. The manuscript in which it survives is damaged, and about a third of the text is lost.

1. *Postumius Terentianus*: Identity unknown.
2. *Caecilius*: A rhetorician and historian of the first century BC. He came from Caleacte in Sicily.

3. *Demosthenes*: The great Athenian orator, 384–322 BC. The reference is to *Oration* 23.113.

4. *Quell . . . strain*: Dorsch here adopts the translation provided by A. S. Way for the edition of Longinus by W. Rhys Roberts (Cambridge 1907), since it brings out so well the bombastic, pseudo-tragic quality to which Longinus takes exception. The lines probably come from a lost *Orithyia* by Aeschylus. The speaker is Boreas, the north wind.

5. *Gorgias*: The Sicilian sophist and rhetorician (*c*. 485 – *c*. 380 BC), discussed in the *Introduction*, section 3.

6. *Callisthenes*: Nephew of Aristotle and historian of Alexander the Great (d. 327 BC).

7. *Cleitarchus*: Another historian of Alexander.

8. *Amphicrates and Hegesias and Matris*: All are Hellenistic authors of whom little is known. Amphicrates fled from Athens to Seleucia in 86 BC, but we know nothing about his writings. The style of Hegesias (third century BC) was severely criticized by classicizing writers.

9. *Theodorus*: A first–century-BC rhetorician from Gadara.

10. *Timaeus*: A Sicilian historian from Tauromenium (*c*. 350–260 BC) who was so fond of finding faults in the work of other writers that he was nicknamed Epitimaeus, i.e. 'fault-finder'.

11. *Isocrates*: The great Athenian orator and rhetorician (436–338 BC). In his *Panegyric* (380 BC) he urged the Athenians and the Spartans to lay aside their rivalry and unite against Persia. The Spartans conquered Messenia in the eighth century BC.

12. *Athenians . . . Sicily*: In 413 BC. The mutilation of the statues of Hermes in Athens took place immediately before the expedition departed for Sicily in 415.

13. *Zeus . . . Heracleides*: The genitive of Zeus is Dios, and Longinus ironically bases on this a conceit in the manner of Timaeus' far-fetched pun on Hermes and Hermocrates the son of Hermon.

14. *Maidens in their eyes*: The word *kore* meant both 'maiden' and 'pupil', presumably because the pupil reflects a tiny image of the person gazing into it. Xenophon uses instead the word *parthenos* which means 'maiden'. On Amphicrates see n. 8 above.

15. *You drunken . . . dog*: Iliad 1.225, Achilles' words to Agamemnon.

16. *They will inscribe . . . temples*: Plato, *Laws* 741c. The following quotation is from *Laws* 778d.

17. *Tortures for the eyes*: Herodotus 5.18.

18. *Keenly . . . accomplished*: Odyssey 11.315–17.

19. *Ajax . . . Dead*: At *Odyssey* 11.563–4 Ajax turns away from Odysseus in Hades without speaking to him.

20. *Alexander's reply*: According to the story reported in several sources, Parmenio said that if he were Alexander he would be content to end a war on the terms offered, to which Alexander replied that if he were Parmenio, he would too.

21. *Strife*: Evidently Longinus has referred to Homer's description of Strife, whose feet are on earth and whose head is in heaven, at *Iliad* 4.442.

22. *Rheum . . . nostrils*: *The Shield of Heracles* 267.

23. *And as far . . . gods*: *Iliad* 5.770–72.

24. *And round them . . . abhorrence*: A conflation of *Iliad* 21.388 and 20.61–5.

25. *And the far-stretched . . . flew*: Another conflation: *Iliad* 13.18; 20.60; 13.19 and 27–9.

26. *So, too, the lawgiver . . . land*: This reference to the book of Genesis has often been suspected as an interpolation. But scholars now argue that it makes good sense where it is, and that there is no reason why a pagan author of the early empire should not know something of Jewish literature. The passage was enormously influential in the eighteenth century in stimulating literary approaches to the study of the Bible.

27. *Father Zeus . . . destroy us*: *Iliad* 17.645–7.

28. *Is raging . . . lips*: *Iliad* 15.605–7.

29. *There lies . . . son*: *Odyssey* 3.109–11 where Nestor is telling Telemachus about the siege of Troy.

30. *The wine-skin*: In which Aeolus imprisoned the winds, which were then released by his companions: *Odyssey* 10.19–20.

31. *Zoilus*: Cynic philosopher and critic of the fourth century BC, who was nicknamed 'Homer's scourge' for his carping criticism of Homer. The following references are to *Odyssey* 12.62, 12.447 and book 22.

32. *A peer . . . dying*: This famous and much translated ode of Sappho, whose work dates from the sixth century BC, is preserved only here.

33. *Arimaspeia*: This lost epic poem on the peoples of the far north was attributed to the legendary figure Aristeas of Proconnesus. See Herodotus 4.13ff.

34. *And he fell . . . death*: *Iliad* 15.624–8.

35. *And . . . destruction*: Line 299 of the *Phainomena* of Aratus, an Alexandrian poet writing in the first half of the third century BC.

36. *Archilochus*: See above on Horace, *The Art of Poetry*, n. 5. It is not certain which lines of Archilochus Longinus has in mind. The Demosthenes passage is from the *De Corona* 169, where the panic at Athens following the news of Philip's capture of Elatea (in 339 BC) is described.

37. *Those, therefore . . . satisfied*: *Republic* 9.586 with some adaptations.

38. *Stesichorus*: The sixth-century-BC lyric poet, who could be described as Homeric in his use of epic themes and vocabulary. On Archilochus see Horace, *The Art of Poetry*, n. 5.

39. *Ammonius*: A pupil of Aristarchus at Alexandria (second century BC) who wrote commentaries on Homer.

40. *This strife . . . mortals*: *Works and Days* 24.

41. *Mother . . . upon me*: Euripides, *Orestes*, 255–7.

42. *Ah . . . fly*: Euripides, *Iphigenia in Tauris*, 291.

43. *He lashes . . . fight*: *Iliad* 20.170–71.

44. *And do not . . . wheel*: This and the following passage are taken from the lost *Phaethon* of Euripides.

45. *Yet . . . horses*: From another lost play of Euripides.

46. *Seven . . . blood*: *Seven against Thebes* 42–6.

47. *Then the house . . . frenzy*: From a lost play by Aeschylus on the subject of Lycurgus' resistance to the cult of Dionysus in Thrace. The line with which this is compared is Euripides, *Bacchae*, 726.

48. *Sophocles*: The references are to *Oedipus at Colonus* 1586–1666 and to the lost *Polyxena*. The poem in which Simonides describes the same episode is also lost.

49. *Be off . . . hell*: Euripides, *Orestes* 264–5.

50. *Demosthenes*: The example is from *Against Timocrates* (*Oration* 24, 208).

51. *Hyperides*: A distinguished Attic orator of the fourth century BC. See chapter 34. The Athenians were defeated by Philip at Chaeronea in 338 BC.

52. *You were . . . Plataea*: *De Corona* 208. Demosthenes is defending, by reference to the past, his aggressive policy which resulted in the Athenian defeat at Chaeronea.

53. *Eupolis*: A comic poet contemporary with Aristophanes. The quotation is from his lost play, *The Demes* (produced in 412 BC), in which heroes from the past came up from Hades to give advice.

54. *Demosthenes*: The following passages are from the *First Philippic* (*Oration* 4.10 and 44).

55. *Xenophon*: *Hellenica* 4.3.19.

56. *We came . . . palace*: *Odyssey* 10.251–2.

57. *For the aggressor . . . his voice*: *Oration* 21.72.

58. *Isocrates*: See n. 11. His disciples included Hyperides (see chapters 15 and 34) and Theopompus (see chapters 31 and 43).

59. *Herodotus*: 6.11.

60. *Polyptota*: Strictly speaking, polyptoton is the use of more than one case of the same word, but Longinus seems to apply it also to rhetorical effects gained by changes in number, person, tense, or gender.

61. *Straightway . . . Tunny*: Author unknown and text uncertain.

62. *O marriages . . . men*: *Oedipus Tyrannus* 1403–8.

63. *Forth . . . Sarpedons too*: Author unknown.

64. *Plato's passage*: *Menexenus* 245d.

65. *Demosthenes*: *De Corona* 18.

66. *And when Phrynicus . . . tears*: Herodotus 6.21.

67. *Xenophon*: *Cyropaedia* 7.1.37.

68. *You would say . . . fray*: *Iliad* 15.697–8.

69. *Do not . . . ocean*: *Phaenomena* 287. On Aratus, see n. 35 above.

70. *From the city . . . Meroe*: Herodotus 2.29.

71. *But you . . . fought*: *Iliad* 5.85.

72. *And with . . . death*: *Iliad* 15.346–9.

73. *Hecataeus*: Historian and geographer from Miletus, writing *c.* 500 BC.

74. *Aristogeiton*: *Oration* 25.27–8, a work not now thought to be by Demosthenes.

75. *Penelope's speech*: *Odyssey* 4.681–9.

76. *Funeral Oration*: *Menexenus* 236d.

77. *Xenophon . . . as praise*: *Cyropaedia* 1.5.12.

78. *Herodotus*: 1.105.

79. *Plato*: *Laws* 801b.

80. *No longer . . . filly*: From a fragment of Anacreon, the sixth-century-BC lyric poet. The word 'filly' used here is derived from a conjectural emendation which is suggested by the context.

81. *Theopompus*: A historian of the fourth century BC, see n. 58.

82. *Herodotus' expressions*: These are from 6.75 and 7.181.

83. *Men . . . integrity*: *De Corona* 296.

84. *Xenophon*: *Memorabilia* 1.4.5.

85. *Plato*: The descriptions are drawn from the *Timaeus* 65c – 85e.

86. *For it is not easy . . . drink*: *Laws* 773c.

87. *Lysias*: The celebrated Attic orator (*c.* 459 – *c.* 380 BC), known for the purity of his style. He appears as a character in Plato's *Phaedrus*.

88. *Eratosthenes*: A versatile Alexandrian author and scholar of the third century BC. The *Erigone* is a learned elegiac poem based on the story of the death of Icarius and the suicide of his daughter, Erigone. On Archilochus, see Horace, *The Art of Poetry*, n. 5.

89. *Ion of Chios*: Poet and prose writer of the fifth century BC. None of his tragedies survive.

90. *Story of Leto*: In the now lost *Deliacus*. The *Funeral Oration* is *Oration* 2. On Hyperides, see n. 51 above.

91. *Phryne or Athenogenes*: Hyperides' defence of the courtesan, Phryne, is now lost, but a large part of his speech *Against Athenogenes* (*Oration* 3) was discovered in the last century on a papyrus.

92. *As long . . . flourish*: Quoted in Plato's *Phaedrus* 264c as part of an epitaph on the tomb of Midas.

93. *Colossus . . . spearman*: The reference may be to the Colossus of Rhodes, which was damaged by an earthquake about sixty years after it was set up at the beginning of the third century BC. But this is by no means certain. The statue of the spearman (the Doryphorus) by the fifth-century-BC Argive sculptor, Polyclitus, was regarded as a model of beautiful proportions.

94. *Unless . . . heels*: From a work at one time ascribed to Demosthenes, *Oration* 7.45.

95. *Isocrates*: See n. 11 above. The passage quoted is from *Panegyric* 8.

96. *For the Syracusans . . . fighting for*: Thucydides 7.84.

97. *In this place . . . with missiles*: Herodotus 7.225.

98. *The field . . . letter*: Author unknown.

99. *This decree . . . cloud*: De Corona 188.

100. *Philistus*: A Sicilian historian of the fourth century BC.

101. *I am loaded . . . more*: Euripides, *Hercules Furens* 1245.

102. *And wheresoever . . . now that*: From the lost *Antiope* of Euripides.

103. *The storm in Herodotus*: 7.188, 191 and 8.13.

104. *Theopompus*: See nn. 58 and 81. The passage quoted describes the expedition of Artaxerxes Ochus against Egypt in the mid fourth century BC.

105. *As Xenophon says*: Memorabilia 1.4.6.

106. *The day . . . manhood*: Odyssey 17.322–3.

107. *It is best . . . be*: Euripides, *Electra* 379.

PENGUIN CLASSICS
www.penguinclassics.com

- *Details about every Penguin Classic*

- *Advanced information about forthcoming titles*

- *Hundreds of author biographies*

- *FREE resources including critical essays on the books and their historical background, reader's and teacher's guides.*

- *Links to other web resources for the Classics*

- *Discussion area*

- *Online review copy ordering for academics*

- *Competitions with prizes, and challenging Classics trivia quizzes*

PENGUIN CLASSICS ONLINE